Night & Day

the book playlist

This book comes with its own Spotify playlist, featuring all the songs mentioned in the story, and others I imagined would have been on Izzy's playlist. The first one on the list is a new song from my sister Aini, a Finnish singer-songwriter who wrote the song 'Under My Spell' specifically for this book.

You can find the playlist here:
tinyurl.com/night-and-day

Chapter 1

Mia gazed up at St Patrick's Cathedral, her mind burning with questions. Surely, if there was a God up there, those pointed gables piercing the blue sky served as connection points. She filled her lungs with the exhaust fumes of Auckland Friday afternoon traffic and scanned the momentarily empty footpath. This was her chance.

Adjusting the soft guitar case on her back, Mia propped her handbag on top of her suitcase, spread her arms, and closed her eyes. When you rarely prayed, it was best to make a gesture. She needed guidance. So far, her Eat Pray Love trip had only included eating. The way the waistband of her shorts dug into soft flesh bore testament to New York pizza, Hawaiian ice cream and Australian pies. This morning, she'd made it to Auckland, the last stop on her round-the-world journey, the furthest away from home she'd ever been. She'd have to fast for the rest of her journey to avoid those sideways glances from Mikko, her boyfriend of three years. He'd shake his head in disappointment at her lack of self-discipline. He'd made that same face when she hadn't jumped at the chance to join his start-up company. She'd told him she needed time to think, insisting that this trip would give her clarity. A vision. Now, five days before her returning flight, she felt even more confused than before.

A shadow flickered somewhere to her side and she heard a rustle, just loud enough to rise above the traffic noise. What was it? Mia cracked her eyelids, checking her surroundings. The footpath seemed empty. She closed her eyes again, anticipation making her skin bristle. Was this one of those God moments? Nobody had called her by name, but maybe her faith wasn't strong enough for manifestations like that. Maybe lapsed Lutherans only heard a rustling sound, like a broken radio.

Mia squeezed her eyelids tighter, focusing all her energy on the divine connection. There it was again. The rustle. She concentrated harder, letting the sun heat her face. The guitar case felt hot and heavy against her back, a perfect contrast to the chill that travelled up her bare legs.

No, it wasn't only a chill. Something brushed her leg, making every hair on her body stand up. Okay, this was officially spooky. With her heart thundering in her chest, Mia opened her eyes and looked down. There was nothing there. Absolutely nothing. In a fraction of a second, her brain registered what was wrong.

Her suitcase and handbag had vanished.

Mia whipped around and surveyed the street. The footpath

was empty, but one car had stopped a few steps away. As her gaze landed on its silver frame, it tore off down the road, the back door slamming as it went. Mia ran after it, the guitar case flapping against her back, panic moving her feet before her brain caught up, but the car sped away, far out of her reach, running a red light in the distance.

After it finally disappeared behind a street corner, Mia thought of the licence plate. She hadn't even glanced at it.

She had nothing.

Nothing but a cheap guitar in a soft bag and a stick of gum in its front pocket. Her handbag held her phone, laptop and wallet, and her suitcase all the rest. For no logical reason, she dug up the gum, storing it in the pocket of her micro shorts for safe keeping. In her flowery loose top, she wasn't dressed for the weather. December – early summer in New Zealand – had greeted her with a cool breeze, a surprise after sweltering days in Australia, and she'd been contemplating changing into jeans. Well, too late now. The realisation arrived like a slowly building cascade, a slideshow of things she needed but no longer had.

Voi vittu! Mia cursed in her native tongue, Finnish, clenching her fists tight, looking for something to punch. She couldn't even throw her handbag.

She walked in circles, the fury that had nowhere to go shaking her body, eventually fizzling out as her brain gradually accepted the new reality. There was no one around to receive her anger. Not knowing what else to do, she eventually sat in the shade of the church's cast iron fence, her whole body shaking. A flush of panic and shame constricted her throat, stealing her breath. How could she have been so stupid? She'd let go of her bags and closed her eyes. It must have looked like she'd been advertising her belongings to any thief out there.

She'd only been in the country for two hours. Until this moment, she'd thought the food poisoning in Hawaii had been the low point of her journey. But no. She'd happily exchange this experience for two days of throwing up. To anything, really.

Nothing around her had changed; spring leaves in the trees across the road, the geometric pattern crisscrossing the footpath, the beige apartment buildings with their windows glinting in the bright sun. The storm cloud that brewed over her life wasn't visible to anyone else. Occasional pedestrians scuttled past her, paying no attention. Hugging her chilled knees against her chest, Mia fought to fill her lungs, waiting for the familiar pain to fill her chest – the swell of emotion that burned somewhere deep inside but never rose to the surface, never escaped. She wasn't sure how it had started, or why. Was she controlling her body or her body controlling her? Either way, she hadn't cried in years.

Shivering to the bone, with nothing but her knees to hold on to, she ached for tears to blur her vision and wash away the shame. She hung her head, drawing in ragged breaths until her head felt light and woozy. The emotion only built up pressure and burning in her chest, offering no release. She had to get up and do something. She needed her rational brain – the one part of her, unlike the tear ducts, that still worked. In fact, she was known for her smarts, for her uncanny ability to keep cool under any circumstances. She was tiny and blonde but fierce, with a piercing pair of big blue eyes that usually missed nothing. This shouldn't have happened to her. Anyone but her. But arguing with her fate changed nothing.

Mia straightened her spine, picked up her guitar, and surveyed the street. There must be a police station somewhere within a walking distance. She'd walk there and make her case. Maybe they could help her contact someone back home to send money and find out her insurance details. There had to be a way out of this mess.

Chapter 2

Izzy put down his guitar and sighed. He recognised the footsteps on the stairs, the sound of a client approaching. Henry, the 60-year-old non-profit CEO carrying a leather briefcase, ducked his head – which was never anywhere near hitting the beam – and stepped into the basement office.

"How're you doing?" he asked, as usual, taking the extra chair and scooting closer to Izzy's computer screens. "Get any sleep last night?"

"Yeah, all good." Izzy nodded, running his hands through his wildly overgrown mop of dark curls. Yes, he did have permanent bed head, but not from tossing and turning.

"Have you been outside? It's getting warmer."

"Yeah, I went for a walk yesterday."

Henry gave him an examining look. "It was raining yesterday."

"It must have been the day before, then."

"Yes! Tuesday was nice." Henry's head bobbed in agreement. "I'm glad you got some sunshine. Vitamin D, mental health…" He opened his briefcase and dug out a pile of printouts. "I have the latest figures here with me so we can update the infographics."

Izzy took a deep breath, trying to squash his frustration. Henry was a lovely guy, but he was also the one client that made him want to scream into a pillow. A true boomer, he insisted on printing everything and visiting in person to watch Izzy input numbers on the screen. An hour's work that could have been achieved in five minutes by sending a simple email.

Izzy opened the correct video project and brought up the graphics – suicide statistics from last year. Numbers were on the rise.

"We'll be okay," Henry said, awkwardly patting him on the arm. "I know this is hard."

Izzy coughed, trying to dislodge the lump that always appeared in his throat when he saw Henry. Their joint loss had brought them together and led them to suicide prevention work. 'How fortunate that something good could come out of a tragedy,' as Henry put it. Except he would never get over losing his daughter. His only child.

Izzy had lost a girlfriend – one he'd struggled with, not that he'd ever admit that to Henry. With the gift of hindsight, he could see how destructive their relationship had been, draining the life out of him before her tragic, abrupt death stole his future. He'd mourned, but he could never match the depth of Henry's sorrow. Over the years, his own sadness had faded, turning into a niggling memory, like a scar that only hurt if you deliberately poked at it.

So many tears had been shed, enough for a lifetime. He'd learned his lesson and stayed away from women, away from potential heartbreak and more tears. But he no longer felt the loss, not like Henry did. Izzy had slept fine for five years, albeit in complete solitude.

"Yeah, it's hard," he replied dutifully, mustering a catch in his throat that was expected, and began typing numbers into the cells to update the bar graph.

He felt like an imposter. Every time Henry came around, Izzy went through the motions of pain and sorrow, sat through the heavy sighs and long silences, discussing suicide prevention. When it came to the topic, Henry was a force of nature, pulling together resources to build educational programmes and trying to craft 'viral videos'. He'd raised funding and put together a passionate team with lived experience – partly ongoing experience - which meant he constantly worried about his staff's mental health, along with Izzy's. Unfortunately, the collective passion also produced strong opinions, which in turn led to much negotiating and incessant changes to the videos Izzy edited for them.

Henry cleared his throat. "I'm sorry to tell you, there's another change. That last image of the beach has to go. Miranda pointed out that seeing a body of water can bring up suicidal ideation in those vulnerable."

Izzy nodded, wondering what else he could use. They'd done the unfurling silver ferns from every angle. It was ironic how working on suicide prevention could make you want to die.

After the graphics were updated, Henry got up. "I'll let you get on."

"Yeah, thanks." Guilt stabbed at Izzy's chest as he angled himself away, focused on his screen.

He should have offered Henry a cup of tea, asked him to stay awhile. The old man loved to drink tea and reminisce. But today, he couldn't take it. The sooner he got the guy out, the sooner he could put on his headphones and listen to his favourite soundtrack, clear his mind of those memories and escape into his story. An imaginary world. Nothing beat an alternate reality.

Henry hovered at the foot of the stairs, a friendly smile softening his drawn face. "How's the film coming along? Are you going to be at the Oscars next year?"

Izzy rewarded the painful joke with a forced laugh, as he stretched his arms behind his head. "The computer crapped out, and I have to order some new gear."

"Oh, really? But, it's working? You can still edit our videos?" Henry pointed at the screen.

Bless his cotton socks. Izzy nodded. "Yeah, the iMac is fine. It's just that rendering 3D environments takes a lot of processing power."

"Of course. Of course. Well, I hope you get it sorted. The

world needs to see some uplifting stories right now."

"Yeah. Sure." He'd told Henry little about his film project, only that the story dealt with suicide in an uplifting way – a statement he felt was likely untrue. Was it even possible to achieve such an oxymoronic outcome? Probably not.

"Don't suppose you want to join us for pizza night next Monday? Got a couple of new people starting at the helpline. Younger people."

Izzy clicked on an email he had no interest in. "No, sorry, I have quite a bit of work to get through." He wondered what had brought this on. Henry hadn't asked him to join any social outings in months. After all, he'd been consistent with his vague excuses for years. Everyone else, including his family, had learned their lesson.

"Of course." Henry lifted his hand in farewell and tackled the stairs one at a time, pausing on each step. He needed a hip replacement but refused to use health care resources 'on frivolous things', so he refused the surgery. Everything this man did put Izzy to shame.

When Henry finally made it to the second level, Izzy abandoned his computer and threw himself on the couch, letting air drain from his lungs. If he ever finished this film, Henry would be disappointed with it. Or shocked to his core. Possibly both. He hadn't quite figured out the ending yet, but considering that the story took place in the afterlife and he couldn't really raise the characters from death... no, that would never work. It wouldn't be authentic. People who died stayed dead, without fail. Just like Erin, since she'd leapt into the dark Waikato river.

Izzy looked at the overgrown garden behind his window, wondering for the hundredth time why he'd stayed so close to the river. He could have left it all behind, if he'd done it straight away. Everyone would have understood. If only he'd done it back then, when nobody had expected anything from him. But he'd always been the responsible one, and when Henry's organisation got the funding, he felt obligated to help. It paid well enough and gave him the chance to do his own thing on the side. That's why he did it, he reminded himself; To fund his art, the film he wanted to create. It was all worth it, as long as he figured out the ending.

Izzy snapped the cordless headphones on his ears, picked up his phone, browsed Spotify for the right playlist, and closed his eyes. As soon as he heard the first notes of the classical instruments, his mind was transported into a world, the music making the imaginary world appear behind his eyelids like a painter's brush that swept across a canvas. How did the story end? What was beyond Limbo, the ominous transportation hub of the afterlife? Where did the doors lead?

The answers would come to him if he freed his mind and drifted into that state between conscious and unconscious. It was right there, within his grasp, eluding and teasing him like a forgotten word on the tip of one's tongue.

Chapter 3

"Can you give us a visual description of the thief? Tall, short, dark, fair?"

Mia stared into the pair of sharp eyes behind blue-rimmed spectacles and a wall of bulletproof glass and swallowed a sour lump. "I didn't see them."

"You didn't see the person who mugged you?" The middle-aged receptionist repeated, blinking rapidly. Her blue vest matched her glasses and her ponytail seemed too tight for comfort.

"Mugging is probably not the right word..." Mia hesitated, her brain drawing blank after blank. What was it called when someone mugged you without touching or even threatening to hurt you? Or even being seen? Like a ghost. "Someone took my luggage when I wasn't looking."

"Did you leave your things unattended? Someone might have taken them to lost and found."

The woman pointed to her left, rattling out directions to the said lost and found. Mia shook her head. "No! I was standing right there. I just… closed my eyes for a second."

"At 43 Wyndham Street, in front of the Cathedral of St Patrick and St Joseph?" She read from her screen, then flicked her penetrating gaze back at Mia, who felt heat rising her cheeks.

"I was praying," she muttered.

The woman nodded slowly and the corner of her mouth twitched almost imperceptibly. "Next time, it might be safer to pray *inside* the church. Especially if you have a lot of valuables on your person."

Mia scoffed. Like she was ever going to pray again. God obviously didn't like her very much. In fact, God seemed to have a cruel sense of humour, much like this receptionist, who was still eyeing her with barely concealed amusement.

"Is there a computer I could use? Or a phone?"

The woman gave her an odd look. "No. This is a police station. There's an internet cafe two blocks away if you need one."

"But I don't have any money. I have nothing!"

"What's on your back?"

Mia sighed, lowering the guitar case on the floor so it was fully visible. "It's an old acoustic guitar, not worth much. I could sell it, just don't know how or where…"

The receptionist's mouth twisted in half-hearted sympathy. "Maybe you can get your bank to send you a new card?"

"Yes, but how do I contact them? I have no money for the

internet cafe."

"What about your accommodation? Can't they help you?"

Mia's forehead creased. "I haven't checked into the hotel yet. I don't know if they'll let me do that without a credit card. I don't think they've even charged me yet."

The receptionist's lips puckered reproachingly, as if this was all very poor planning on Mia's part. "So, you have nowhere to stay? And no money on your person?"

Mia shook her head, feeling utterly worthless. She clutched her guitar case, wondering if the cruel woman would suggest she go busking outside the supermarket. The thought filled her with dread. She'd never played live for anyone and only used the old guitar to play with song ideas that seemed to drift in whenever her mind was idle. Mikko had called her song writing 'meditative ideation', comparing it to his own bathroom breaks. Apparently, he got his best ideas on the can. Mia accepted the premise, trying to dismiss the fact that she'd never had a useful business idea when strumming her guitar. At least her boyfriend was kind of supportive of her musical hobby. Maybe one day, she'd have a stroke of genius when humming a new melody.

Mia hadn't told Mikko she'd packed the guitar on this trip. She wouldn't have been able to tell him why – it was cumbersome and problematic on flights. She'd made her own way to the airport with her *soft* guitar case (Mikko would have ridiculed it to no end), awkwardly bumping into doorframes and other travellers. Right now, she was grateful for the little Landola, though. It had survived the flights, mostly in overhead bins along with hand luggage because the crew took pity on her, and was still in one piece for her to hold. The idea of selling the guitar made her feel a little sick.

The receptionist turned to catch the attention of her colleague. Mia couldn't hear every word, but guessed from the tone this was about bending the rules. After a moment, the lady turned back to her, adjusting her glasses. "You can come around and use the phone or the computer."

After a moment, the side door flung open and Mia stepped in. The receptionist gestured at the phone on her desk, then at an unoccupied PC in the corner. An easy choice. The only phone number Mia could remember by heart was her own. She sat down and propped her guitar case against the desk.

The receptionist handed her a pen and a blank notebook. "If you need to take notes."

"Thank you."

She'd already reported her passport stolen, but she had to get it replaced with an emergency travel document to get on her last flight in five days. A quick Google search made Mia's stomach plummet. The Finnish Embassy of New Zealand was in Yarralumla, Australia. That couldn't be right. After a bit of searching, she found the contact details of a local consulate. Her stomach dropped further. The Dutch embassy handling emergency passports for Finnish citizens was in Wellington. Based on her limited knowledge, that was at the other end of North Island. But at least she could travel there without a passport.

The next order of business – contacting someone back home to get money. Maybe she could find Mikko's phone number in her email. He hated speaking on the phone, so it wouldn't be on the website. As Mia navigated to the Gmail home page, her whole body seized in terror. What was her password? She'd changed it at some point last year, but her laptop logged in automatically, never asking her to type it in. Before leaving Finland, she'd resigned from her job and the company had promptly disabled her work email account. All she had was Gmail, but if she couldn't get in, then what?

Steeling her nerves, Mia launched her fingers on the keyboard and punched in several possibilities. Soon enough, Gmail warned her about disabling the account. Five minutes later, she'd tried all her social media accounts. Instagram told her the password she'd typed in was an old one. Facebook wanted her to verify her sign-in by logging into her email. For crying out loud!

Mia took a deep breath, her hands falling into her lap. Was there any website she could log into? Before leaving, she'd helped Mikko set up a mailing list for his start-up. If she could get into that account, she could send an email campaign. It was a cheaper service, not one with layers of security like Mailchimp. It was a long shot, but worth trying. To her surprise, the password worked.

Dread quickly replaced the relief of gaining access. Who should she try to message? Her parents' English wasn't great, so they wouldn't be of any help with overseas money transfers or other complicated manoeuvres. Her sister was in her eighth month of a high-risk pregnancy, a reason she'd booked her return for less than a week, to make sure she was back home to help her through the first weeks and months. Kati didn't need any extra stress. She'd have to message Mikko.

Mia created a new email template and typed a short message, asking Mikko to respond by creating another draft email campaign.

Please don't change this password! This is the only account I can log into at the moment.

Mia pressed 'send', the hopelessness of her quest hitting her. The email wouldn't land in Mikko's primary inbox. It'd be lost amongst other newsletters from motivational speakers, pitch deck tutorials, and whatever else he subscribed to. Staring at the campaign confirmation on the screen, a fresh wave of hopelessness coursed through her. When had she ever seen Mikko browsing the promotional tab on Gmail? She had to get into his inbox some other way.

Mia turned back to the receptionist. "Excuse me?"

The woman swivelled her chair. "Yes? Did you get your business sorted?"

Mia bit her lip. "Not, really. I can't remember my email password. But if you could send an email from your email account to this address..." she wrote Mikko's email address on the notebook. "And if you could let him know what happened, and ask him to check his promotional messages for an email campaign with my name in the subject line?"

"You can't access your email, but you sent him an email *campaign*?" The receptionist cast her a suspicious look.

Mia sucked in her lips. "I know it sounds weird but yes. I got into his newsletter account." She extended her hand, desperately dangling the piece of paper with an email address at the suspicious woman.

The receptionist picked up the note with two fingers like a used napkin and turned back to her computer, shaking her head in disbelief. She opened her email, painstakingly typed in Mikko's email, then spent a good five minutes composing a one-line message. Finally, she sent the message and turned back to Mia. "So, you really have nowhere to go?"

Mia shook her head, squeezing her eyes closed. This is where tears might have actually helped. She could tell the receptionist doubted her story. Anyone else in her situation would have been crying. Mia fought to fill her lungs against the pressure that had sat in her chest since the robbery. Why couldn't it morph into a proper heart attack? That would at least get her a hospital bed.

The receptionist released a heavy breath. "I can call a couple of women's shelters to see if they have room for tonight?"

Please, no.

"And if that doesn't work," she continued, "there might be a holding cell available."

No, no, no.

"Unless you have any contacts in the country? Anyone at all? You can use the phone."

"I don't know anyone from..." That's when Mia remembered the name. She'd last emailed him maybe three months ago, requesting a shorter edit of an immigration video they'd produced for the Finnish government. Isaiah McCarthy, video editor. Some of her colleagues had thought it strange she commissioned an editor located so far away, but it made sense. He'd been cheap, talented, and fluent in English. The perfect contractor. Being in an opposite time zone, McCarthy could turn around urgent jobs overnight without charging extra. He'd been friendly, expressing gratitude for her clear notes and swift decision-making, always signing with 'If you need anything else, please don't hesitate to ask'. His phrasing had felt over-the-top, but she'd chalked it up to cultural differences. Now those words floated back, giving her a nudge of courage.

"Isaiah McCarthy."

The receptionist looked up in surprise. "And where is he located?"

Mia held her breath, trying to remember anything the editor might have mentioned. His emails had been short and to-the-point. She liked that he didn't waste her time on idle chitchat. As an editor, he had an exceptional ability to condense time without losing the essence of the story, and decent file-naming conventions – none of that 'final-final-final-v3' shit. Mia rubbed her forehead, wading through useless trivia for something that could help her find the guy.

"Can you please google his name plus Maven Productions? That's the name of his business, I think."

The lady turned back to her computer. Over her shoulder, Mia saw a glimpse of a dark blue website that loaded on her screen. She recognised the simple logo. "That's the one!" A ray of hope shot through her for the first time in hours.

"This company is in Hamilton," the receptionist said as she opened another page with a map. "There's a mobile number here for Isaiah McCarthy. You can use our phone to make a call."

Mia's stomach lurched. "Where's Hamilton?"

The receptionist lifted a shoulder. "About ninety minutes South."

That didn't sound convenient, but it wasn't impossible. Mia's gaze flicked to the landline phone on the desk. Could she take the phone somewhere private to make the call? Probably not, judging by the way the receptionist's eyes tracked her every movement. She'd just have to steel her nerves and ignore the woman.

Her breath quickening, Mia reached for the offered phone. Placing the receiver against her ear, she realised it was already ringing. The receptionist had dialled the phone number.

After a long moment, she heard a grunt.

"Hello? Is this Isaiah McCarthy?"

"Yeah."

"Great! My name is Mia Forsman. I used to work at Lounatuuli Productions. We did some business with you I believe?"

"Yeah."

Mia swallowed, panic tightening her throat. She couldn't tell if the gruff voice was angry, indifferent, or belonged to someone who disliked phone calls. She forced herself to continue. "This isn't a work phone call. I just didn't know who else to call. I just arrived in New Zealand and got mugged... well, not mugged but robbed." she sucked in a breath, her voice turning a bit squeaky. "Anyway, since I don't have a passport or my credit card or anything, I'm in trouble right now. I was wondering if you could help. I'll pay you back later, I promise!"

The line was quiet for a couple of seconds, long enough for Mia's heartbeat to skyrocket. Then Isaiah cleared his throat. "Where are you?"

"At the police station in Auckland, in the city centre. I mean, I'm not under arrest or anything. I had to report the theft—"

"Stay there. Give me ... two hours."

"Okay." Mia's voice trembled. "Thank you so much," she continued, but realised Isaiah had already ended the call.

Mia handed back the phone and sunk into the office chair, feeling like she'd been punched in the stomach.

"Did you get hold of him?" The receptionist asked.

"Yeah, he's coming here, I think."

Mia took her guitar, thanked the receptionist, and snuck through the side door, settling into one of the seats in the waiting area. Its minimal padding and general discomfort reminded her of airports.

Okay. She'd done this before. She was an expert at hanging in airports by now. But without her phone, laptop, or even a book to read, her hands began to fidget. Mia sighed, wiggling on the seat to find a more comfortable position. Eventually, she lay across two seats, her arms wrapped around the guitar bag. Exhaustion from the interrupted night and the heightened excitement of the day flowed down her spine, making her limbs heavy. Maybe she could shut her eyes for a bit.

As her eyelids fluttered, Mia's mind travelled to the moment of the robbery, and a shot of alarm threw her eyes open. No, she reminded herself, closing her eyes again wouldn't bring in any new misfortunes. She was at the police station with nothing left to lose. Comforted by the almost liberating sense of emptiness, she rested her head against the crook of her arm and allowed herself to drift off.

Chapter 4

Reversing into the visitor carpark, Izzy flipped the visor and stared into the little mirror. Was he presentable? He hadn't shown his face in public for a week, since he'd visited the gym to cancel his membership. His home gym had better equipment with no waiting times, so why pay for the inconvenience? Not leaving the house also meant he didn't have to care about his appearance. Unsurprisingly, the face staring back in the mirror had been taken over by an unruly beard. Was it really that long? Holy shit.

Izzy shook his head, grabbed his keys and wallet, and headed for the front doors. The imposing glass building looked brand new, nothing like the old police station he remembered. Although he hadn't visited Auckland in years.

Stepping into the reception area, Izzy scanned the room for a familiar face. On the way, when traffic drew to a standstill around Drury, he'd quickly googled the Finnish woman. A pretty blonde with one of those edgy, short haircuts. She'd been easy to work with, prompt and appreciative with clear, short briefs. Meandering, indecisive clients were the worst. He'd hoped for more work from Lounatuuli Productions, but hadn't heard from them in months. According to LinkedIn, Mia no longer worked there, just like she'd said on the phone.

At first, his gaze landed on two excessively tattooed gentlemen by the door. He brushed past them, offering a respectful chin-lift. In the far corner of the room, he noticed the sleeping figure. She looked tiny, like a lost child, curled up across two seats, her arm draped over a soft guitar case. Her hair looked longer than in the online photograph, the shaved sides grown into wispy waves that swept over her ear. She had delicate features, like a little fairy who might sprout wings at any moment.

Izzy stopped a few steps away from the strange creature, his breath catching. He didn't believe in love at first sight, not anymore, but something about this woman made his body seize. She hadn't noticed him yet. Revelling in the unique opportunity, Izzy studied her face and body, imagining what kind of character lurked underneath.

When she stirred, Izzy retreated half a step and arranged his features into a smile. He hadn't driven all the way here to freak her out. She must have been pretty freaked out already, stranded in a strange country without her belongings.

"Excuse me. Miss?"

Mia rattled awake like she'd heard a gunshot, springing to her feet. The guitar case slid off her grasp and Izzy lunged forward, catching it just before it made contact with the floor. Mia reached for it simultaneously, their skulls clanking together with a loud thud. Her yelp gave him a jolt.

"Sorry." He handed her the instrument.

"Thank you." She hugged the black guitar-shaped bag and blinked at him, rubbing her forehead. "Sorry about taking up so much space. I didn't mean to fall asleep. I was just waiting for someone." She gestured apologetically at the seat she'd used as a daybed.

Izzy rubbed his own forehead, trying to catch up with the situation. Did she think he was after her seat?

"Are you… Mia? Sorry I took so long."

Her face lit up in recognition, cheeks reddening as her mouth fell open. "Oh, right! Sorry, of course. Isaiah?"

Mia set the guitar case against the floor and offered him a delicate hand with clear nail polish. Izzy shook it, careful not to squeeze too hard. "Call me Izzy. Everyone else does."

"You… look different from the photo." She peered up at him, sucking on her bottom lip.

Izzy ran his hand over his beard to tame the yeti look. He felt heat pushing up his face. Any photo of him online would have been about five years old, and right now, he wasn't at his most presentable. He hadn't showered before leaving, not wanting to make her wait – well, any longer than she would have to because of geography. She'd sounded so distressed he'd grabbed his phone and keys and leapt into his car, only giving a moment's thought to the absolute necessities such as having enough petrol in the tank. Hence the worn-out army-green T-shirt and grey slacks.

A dusty, soapy smell drifted into his nostrils. Finding an old stick of deodorant in his glove compartment had been a happy surprise, but he'd probably applied it too generously. There was a chance deodorant didn't stay fresh for ten years, especially when it was cooked in a hot car every summer.

Izzy wagged his finger at the reception desk. "Are you waiting on something?"

"No. I filed the report, and there's nothing else I can do here."

She gripped her fingers around the guitar neck, her bare legs sporting goosebumps. Izzy glanced around, instinctively looking for a suitcase or bag, before he remembered. "So, you have nothing else? Not even a jacket?"

Mia shook her head, pink blotches appearing on her cheeks. Was she about to cry? Instead of tears, he heard a sharp intake of breath as she stared back at him, shaking her head.

"That's okay," Izzy said quickly, guiding her towards the doors. As they passed the reception desk, the woman behind it nodded at Mia.

Izzy led her to his car – an old, silver Toyota Corolla that looked terrible but passed its WOF with relative ease year after year. He'd never contemplated upgrading. Well, until this very moment.

"The A.C. isn't great, but it kind of works if we keep the back windows cracked. Hope that's okay?" He opened the passenger side door. "You can put the guitar on the backseat."

She stumbled backward, clutching the instrument. "Where are we going? I don't mean to be rude, but I called you because I need to borrow some money. I'm good for it, I promise."

Izzy froze, dumbfounded. "So, I give you money and then what?"

She swallowed. "Then you can go home. I'm so sorry you had to drive all the way here. I'll pay you back with interest, of course. Is twenty percent acceptable?"

Izzy blinked. He could barely follow the woman's logic. "Twenty percent? What am I, a loan shark? I came to pick you up, so you'd have somewhere to stay and I can help sort you out."

Mia's jaw dropped as she studied his face. "But you don't know me. I couldn't ask you—"

"I'm offering. Take it or leave it." He yanked open the car door, gesturing with his head. The constant traffic noise from the street behind them was giving him a headache, and this woman's pointless resistance to his help was making it worse. "Let's just get out of here. If you don't like my house, we'll book you into a hotel. How's that?"

Mia flushed pink. "No! I didn't mean... You have a house?"

Izzy lifted a shoulder. "Yeah. I look like I sleep under a bridge but—"

"No! I meant... a house, not an apartment? I don't know anyone my age who lives in an actual house. Only wealthy people or families out in the countryside."

"It's really not that unusual around here. And it's nothing flash either, so please adjust your expectations." He tried to smile to lighten the mood, thinking of how badly the house needed maintenance.

"Okay." She nodded to herself, still staring at the car. "I suppose it would solve one of my problems right now, if you really don't mind."

"I really don't mind," Izzy confirmed, still holding the door and his breath. He felt like he was trying to catch a runaway budgie, coaxing it closer until the cage came down. When she finally lowered herself into the seat and wiggled her guitar onto the backseat, he slammed the door, trapping her. A confusing mix of shame and excitement coursed through him as he circled the vehicle to the driver's side.

Once behind the wheel, he risked another glance at the peculiar woman. Sunk into the fluffy seat cover he'd bought to extend the life of the furnishing, she looked even more like a fairy – a lightweight, magical creature he'd inadvertently captured. She tucked her hands under her bare thighs, holding herself rigid, as if to avoid relaxing against the seat. Was she afraid of him? He might have been twice her size, but he hadn't lured her into his car. She'd called him. Technically, they were work colleagues, although he had to admit, working remotely across the oceans didn't facilitate much closeness.

They'd only exchanged a few emails discussing a job

he suspected neither of them had any genuine interest in. He'd noticed the careful way she worded her feedback, so it neither offended nor expressed particular excitement for his creative choices. Facing a roadblock, she'd quickly chosen the fastest way forward to make sure they met the deadline. So efficient and flawless she could have passed for a very sophisticated bot.

Looking at her now, Izzy felt ashamed for his initial assessment. Mia was definitely human. A distressed human. As he navigated through the city centre towards the motorway ramp, her body remained stiff, her unblinking eyes staring out the window, recording every landmark like she was expecting to be thrown out of the vehicle at any moment and having to find her way back.

Izzy racked his brain for the right words. He should have known how to deal with distress. How did he work on all those suicide prevention videos without absorbing any actionable knowledge? What did B.R.A.V.E. stand for? Was B for being there, or breathing? Izzy filled his lungs, hoping oxygen would somehow unlock the rest. In truth, he'd stopped really listening years ago. Besides, this woman wasn't necessarily thinking of ending her life.

"Is it a long drive?" she asked as he accelerated down the motorway ramp.

"Ninety minutes, if we're lucky."

"Lucky, how?"

"If we don't hit traffic. I consider that very lucky in

Auckland. Especially at this time of day."

He glanced at his wristwatch. 5:30pm. This was not a lucky time. Mia nodded, but still wouldn't lean back against the seat. Instead, she folded her legs against her chest, locking her arms around them like an Olympic diver somersaulting through the air. Maybe she felt she was in free-fall. How long could she hold on like that before her arms cramped?

"You must be quite shaken," Izzy said.

"Uh-huh." It was but a whisper.

"So, what happened? How did you lose your stuff?"

Mia's breathing turned into a shallow wheeze and she turned away from him, hiding her face from view.

Izzy scanned the view outside, not sure what to do. They were on the motorway with nowhere to stop. "Are you okay? Please, calm down. Just breathe."

She wheezed a few more times, avoiding his eyes. Gradually, her shoulders dropped and her breath settled.

"Do you have asthma?" He asked.

"No. I can't cry and my body does this instead."

She kept her gaze on the window, her neck flushing pink. Izzy couldn't help his voice creeping up. "You can't cry? You mean you've never..."

Mia shook her head. "No, of course I cried as a baby, and in my youth. I don't know when I stopped. It was some time in the last five years."

"Oh, wow." Izzy shifted in his seat, suddenly uncomfortable. He'd teared up last night when listening to music, not even sure why, but it probably wasn't the right thing to advertise right now.

"It's okay." Mia drew a shuddering breath. "At least I'm not gaining sympathy points or using my femininity to get ahead."

Izzy braked, realising he'd crept far too close to the white Mazda ahead of them. He'd never met anyone concerned about such a thing. "Your English is amazing," he said, hoping to find common ground.

"Are you uncomfortable with a woman who can't cry?" Mia turned to him, her eyes burning bright and guileless.

Izzy glanced at her, then whipped his attention back to the road. Too late. The look in her eyes was already imprinted on his corneas, an open gaze that held no politeness or placation, offering him no escape. Thank goodness he was behind the wheel. Staring into those eyes for any length of time rattled him.

"I don't know. I'm a little uncomfortable right now." He expelled a hollow chuckle.

"That's okay. You're honest." Mia's voice softened. "I know I make men uncomfortable. I can't help it."

"Is that right?"

"Yes. They called me ice queen at work. I know I can be intimidating."

Laughter bubbled up in Izzy's chest. Did the little garden fairy really think she was intimidating? Intriguing, sure. Puzzling even. She was so small, so deeply troubled that he felt like he'd stumbled on a wounded bird. She may have flapped her wings and attempted to limp away, but she needed help. His help.

Chapter 5

Mia stared at the big, bearded man. His soapy scent filled the car, sucking the air out of her lungs. Was she not getting enough oxygen? That could explain why she'd already spilled her guts to this stranger. Now he knew she wasn't normal. Mia, the ice queen; always in control, with an answer to everything. Sometimes, they dressed the sentiment up as a compliment, but she knew what they meant. She was cold and creepy. After all, who else did she know who couldn't cry?

Sunken into her dark thoughts, it took Mia a moment to notice Izzy's amusement.

"What are you laughing about?" She demanded, her stomach winding itself into a knot. A double Windsor.

Izzy tried to straighten his face, running his huge hand through the mop of overgrown dark hair that fell onto his shoulders. Together with the untamed facial hair, it covered most of his skin from the neck up. Mia wondered what he looked like under that stranded-on-a-desert-island look. A flash of white teeth peeked through his full lips as he laughed. "Who says you're intimidating?"

"Um... my boyfriend."

Izzy's smile vanished.

"We're kind of on a break right now," Mia added, uneasy. "Since I'm travelling around the world by myself and all." She twined her fingers so tight they hurt. He must have injected her with some kind of truth serum. "He asked me to get involved in this start-up business he's working on... it's a huge deal, big investors, lots of money and so much pressure... and I said I needed time to think, so I booked this trip."

"Wow. And how's it going?"

She lifted a brow. "Do you have to ask?"

"I mean before getting robbed. Was it going okay?"

Mia's chest ached. She could feel the wave of emotion welling under the surface again. She hadn't felt this close to crying in a long time. Maybe the tears would eventually break through. Either that or her chest would explode. "Not really," she whispered. "I wasn't any closer to a decision. And this is my last stop."

"Is this your first time in New Zealand?"

"Yes."

"I'm so sorry." Izzy's voice filled with regret. "Honestly. I swear we're better than this!"

His needless apology soothed her nerves. "It's not your fault. You didn't rob me."

"So, what do you need to do? Get a new passport, find your flight tickets?"

"Yes. The Dutch embassy handles the emergency passports for Finnish citizens in New Zealand." Mia swallowed. "But it's in Wellington."

"Don't worry. We can drive there." Izzy cast her an encouraging look that tightened her stomach even further.

"No! You don't have to drive me around! If I can borrow some money, I'll go there and get it sorted, maybe get on an earlier flight. I can sort out everything else when I get back home."

"Or… you could look at this as an opportunity?" Izzy's voice sharpened, making the air between them bristle. "You're on this trip to figure things out. Maybe this is God's way of telling you to take a break."

Mia's laugh took on a sad tinge. "No, I think God, if He exists, doesn't like me very much."

"What do you mean?"

Mia bit her lip. After the mortifying encounter at the police station, she didn't feel like discussing the details of her stupidity, but her mouth opened anyway. "I… I was kind of praying, with my eyes closed, when I lost my bags." Heat engulfed her face as she thought back to the moment. "I never saw the thief. I only saw a car driving away."

Izzy kept his gaze on the road, but his eyes widened into saucers. "Where were you?"

"Outside a church—"

"Hang on. You stood on the footpath, closed your eyes to pray and all your stuff disappeared?"

"Yes." Mia wanted to kick herself, regret filling every cell in her body. If she could only go back in time, undo—

"Don't you think that's just a little... unbelievable? I mean, the timing of it. Unless you prayed for hours?"

Mia frowned. "No. Maybe thirty seconds."

"Wow. I have chills. Literally. Goosebumps. Look."

He peeled his T-shirt sleeve up to reveal a huge, solid bicep. Mia couldn't detect any goosebumps, but her stomach flipped at the sight of his muscles. This guy was like a marble statue. Reluctantly, she tore her eyes away. "What do you mean?"

"Well, you didn't say what you prayed about, but that sounds like an answer."

Mia huffed in disbelief. "Are you suggesting I prayed for God to beam up all my stuff? Like some sort of reverse rapture?"

His rumbling laugh resonated in her body and she longed to join in, to feel that light. She couldn't imagine her stomach ever unwinding itself, not until she got her life sorted and made it out of this cursed, backwards-ass country.

"I'm sorry," Izzy hiccupped, wiping his eyes. "I know it sucks, but one day you might look back and see this as a really good story. It's got drama, divine intervention, everything."

Mia watched the glistening teardrops spilling from the corners of his eyes, jealousy tightening her chest. He laughed and cried so effortlessly. What was wrong with her that she couldn't do the same?

Chapter 6

Izzy sped along the motorway as it wound between the river and the blue-green Taupiri mountains, enjoying the open road after Auckland's congestion. He wondered what Mia might have thought about the views had she been awake. She'd admitted spending the previous night at Sydney airport, and dozed off around Pokeno. He couldn't stop glancing at the sleeping woman, holding his breath every time she sucked in a sudden inhale, shoulders fluttering.

Izzy wondered if sleeping this early in the evening would mess up her circadian rhythm, but he didn't have the heart to keep her awake. She'd made it clear she wanted out of New Zealand on the first available flight, so it probably didn't matter when she slept. Still, he hoped the passport and other matters would take a little longer. Maybe he could show her around and change her mind about New Zealand. He couldn't let her leave thinking his home country was some kind of crime-infested hellhole. Her experience may have been typical in some other countries, but not here.

Gradually, the green hills levelled into flat, green fields as they approached Hamilton, the dairy central of New Zealand. Tractor dealerships and workshops flashed by as they entered the ugly side of town, dominated by a hotchpotch of small businesses with sun-faded signs. Izzy negotiated each roundabout and traffic light smoothly, hoping Mia would sleep through the unflattering introduction. To his relief, he made it past the hospital (also ugly) and into the rundown but reasonably leafy suburb of Bader.

Izzy pulled into his driveway, exhaling in despair. The golden late evening light did nothing to hide the state of his crumbling rental. Apart from one film school buddy who'd been practically homeless, he hadn't entertained guests in years. Whenever his family brought it up, he argued that the rent was cheap. Not that it excused the chipped paint and cracked concrete steps.

As Izzy killed the engine, Mia woke with a start. "Is this where you live?"

"It's better inside," Izzy grumbled.

He got out and circled the vehicle, but before he reached the handle, the door flew open and Mia stepped out, crashing into his chest.

"What are you doing?" she asked, brushing her shirt, cheeks flaming bright.

"Sorry." Izzy took a step back. His heart pounded as if in the middle of a gym workout, every fibre of his body on high alert. Nobody had invaded his personal space in years. "I was going to open the door for you."

She stared at him, her eyes huge. "Nobody opens the door for me."

Izzy frowned, trying to follow her logic. "You mean nobody is *allowed* to open a door for you?"

She blinked in confusion. "No, I mean, it doesn't happen to me." She paused, looking past him. "I don't think it happens to anyone in the twenty-first century. I'm not a damsel in distress."

A wayward smile tugged at Izzy's mouth. "Well, actually..."

Mia folded her arms, sticking her chin out. "Come on! I know I'm in trouble, but I didn't expect to be rescued. I only wanted to borrow some money."

Izzy felt irritation brewing in his gut. Hadn't they covered this already? "If you're expecting me to throw you some cash and walk away... That's not how we treat visitors in my country. That's not how I was brought up. You called me asking for help, which makes you my personal responsibility. I don't take that lightly."

Mia opened and closed her mouth without producing a sound. To his relief, she dropped the subject, fetched her guitar from the backseat and followed him to the door.

Chapter 7

Huddled under a woollen throw, Mia curled her fingers around a steaming teacup, examining Izzy's dining table. Its peeling melamine top resembled the moon's surface. You couldn't buy this kind in a shop, not even a second-hand shop. The inside of the house felt colder than the air outside. After shivering for a few minutes, waiting for Izzy to boil the jug and search his pantry for something to offer, she'd given in and asked for a blanket. She'd have to find some warmer clothes.

"Thank you," she said, accepting a plate with a hard, round biscuit which was broken in half. "Is this your last one?"

Izzy balled up the wrapper, smiling apologetically. "Yeah. We can go shopping. I usually order groceries, but"—he glanced at the wall clock—"tomorrow's delivery slots are probably full by now."

"You order groceries online? How far away is the shop?" Mia regretted sleeping most of the drive, since she now had no idea of her current location. If he turned out to be a psychopath and she had to call for help... she didn't even want to finish the thought. No phone, no money, no location. She was officially at his mercy.

Izzy sat across the table and huffed an embarrassed chuckle. "A five-minute drive." He looked away, clearing his throat. "I know it sounds odd. I've been busy working on something and ordering online saves time."

Mia shrugged. "I've never enjoyed grocery shopping either. In Finland, I lived on the fourth floor with no lift so it was good exercise, but it's not really deep and meaningful social interaction, is it?"

Izzy's eyes brightened momentarily. "Exactly! That's what I've been telling my…" The conviction escaped his voice and he looked away.

"Telling who?"

"Never mind."

Mia observed his hunched shoulders, wondering what he was hiding and why. She decided not to ask. If he turned out to be dangerous or creepy, it was probably best not to trigger him.

Izzy cleared his expression and raised his coffee cup. "Here's to better days in New Zealand?"

Mia lifted her teacup. "I'll drink to that." She tried to smile. Things could be worse, she reminded herself. She could have been stabbed or shot.

The black tea trickled down her throat, calming her nerves with its universally familiar taste as she studied her hairy host. Despite his unkempt appearance, he didn't smell bad and neither did his house. Its worn-out, tidy interior further settled her fears, offering no unsettling clues – no giant chest freezers or pagan altars. Isaiah McCarthy probably wasn't a serial killer.

"We'll find you some extra clothes," Izzy promised as she tugged on the blanket to stop it from sliding off her shoulders. "My brother's fiancé is about your size, and might be able to lend you a few things."

Mia nodded, fighting the shot of discomfort. She didn't want to dress up in a random woman's clothes, but what choice did she have? Based on Izzy's home, she suspected he didn't have that much money to lend her. Maybe that was why he'd brought her here, to offer her the only thing he could – a place to stay.

The kitchen had seen better days. Or decades. The fifties style cabinet doors reminded her of her grandmother's apartment in Helsinki, except these had been painted over several times. One particularly worn out corner revealed bits of electric blue and dirty orange peeking from under the latest choice of beige. The paint job itself was so shoddy she doubted they'd even attempted sanding the doors before slapping on another layer.

Izzy followed her gaze. "I know. It's the worst home reno in history. The owner is a lawyer who fancies himself as a handyman. He doesn't like paying the professionals."

"So you're renting this place?"

"Yeah. That's why I'm not too fussed about maintenance.

I don't feel like adding value to that guy's investment. He's a dick." Izzy stood up, placing his cup in the kitchen sink. "I've done a bit more downstairs, though. That's where I spend most of my time." He cocked his head at the doorway. "Wanna see it?"

Mia followed him to a narrow hallway. At the far end, Izzy disappeared down a flight of stairs, swallowed by darkness. Mia stalled on the first step. Following a stranger into a dark basement had an added creepiness factor, but there was no odd smell and the air felt dry and warm. It probably wasn't a rat-infested dungeon with meat hooks hanging from the ceiling. Probably.

A light flicked on in the room underneath. "There you go." Izzy's relaxed voice echoed in the stairway. "Don't trip on the last step. It's shorter!"

As Mia descended the stairs, her breath caught in her throat. The walls were painted dark teal. The ceiling was higher than she'd expected and as Izzy pulled the curtains, the floor-to-ceiling windows flooded the room with evening light, revealing an overgrown backyard bursting with vivid green.

"Wow. This doesn't look like a basement!" Mia crossed the red-and-blue oriental rug to where Izzy stood in front of an endless display of computer screens.

"No, it's not like a bunker inside the ground or anything. The section slopes down to a gully," he explained, gesturing at the view behind the window. "Lots of mosquitos but no neighbours. Some of the recent developments in Hamilton are so back-to-back that you can only see your neighbour's wall. My brother used to build those."

"Did you paint this room yourself?" Mia asked, turning to marvel at the strange, deep colour surrounding her. Even the ceiling was dark. "In Finland, all the rentals are white and you can't do anything to them."

Izzy laughed. "Same here! I had to negotiate with the owner."

"You've done well."

The room felt completely different from the upstairs. It wasn't just colour. It sounded different, softer and cosier. That's when Mia noticed the acoustic panels on the wall – and the guitar in the corner, behind his workstation. "Do you play?" She asked.

Izzy turned to look at the guitar, his face widening into a grin. "Yeah. Maybe we can have a jam later?"

"Maybe." Mia swallowed. She didn't jam with other people. No wonder Mikko compared her musical hobby to sitting on the toilet. She'd been pretty much as private about it as her bowel movements.

She wandered across the room, noting the worn leather couch, heaving bookshelves and the rack of Olympic level weights. So, that's how Izzy kept himself looking like the Hulk.

At the far end, a half-open doorway gave a glimpse to another room. Propelled by curiosity, Mia peeked in. "Is that your..." Oops, it looked like a bedroom. A pile of laundry perched on an unmade bed.

"Sorry." Mia backed away, bumping on Izzy's chest as he reached her at the doorway. "I didn't mean to snoop."

He steadied her with a hand on her upper arm, a touch so brief it should have barely registered, yet it fired up her every nerve ending. Izzy took a step back to reinstate a respectful distance. "All good. You'll have to go in there if you want to use the bathroom. The other one upstairs is my flatmate's territory. You may not want to go in there."

Mia whipped around. "You have a flatmate?"

"Yeah. Don't worry. Deke's okay, but his bathroom's just a bit gross."

"How come?

Izzy chuckled. "He collects... um... vintage porn. Which means there's a stack of magazines with pages stuck together. And used tissues. I've told him to clean—"

"I get it. In fact..." She nodded at the door. It seemed her kidneys were done with the tea.

Izzy opened the door, and she padded through the bedroom and into the en-suite. To her relief, she discovered it in order with no magazines or stiff tissues. A sad bar of soap sat on the edge of the sink and a milk-bottle sized shampoo in the shower cubicle, but nothing else. He must keep his personal grooming products, if he had any, hidden in the tiny vanity. No. She wouldn't snoop through his stuff, she decided, no matter how her fingers itched to explore everything in his house.

On the way out, she allowed herself to survey the bedroom. Apart from the laundry pile, the room appeared tidy, nearly as spartan as the bathroom. The eclectic mixture of furniture had a student flat vibe, complete with a pile of books on the nightstand. After days of airports, hotels and other public spaces, Izzy's house felt a like a hideout. Behind the partly drawn, thick curtains, a huge bush full of pink flowers grew against a tall fence, adding to the sense of privacy.

Mia found Izzy at his computer with several browser windows open across his three screens. "Do you have work to do?"

Izzy minimised his inbox. "I edit videos for a suicide prevention charity and they're quite particular about some stuff. I have to cut all beach footage from the latest video."

Mia blinked in confusion. "Why?"

"Because, apparently seeing a body of water may incite a vulnerable person to drown themselves." Izzy offered her a rueful smile. "They're very risk averse."

"Okay. If you need to do that now, I could go for a walk or something."

She gestured at the stairs, but Izzy shook his head. "That's probably not a good idea. What if you get lost? You don't have a phone." He pulled another browser window from the side screen to the middle one. "Anyway, I was just looking up the Dutch embassy you mentioned, and where we could stay in Wellington."

"We?" Mia's heart picked up speed and she lowered herself

into the closest armchair. "I can't ask you to take time off to escort me to Wellington. I've already gone around the world, so I can make it there and back. Or maybe I don't have to make it back if I can change my flights."

Izzy cocked his head and a small frown appeared between his brown eyes. They were so kind and soulful she nearly lost her train of thought. And those solid arms, propped on the arm rests of the chair, muscles bulging out of that flimsy T-shirt... Again, her mind drifted to Greek statues, and she looked away, trying to compose herself. If he knew what was going on in her head, he'd think she was nuts.

"You're fascinating."

Izzy's words shot through her, forcing her attention back to him. The low rumble of his voice made her insides vibrate. She'd noticed hints of it in the car, but with the thrum of the engine, it was hard to tell. Here, in a silent room with soft acoustics, her body responded to the frequency of his voice like an instrument vibrating throughout. Mia drew in a sharp breath, grateful she was sitting down. "What do you mean?"

Izzy shifted closer. "I can't figure out if you're trying to be incredibly polite and no trouble to anyone, or if you really are uncomfortable around me." A smile tugged at his mouth as his gaze drilled into her like a laser.

A warm flush spread across Mia's chest. Definitely a new experience, she noted, trying to control her breathing. "I have no reason to be uncomfortable around you," she half-whispered. "You've been very accommodating."

But he was right. She wasn't comfortable. She felt terrified or excited. Maybe both. Being alone with a stranger in his basement, she should have been afraid, but there was something dependable about this man, even if his deep voice and brown eyes cut through her defences, making her unsettled. He hadn't made a move on her, not even jokingly. She had to get her body under control and focus on solving the issues life had thrown at her.

The sound of a door banging echoed from somewhere upstairs. Mia glanced at the stairs, her muscles tensing.

"That would be my flatmate, Deke."

Just as Izzy said it, the muffled sound of conversation carried from the upper level. "Does he have company?" Mia asked.

A flicker of confusion crossed Izzy's eyes. The medley of voices rose in volume. A group of people. Their footsteps echoed in the hallway.

"Izzy? Are you there?" The male voice bellowed from the top of the stairs.

"Yeah," Izzy called back. "Who is it?"

"Your... family," another voice called back. "Should I send them down?"

"Just a second!"

Izzy turned to Mia, his eyebrows raising in alarm. "Sorry. I don't know what they're doing here. You must be tired. Would you rather wait in the bedroom?"

Politeness and exhaustion warred in Mia's mind. The

overlapping voices above them grew into a medley that sounded like a fleet of ten. Her introvert heart began tying its sneakers, ready to sprint for safety. As much as she thought of herself as a capable person, part of her wanted to crawl into a hole. And Izzy was offering her an out.

She bolted from the armchair. "Yeah, I'll hide in there, if you don't mind."

"No, all good." Izzy followed her to the bedroom and hastily gathered the laundry off the bed, dumping it into a nearby basket.

Mia waved her hands to make him stop. "I didn't mean in your bed! I can sit behind the door and read."

She swiped two books off his nightstand and scooted onto the floor behind the half-open door. Judging by the sounds, the family had descended the stairs.

Izzy flashed Mia a quick smile. "I'll get rid of them," he whispered and disappeared, leaving her perched behind the door holding *Grapes of Wrath* by Steinbeck, and a black book with no title on it. She opened it on a random page and found it full of handwriting. Was it a diary? There were no dates, only a long-winded sentence describing a strange, otherworldly scene.

Mia's fingers hovered on the page, torn between curiosity and respect for her host. But it wasn't respect that made her close the book – it was the scene unfolding behind the door.

Chapter 8

Izzy took his office chair, leaving the couch and armchairs for his family members who poured down the staircase one after another. What on earth were they all doing here? Why now? Did they know he had a visitor? How could they have possibly found out?

His mother Sue sat on the couch, a nervous smile puckering her papery skin. His father John joined her, leaving the armchairs for his brother Mac and Mac's fiancée, Shasa. They all smiled with such effort Izzy's stomach heaved. "What's up?"

"Sorry about barging in like this," Mac said. "Mum's been saying we should all visit you and since you're usually home..."

Izzy nodded at the thinly veiled reproach. "Yeah, I work from home."

"Mac told us you're ordering groceries online," his mother added, eyes widening with worry.

"And now you work out from home?" Mac glanced at his

stack of weights.

Izzy shrugged. "So, what? I don't like shopping and the gym just raised their fees."

"Surely you can afford a bit more," his father suggested. "Is your business in trouble?"

"No!" Izzy tugged at the neck of his shirt, confirming that the collar wasn't restricting his airflow. This conversation was. "No," he repeated quieter, hoping the others would match his volume and he could somehow avoid Mia hearing every word. This was the worst introduction in the history of introductions.

"That's good." His father relaxed against the couch, content to stop talking. He was more of a listener, like Izzy himself. The others had likely dragged him along against his will.

"The reason we're here" —Sue glanced at Mac and Shasa for support— "is that we really care about you. We'd hate to see you wake up full of regret one day because you let life pass you by."

She fanned herself with a pamphlet, *Wintec Prospectus 2022*. "We'd like to contribute towards the cost if you want to do some further studies, in any field, anything at all you'd like."

Izzy took the brochure and dropped it on the coffee table. "I have a film degree. I'm qualified to do what I do and I'm making a living. I can upskill myself online. Why would I need to go back to school?"

He could sense their answer, and it occurred to him, far too late, that asking the question would lead to his hidden house guest hearing what he himself didn't want to hear.

Shasa stirred in her chair, her forehead wrinkling. "For the record, I thought the study idea was a bit off topic, but I have a friend I'd love to set you up with." Her voice raised like a question, her smile turning apologetic.

"She's hot," Mac added with a wink.

Sue's eyebrows shot up. "I think that's a great idea! It doesn't have to be study, as long as you're open to something a bit more ... social. We're all worried about you. Isolating yourself is a sign of depression, you know?"

Izzy took a breath, waiting for the hot ball of anger in his gut to fizzle out. "Of course I know. I edit suicide prevention videos."

Sue's mouth twisted in disdain. "It's such a morbid subject to spend your days with."

Izzy sighed. Sometimes, working on suicide prevention indeed tested his will to live.

"It's important work for sure," his father added absent-mindedly, leafing through a film magazine.

"We're not saying there's anything wrong with what you do for a living, or even working from home," Mac rushed to add. "But bro, let's face it, you need to go out and spend some time with humans. See some friends. Find a girl. Stop punishing yourself for what happened five years ago, it's—"

"I'm not!" Izzy roared, desperate to shut him up. Was it really necessary to advertise every aspect of his emotional baggage? They wanted him to go out on a date with Shasa's friend, or join a club to meet people? Fine! But why did they have to gang up on him like this? He stared at the delegation in his lounge, a cold sensation trickling down his spine. "Wait... Is this an intervention?"

Mac's eyes flashed with guilt.

"We didn't want to use that word," Sue said, weaving her fingers together so tight her knuckles cracked. "It sounds so invasive."

Izzy cast her a firm look. No shit? This felt invasive.

Shasa's apologetic smiles mirrored those of his mother's. They all cared about him, but they didn't understand. He had a plan, and it simply didn't include mindless socialising, dating or starting a family. Not yet. Right now, he was ready to sacrifice everything, save every penny, and put it towards the film project he was working on. On some days, his life felt empty, even unreal, but when he stepped into a world of his own creation, it all made sense.

"I'm okay, mum," he said quietly, holding her gaze. "I don't intend to stay here forever and I will join the living. I've just been busy working on something and I'm quite excited about it."

"Is it that suicide story?" A deep V appeared between Mac's eyebrows.

Izzy shot silent daggers at his brother. Wording it like that did him no favours. "It's a paranormal thriller. Constantine meets Mad Men in hell."

Sue's face turned white. Izzy clamped his lips, sighing

from frustration. Scandalising his deeply religious parents didn't help his case. He loved them, but at that moment, he felt like he couldn't breathe. He had to get them out of the house. Or at least out of this room.

He jumped to his feet. "Coffee or tea, anyone?"

Not waiting for a reply, he headed up the stairs. His family followed, congregating around the dining table as he served cups of tea to his mother and father. Mac and Shasa declined.

"I really hope we haven't offended you." Sue fiddled with her spoon.

Izzy smiled. "It's okay. What I was trying to say is"—he filled the teacups with steaming water—"You don't have to worry about me. I'm fine. I know I've spent a lot of time in the basement lately, but I'm not a total hermit. I'm ... seeing someone."

The lie left his lips before his mind could reel it in. His mother's face lit up with relief.

Mac threw out his arms. "You are? Since when?"

"It's new." Izzy swallowed down the acidy taste rising in his mouth.

"We'd love to meet her!" Mum enthused, and the others nodded along.

"I'm sure you'll meet her one day," Izzy replied obligingly. Obviously, this fake relationship would crash and burn before that day ever arrived.

While dishonesty niggled his conscience, the lie worked better than Izzy had dared to hope. His parents finished their tea and got to their feet, looking far more relaxed than they'd done on their arrival. He walked them to the door, making multiple promises to introduce his girlfriend when the time was right.

He could understand their worries, and maybe that was the worst part. It wasn't like he'd set out to become a social outcast. Had it been possible to have it all, he would have. He got lonely and tired of his own hand. His instant physical reaction to Mia bore evidence to the long drought. Of course, he'd rather be with a woman, but everything came at a price. He would have had to put his dreams aside and focus on making himself and his life presentable to the opposite sex. The thought exhausted him. It didn't mean he was punishing himself for anything, did it? He simply preferred his life this way, without the demands and distractions of civilised society. Staying in his own, tiny kingdom, he could pour all his energy into creative projects and achieve something.

"Was great to see you, bro! Are you coming for Sunday lunch? We're test driving the new barbecue." Mac gave him a quick hug.

"Sure, maybe. I'll let you know."

His brother cast him one last look that said 'I'll hold you to that', then released him with a smile and turned to Shasa. "Let's go, before the babysitter burns down the house."

After everyone else left, his mum lingered at the doorway, a dreamy look in her eyes. "What's her name?"

Izzy's mouth went dry as his mind went blank.

“Mia,” he finally answered. “Her name is Mia.”

Satisfied with his answer, Mum skipped down the driveway. Izzy blew out a breath, discomfort tightening his guts. It was the natural solution, wasn’t it? If he could get his surprise house guest to agree to this ruse, he could get his family off his back. Some peace and quiet without any interventions or matchmaking.

If Mia said no, he’d invent a really bad stomach flu and cancel last minute. Izzy stepped back into his house, his nerves vibrating. The poor woman had lost everything. How could he ask her for this?

Chapter 9

Mia leaned back against the door, her ears burning. This was the most uncomfortable crash-course into another person she'd ever endured, yet she could barely contain her curiosity. Hearing footsteps, she shifted closer to peek through the doorframe. It was Izzy, and he was alone.

"Are they gone?" she stage-whispered from the door.

Izzy crossed the floor and entered the bedroom, his wide chest looming over her. "Yeah. They left. Are you okay?"

Mia scrambled to her feet and snuck the books back onto the nightstand. "I'm sorry, I accidentally picked up your diary. I didn't read it. I read a bit of the other one."

Izzy glanced at the books, his body tensing. "It's not a diary. It's a project I'm working on. I use that book to write down dreams... or ideas." He cleared his throat, looking away. "I'd be surprised if you could make any sense of it."

Mia shot him an earnest look. "Honestly, I didn't read it. If you don't believe me, ask me about *Grapes of Wrath*. I'll summarise the first chapter."

He laughed. "That's okay. I'd rather you read the screenplay I'm working on."

"You're working on a screenplay?"

"Yeah. I'm also putting together a film trailer to use for pitching, but it's all computer generated and I have to update my equipment to finish it."

Mia stared at him in disbelief. "Seriously? Who're you working for?"

Izzy blinked. "Myself."

"Oh. It sounds like a big project. I thought you must have… funding." Mia shook her head, feeling hot. Had she offended him?

Izzy gave her a curt nod. "That's okay. Lots of people think I'm weird, but I have this vision I can't get out of my head, so I decided to see where it leads, you know? We only have one life."

Mia followed him to the living room, the words ringing in her ears. What was she doing with her one life?

He paused at the foot of the stairs. "You must be hungry? I'm starving."

Mia nodded, grateful that she didn't have to raise the issue. With no money on her, she felt like a leech, and the thought of asking for anything, no matter how elemental, made her uncomfortable.

"I'll order something. Do you like kebab? There's a decent place nearby." Izzy picked up his phone and sat down in his computer chair. His screens had gone to sleep, displaying the hypnotic black-and-green Matrix animation.

"Sounds great, thanks."

Feeling at a loose end, Mia sunk into the one armchair she was already familiar with. The light outside had dimmed and someone had turned on an orange floor lamp that filled the room with a cosy glow. If she didn't think about the last few hours, she could almost relax. "What kind of screenplay are you working on?"

Izzy looked up from his phone. "I'll show you later. Anything you don't eat? Onions? Chili?"

Mia shook her head. "Anything goes." She wasn't going to be picky.

Izzy held her gaze, his eyes slightly narrowed. "Anything? They make this horrible, dry falafel that sticks to the back of your throat. But if you say 'anything', I'm just going to order you that with extra jalapeños."

Mia shrugged. "Order whatever you want." The falafel sounded pretty yuck, but she'd eat it to survive.

Izzy's lips twitched. Did he have to stare at her like that? His brown gaze pierced her, like he'd drawn up and concentrated the room's energy on her. Mia shivered.

"That's ridiculous," he said gently. "I want you to tell me what you really want, and I'll order that. It doesn't have to be kebab."

"Kebab is great," Mia insisted, staring out the window. She could only detect dark shadows against the receding light in the sky. It must have been late.

"Look at me!"

The sudden uptick in volume gave Mia a start, and she obeyed, looking up. Izzy softened his expression with a hint of a smile, but his eyes wouldn't let go of her. "I understand you feel uncomfortable without your things, but there's no need to act like that. I want to help you. We can go out and buy what you need – clothes, toiletries, breakfast cereal. I know I can't replace everything you lost, but I can make you feel a little more at home. Will you let me try?"

His smile was so genuine it made her heart ache. "I'll pay you back for everything, I promise."

"You don't have to."

Mia craned her neck to see his desk. "Can I have a piece of paper and a pen? I appreciate your hospitality, I do, but I'd feel better if I could … record everything."

A shadow of disappointment crossed his face, but he picked up a small notebook, ripped out a handful of pages and handed it to her with a ballpoint pen. "There you go. But you're not allowed to list the cost of the notebook and pen, okay?"

Mia smiled in agreement. "Can I see the menu?" She asked.

Izzy offered her his phone. As she took it, her fingers brushed against his, sending an unexpected shock wave through her body. Mia pulled away and burrowed into the couch. She had to keep her hands off this guy. The chances were he wasn't at all on the same page. The traumatic events of the day had probably made her senses go haywire.

Mia focused her attention on the menu and selected a chicken and rice dish. Her mouth filled with saliva just reading the list of ingredients. It had been hours since her last meal – a tray of watery scrambled eggs she'd had on the plane.

With the food on the way, Mia picked up her notebook and wrote the cost of her meal. Seeing it on paper like a proper loan relaxed her a little. She would pay back every cent. Could she ask him to drive her to the supermarket to get a toothbrush? What about other toiletries? What about makeup? She needed a shower, but the thought of washing away everything on her skin and going completely makeup-free made her nervous. Her skin was smooth, but the combination of her short, flat-chested frame and a wispy, blond bob posed its challenges. Without some eyeliner and mascara, and a wardrobe featuring a bit of lace, she'd look like an adolescent boy. How much money would she have to borrow to maintain a resemblance of style and femininity? More importantly – was she really this high maintenance?

The soft sound of strings broke her concentration. Izzy had picked up his guitar and begun plucking a strange melody. The unassuming instrument had the warmest, richest sound she'd ever heard. Captured by the tune, she momentarily forgot her calculations.

"That's beautiful. Is it… yours?"

Izzy smiled, shaking his head. "The guitar, yes. The song,

no. It's Sufjan Stevens."

"Ah." Mia nodded. "Do you write music?"

Izzy shook his head. "I only have these half-baked ideas."

He closed his eyes and sang softly, gradually surrendering to the song his fingers teased from the strings. Mia's spine tingled. He had a voice like liquid caramel, a euphonious resonance that vibrated through her core. He finished with a single note, leaving it dangling in the air.

"You're definitely a singer," Mia whispered, sudden sadness cascading through her. This was why she had to stop dreaming about a creative career. She didn't have that kind of talent. She was better off staying on the outskirts of creativity, helping others realise their dreams. The world needed organisers, and she was an excellent one. That's what Mikko always said.

Izzy offered her his guitar. "Do you write songs? Play me something."

Mia set down her pen and rubbed her throat. It felt tight as a straw. Would the same dark force that had stolen her tears eventually steal her breath?

Izzy's eyes filled with concern. "Are you okay? Would you rather have your own guitar? I can go get it from upstairs."

Mia shook her head. She tried to clear her head from the crowding thoughts and before she could stop herself, her hands stretched out for the guitar, more to hide behind it than anything else. She was so used to hugging those smooth, wooden curves against her chest, gently fumbling her way through song ideas. Even here, the nauseating self-doubt squeezing her windpipe and freezing her fingers, holding a guitar grounded her.

"I've never played for anyone else. It's just ... meditation," she explained breathlessly. "Just like some people play candy crush or take baths or something, you know? I'm not a musician."

Izzy gave her an encouraging smile. Mia embraced the guitar, which felt much bigger than her own. Her heart thumped so hard she could sense its echo in the wooden chamber. She couldn't play for him.

"Izzy!" A muffled sound carried from upstairs.

Izzy flashed Mia an apologetic grin. "That's my flatmate Deke. I... should talk to him. Do you mind? I'll introduce you a bit later."

"No, that's fine."

Izzy glanced at his phone. "The food will be here soon. I'll bring it with me and we can eat here."

Mia listened to his receding footsteps, grateful for the moment alone. Izzy's presence made her jittery. It wasn't just the current that passed between them through an accidental touch. It was the creative expression all around her – the notebooks, screenplays and music. That someone chose to devote hours, days, and weeks on something so unproductive and fanciful. The thought gnawed at her. Kids did art at school to pass time, but most people had to grow up and become productive members of society, right? She could almost hear Mikko's voice as he rolled his eyes at something to do with arts funding. Sure, they both watched movies that someone had dreamt up, but those people were one in a million. For the rest of them, especially those born in small countries, speaking an obscure language, dreaming of a movie career was a waste of time.

Mia listened to the sound of conversation upstairs, punctuated by laughs. She couldn't make out the words, but the rhythm of it soothed her, bringing back a feeling from her childhood, napping in her room while her mum and dad discussed something behind the half-open bedroom door. The adults were awake, keeping watch, allowing her to drift off, safe and sound.

Her heartbeat settling to a slower rhythm, Mia's fingers found the strings, trying out the familiar tune she'd played for the past couple of weeks. It sounded better on Izzy's guitar, softer and richer. Encouraged by the beautiful tune, she played on, and soon sang the words – a folksy, escapist pop song that had first burst out of her in Hawaii. Playing it transported her back into the small hotel room, the smell of frangipani mixing with the sickly feeling lingering in her empty stomach after the food poisoning. She'd been so relieved to keep down a bit of apple sauce, still too weak to worry about achieving anything or going anywhere. Nobody wished for those moments, yet they often offered the greatest gift – a lull that woke the imagination. She'd felt like someone else, someone with the luxury of time, filled to the brim with words and notes that needed to flow out the same way she needed to breathe.

"Beautiful." Izzy's gravelly voice cut through the room, hitching her breath.

She spun around, her face warming like a hot plate. How had she not heard him approaching? The voice still sounded from upstairs, but now that she focused her ears on it, she could only hear one person. And they weren't talking. They were singing.

Izzy followed her gaze. "Yeah, that's Deke. He sings when he cooks. He sings doing anything, really. He's got a terrible voice, but he doesn't care." Izzy laughed, plonking a large paper bag on the sofa table. "You, on the other hand..."

"I'm not a singer. I—"

"Just take the compliment. I like your sound." Izzy winked, handing her a cardboard container and a plastic fork.

The delicious smell of chicken derailed Mia's thoughts. She slid the guitar onto the couch and picked up a fork. "Thank you."

They ate in silence. The kebab reminded Mia of many she'd had at home in Helsinki. Was there an international formula for this type of meal that produced a standard outcome anywhere in the world?

As her stomach filled, her body relaxed. So what if Izzy had heard her untrained singing voice? Part of her wanted to know what he thought, not so much of her voice but the song. It had a nice hook, a melody that had captured her imagination, and she loved the way it made her feel.

Izzy set down his fork and wiped his mouth with a napkin. "That song you were playing, is it yours?"

Mia nodded, staring at his beard. He'd missed a piece of red cabbage that now hung off his beard like a Christmas ornament. She dabbed on her own face. "You've got something..."

"Do I?" Izzy's mouth stretched into a grin, those intense eyes dancing as he studied her, making no attempt to clean his beard. He stuck his chin forward, proudly dangling the curly cabbage.

Mia raised her hand to snatch the misplaced vegetable, but hesitated before touching him and just pointed at it with her finger. "Yep, right there. It doesn't bother you?"

His grin turned even sillier as he tried to peer at his own beard, eyes crossed. "No. I can't even see it."

Was he daring her to touch his face? Mia's cheeks burned. Why couldn't she feel relaxed around him? She was acting weird about touching him, and he could tell. He was testing her.

Mia steeled her nerves and threw on a bright smile. "Great. It doesn't bother me, either. I think you should add more." Her gaze flicked at the food container on the table. He'd finished the chicken and rice, leaving most of the greens behind.

Izzy picked up another piece of cabbage and tried to hang it on his beard, but as he released his fingers, it started sliding off. Acting on a reflex, Mia caught the falling piece and weaved it into his thick, dark beard. She gasped at the rough texture under her fingertips. As she made contact with his hard jaw, the familiar tingle ran through her and she trembled. She pulled her hand away, leaning back to study Izzy's cabbage-adorned beard. "Looks great!"

"Cheers. Now, play that song." He grinned, miming chords with his left hand.

Mia shook her head. "No. I'm not a singer. I just tinker with these song ideas, but I've never performed for anyone."

His eyes darkened. "Not even your partner?"

"No." Mia sucked in her lips, fighting a wave of anguish. "He... um... never asked me to."

"He knew you were writing songs, but he never asked to hear one?" Izzy stared at her, that strangely meaningful yet obscure look in his eyes. She sensed worlds upon worlds behind them, yet saw nothing, like observing a battlefield through a keyhole.

"We both had our own interests, you know. Isn't that how it goes in a long-term relationship?" Mia lifted, then dropped her shoulder, trying to keep her tone light. "I didn't ask him about cycling, either. I don't really care about bikes and he does."

Izzy leaned in. "But you must have common interests?"

"Yeah." Mia's head flooded with fragments of conversations on the business plan, pitch decks, funding... Had they talked about anything other than work? "He's been working on a start-up business and they finally secured an investor a couple of months ago. It's all been a bit of a blur."

"That sounds… exciting?" He raised his brow.

Mia nodded, a little too animatedly. "Yeah, very exciting. It's a new type of productivity app, very high tech, lots of A.I. I'm supposed to go back next week and start working on their marketing and PR. It's a great opportunity." She nodded once more for good luck, to convince herself. It almost worked.

"But you don't want to?" Izzy concluded, cocking his head like a therapist.

Was it that obvious? Mia huffed, trying to look indignant. "Does it matter? I don't have any better ideas. I'm running out of money."

Izzy held her gaze. "But your heart's not in it?"

Nausea swirled in Mia's stomach, followed by a flash of anger. "Maybe I don't have a heart? I don't even know how to cry."

"Are you sure about that?" Izzy narrowed his eyes. "Maybe you just haven't used that muscle?"

"What muscle?"

"Being vulnerable is a choice. It's pretty uncomfortable, but it's also the only way to do art, so I think it's worth it."

He reached across her to grab the guitar she'd laid on the couch. His arms brushed her knee and his scent invaded her senses. Mia held her breath, waiting for the instant pulsing in her core to settle. This was ridiculous. She was alone in a foreign country with no possessions. She certainly wasn't looking to become *more* vulnerable. Maybe she just needed to get laid. Could she risk getting involved with this guy? Have a bit of fun and then go back home. Heartless girls couldn't get their hearts broken, right?

Izzy lifted the guitar onto his lap and began playing. Mia recognised the chord progression and her heart skipped a beat. It was her song. "How do you do that? How did you just pick it up?"

He shrugged. "I listened. It's a beautiful song, caught my ear." He hummed along as he played, smiling. "I didn't catch the lyrics."

Mia smiled to herself. She'd sung and played so softly it was a wonder he'd picked up anything at all. "You have a good ear. I wish I could do that."

"I wish I could write songs."

He hummed the tune building up to the chorus. Before she could stop herself, the words floated out of her mouth. She sang along to the melody as Izzy plucked the strings, playing it so much better than she had.

A mind that is sleeping is so easy to seduce
Is it the new moon or the orbit surrounding you
I'm longing, longing for something foreign
My eyes wandering along the swaying light

Izzy backed up and played the part again, singing along with her lyrics. His mouth pulled into a lopsided grin on the word *foreign, and Mia swallowed air. Oh, God. But it was too late. The song had swept them both away. He slowed down, then picked up the pace again, progressing to the chorus, his eyebrows arched, eyes pleading for the missing words. Mia kept singing.*

Izzy finished with soft picking of the strings, turning his flaming eyes to her. "Chills." He extended his arm. "Look."

What was this obsession with goosebumps? Mia stared at the solid forearm, thick veins roping under tanned skin. She couldn't detect raised hairs, but her lady parts clearly didn't care, zeroing in on the apparent strength vibrating underneath. Those arms could easily lift her up and pin her against the wall. She took a breath, trying to focus on the song. "You played it much better than I ever have. You make it sound good."

"Don't sell yourself short. I want to hear you play." He handed over the guitar, rolling his office chair right up to her seat.

Mia accepted the instrument, mostly because she wanted to hide the sharp peaks of her nipples poking through her flimsy bra and thin, flowery top. Izzy kept staring, his gaze filled with expectation, so she played the song again from the start, only humming the melody. He listened, leaning his elbows against his knees, eyes rapt, mouthing the bits of lyrics he remembered, urging her to fill in the blanks. After a moment, Mia's mouth followed and words flowed out, filling her stomach with warmth. She'd never played for another person, not like this. No one had ever cared. No one had listened. As she played, her voice grew stronger, buoyed by his undivided attention.

No, nothing familiar, I want to feel new
Lift me higher, to the fiddlers on the roof
Buoyed by the sound, we're orbiting too

Her conscious mind decoded the words as they tumbled out of her lungs, lagging like a lazy interpreter. Had she written about wanderlust, or maybe a desire that travel alone couldn't quench? She needed to feel new, and sitting here in Izzy's cosy basement, surrounded by books, computer screens and instruments, she hardly recognised herself. Was there more to her than an unwavering work ethic? Could she be more than a valued team member? Could she be someone truly creative?

"How do you do it?" She asked after finishing the song with a simple chord, nothing like Izzy's flourish. "How do you write screenplays and make film trailers and play the guitar and not feel unproductive?"

Izzy's eyebrows sailed up. "How is that unproductive?"

Mia bit her lip. "Sorry, that's a horrible choice of words. I just meant in terms of money, you know? There's so much I want to do, but most of those options don't pay anything, so I can't really afford to give them that much time."

"Why not?" Izzy's dark gaze bore into hers, making her insides swim.

Mia swiped a wayward hair out of her eyes, lost for words.

Why indeed not? She'd thrown thousands of Euros into plane tickets and accommodation, on a whim. She worked hard to have enough money for travel and buy things. "Do you travel a lot?" she asked, hoping to change the subject.

Izzy hung his head a little, giving it a slow shake. "No. I don't spend on anything else, really. That's how I can afford to spend my time on these ... passion projects. It's a choice. I can't pretend it doesn't hurt sometimes. I see others going overseas and having those sort of adventures and I know I'm missing out—"

"No!" Mia's hand flew to his arm, their knees bumping together. "You're not! You've found something. You have something here... I'm jealous of it, and I haven't even seen what you do. But you're brave. I can already see that." She squeezed his forearm, her lungs seizing at the hard muscle that twitched under her palm. Was she being supportive or just looking for excuses to touch him? Mia cringed at the stab of her conscience, but held on, her whole body vibrating on high alert like a flat battery plugged into a charger.

Izzy huffed, his gaze on her hand, but held still. Too still. Mia brushed her thumb across his black arm hair. She could see the goosebumps now, and they seemed to transfer onto her own skin. How long could she stay here, locked into his warm skin, enjoying the cascade of heat that pooled in all the right places?

"Would you like to see the movie trailer?" Izzy asked, lifting his eyes up to her.

Mia pulled her hand away on a sharp inhale. "Yes, please!"

Izzy invited her to the computer screens, clicked his mouse and brought up a video window. "Now, this is only three minutes. The whole thing will be about half an hour, but like I said, I just can't render it on this computer. I'm saving for a whole new production suite, like the one Weta Digital used for the Marvel movies."

Mia's eyes rounded. "How much is that going to cost?"

"A shit ton."

"Sounds great."

His mouth curved into a regretful smile. "Yeah, no travel for the next ten years."

He hit 'play' and an image of a dark prison cell filled the screen. A single lightbulb swayed in the middle, illuminating a naked man who lay face down on the concrete floor. He stirred to life, rising to sitting, looking around. His face looked familiar.

"Who's the actor?" Mia asked.

"It's ... not really a person. It's computer-generated."

Mia did a double take, blinking at the screen. The naked young man on the screen was real. There was no question about it. He had to be. "But he looks like a real person. That's a real person!"

"Deke played the part in a motion capture suit, but we put a slightly different face on him—"

"Like a deepfake?"

"Sort of, except the character was created by an artist, so

it's not really any living person. Does that make sense?"

Mia frowned. "Technically, yes. But why? Surely you could get an actor who looks the part to play the role..."

She lost her train of thought, her attention back on the screen. A haggard old man, in a soaking wet uniform, sat on a bunk bed and addressed the naked guy. 'You thought the pain would be over?' he asked. The naked man stared at him, confused.

Izzy pointed at the old guy. "My brother played that part and then we aged him." His face split into a grin. "I know it sounds weird, but I save so much time and money that way."

The video continued with the old guy introducing himself as Friday. 'Born on a Friday, died on a Monday,' he said rather cheerfully. The video screen turned black.

Izzy's shoulders dropped. "That's all I have so far. It took forever to render, and I fried one of my hard drives, so I have to upgrade the gear before I can go on."

"That's amazing! I can't believe that's computer generated. It doesn't look awkward or fake like... you know."

"CGI has come a long way since Polar Express." Izzy laughed, then looked up as a heavy bass vibrated through the building. Someone was playing music upstairs. "Do you want a drink? I think I have a couple of beers. I can introduce you to Deke. You guys should know each other, living in the same house and all."

Living? Mia shook her head at the thought, but followed Izzy upstairs.

Chapter 10

They found Deke at the dining table, eating a massive portion of nachos with store-bought jars of salsa, guacamole and sour cream arranged around his plate. Salsa music blasted from another room and he bobbed to the beat with a cheery grin on his face.

Whatever Mia had imagined, Deke wasn't any of it. He was skinny, with round cheeks and an adorable baby face. His hair resembled a clown wig, down to its orange colour. He wore a shirt, or rather a blouse, with flared arms and a happy sunflower print. It had to be from a women's collection.

At the sight of Mia, Deke stood up, his eyes sparkling with excitement. He crossed the floor in two giant steps and took Mia's hand before she had a chance to extend it. "Wow! You're so pretty!" He turned to Izzy. "Isn't she pretty?" His rough, worn jeans offered an odd contrast to the ultra-feminine shirt, like someone had been playing with two halves of male and female paper dolls.

Izzy cleared his throat. "Sure. Look, Deke, this is Mia.

She's staying with us for a while. I thought I'd introduce you guys."

"Absolutely. Absolutely. It'll be an honour, mi' lady!" Deke performed an awkward curtsy, swirling his hand in the air.

"What's with the shirt?" Izzy asked, his voice a bit wary.

"Ah, this one?" Deke grinned. "Mum Marie Kondo'ed her house and this wasn't bringing her joy, so I took it in case of an emergency."

Izzy opened the fridge, letting out an audible sigh. "What's the emergency?"

Deke returned to his meal, gesturing Mia to join him. "I haven't done laundry in a while." He lifted his nacho plate to Mia, but she shook her head, smiling.

Something about Izzy's flatmate immediately put her at ease, exactly the opposite of how she felt with Izzy. Deke grinned, diving back to his meal. The room filled with the sound of his crunchy chewing, chorused by the Latin dance track that made Mia feel like she was attending a Zumba class. She wondered if Despacito was next on his playlist, and if her body would launch into an involuntary choreography.

Izzy took a seat next to her, handing her an opened bottle of beer. Mia thanked him and took a sip, trying to remember the last time she'd drunk beer. Well, if she was looking for something new, this was perfect. The beer tasted malty and strong, nothing like the watery piss she remembered from her youth; bottles she'd hidden inside woollen socks and stuffed under her bed to keep her parents from finding them before Friday night.

"So Deke, what do you do?" she asked, raising her voice over the music. "I mean, do you study or work or...?" Mia flashed him a nervous smile. Was there a third option?

Deke raised a pair of round, blue eyes at her. "I'm an actor, but when I'm between acting gigs, I do other stuff. Earlier this week, I was a hair model." He pointed at the orange cloud framing his head. "I like to volunteer."

Izzy nodded in confirmation. "Deke's very agreeable. You can talk him into doing pretty much anything."

Deke grinned back. "It's true, but Izzy can talk me out of things as well. He makes sure I don't do anything stupid or embarrass myself. You see, I'm looking for true love and I don't want to miss my chance if I meet the one."

Mia searched his face for hints of sarcasm, but came up with nothing. She glanced at Izzy, who quickly hid his smile. "I don't always get there in time," he explained. "But we've agreed he shouldn't get a tattoo without my written consent." He lowered his voice, giving Deke a meaningful look. "And we've talked about borrowing your mum's clothes, haven't we? Even if they fit. Nothing wrong with cross dressing, but it might signal that you're *not* looking for a girlfriend."

Deke frowned like a hurt toddler. "I haven't left the house, have I? I wasn't expecting female company." Deke eyed Mia with such open interest that she felt a giggle bubbling in her chest and clamped her lips together to stop it from escaping. "But now that I find myself in this situation, I'm happy to change into something... um, butch." He turned back to Izzy, wiping salsa off his chin. "Can I borrow one of your shirts?"

Izzy's face palm was GIF-worthy. "Just do your laundry, man!"

Deke's gaze flicked between the two of them, his smile softening into a look of solemn understanding. "I can see she's taken. I'll back off."

Izzy took a swig of his beer, grumbling something incoherent. Mia wasn't sure what was going on, but her breath came in shallow gasps as she observed his sudden discomfort. Had Izzy just claimed ownership of her? She should have been outraged, but part of her felt inexplicably thrilled.

As if on cue, Despacito burst from the speakers, and Mia's mouth stretched into a ridiculous grin. She set down her beer and let her hands do the dance they remembered, weaving in the air, drawing her shoulders and upper body with them. Something new indeed. Dancing outside of the dance class, even if only with her hands, was so out of character it felt like an out-of-body experience.

Deke dropped a corn chip and stood up. "Oh, please show me the steps!"

He circled the table and grabbed Mia's hand, pulling her up to standing. Captured by his child-like enthusiasm, she danced, her body remembering what her mind would have never recalled. She danced and Deke imitated her movements, picking up the routine fast, moving as gracefully as a scarecrow being whipped around by gusts of wind. They both laughed, holding eye contact. From the corner of her eye, she noticed Izzy sitting up in his chair, his gaze glued to her body. Was he angry with her? Was she not supposed to goof around with his flatmate? Was he jealous?

Mia shook her head at the thought, launching into the quick spins that went with the chorus. Deke followed, laughing as his arm whipped against the kitchen counter. Once he got the steps somewhat down, she turned to extend her hand to Izzy. "Come on, join us!"

A wan smile crossed his face, but he didn't move. "That's okay." He lifted his beer to his lips and held it there, frozen.

Mia turned back to Deke and danced the rest of the song, all the way to the grand finish. Giggling and out-of-breath, she collapsed back into her seat. Well, that was a first.

"I challenge you to a duel over this woman!" Deke exclaimed between bursts of laughter, pointing at Izzy with a kitchen knife.

Izzy whipped his hand away like an irritating fly. "She has a boyfriend."

Deke sat across the table, raising his brow at Mia. "You do?"

Mia nodded, giving him a meek smile. "It's strange," she mused, desperate for another subject. "I've gone to the same dance class for years and I've never danced outside of it. I mean, never those same steps."

"Really?" Deke stared at her with his jaw hanging. "Why not?"

"I felt embarrassed, I think. And you don't really hear this music outside of the Zumba class, so I've never really felt like... you know. Without the music, I wouldn't ever remember the steps."

Izzy's face brightened. "Music is amazing. It literally lights up pathways in your brain. That's how I get ideas... I'm not much of a dancer, but I lie on the ground and just listen to music. Have you ever listened to music under the stars? I drive further out so there's no light pollution and lie in the middle of a field."

"Once he lay on cow shit." Deke chuckled.

Izzy sunk his teeth into his bottom lip. "Yeah. I quickly learned to bring a picnic blanket."

Mia laughed, enjoying the mellow warmth that pooled in her belly. "A blanket sounds like a good idea. I love that... starry sky and headphones. Sounds perfect."

She hid behind her beer, her cheeks hot. Oops. The drink must have gone straight into her head. Was she trying to invite herself to a dark, remote field with a stranger? But he wasn't a stranger anymore, her heart argued, squeezing at the sight of the burly man next to her. She was learning about him and getting more intrigued by the moment.

The playlist ended, filling the kitchen with a heavy silence, punctuated with Deke's chewing. Then a strange screeching sound pierced the air, coming from the hallway.

"Don't worry, that's my parrot," Deke said, swiping the last chip. "I can introduce you—"

"If you need anything from the shops, we should go now," Izzy cut in, an edge in his voice. He gestured to the clock on the wall. "We can take the headphones and go by the field on the way back if you want. Let's see if the sky's clear."

Mia straightened up in her chair, her head spinning. She desperately needed toiletries, clean underwear and some basic makeup. Could she ask for him to pay for all that? She cast an apologetic look at Deke. "I'd love to meet your parrot, but I don't even have a toothbrush."

Deke nodded. "No worries. You should go, everything closes at ten. Don't forget condoms!" Mia's lungs flattened at the sound of his cheery voice, and she fought to keep her composure.

Izzy slapped the back of his friend's head as he traipsed past. "Shut up." He gestured Mia towards the door. "Don't mind him. He carries condoms everywhere." He glanced at the basement stairs. "I'll get my wallet and the headphones and we can go."

"Okay," Mia agreed breathlessly, turning her attention to Deke. This guy baffled her. "I thought you were looking for... true love?"

Deke's round eyes radiated odd sincerity. "Yeah. You never know where it hits you, right?"

"You really think it'll hit you so hard that there's no time to go shopping... for condoms?" Mia bit down her smile.

Deke shrugged. "Could happen." He got up and dropped his empty nacho dish in the sink. Mia stared at his back, wondering what it would be like to possess such unwavering optimism.

Izzy reappeared, slightly out of breath, carrying a large gym bag. Had he run? Mia shot him a questioning look. "Are we staying overnight or something?"

"Nah, this is just the only bag I own." He froze for a second, studying her face. "You ready?"

Mia breathed deeply to calm her nerves and headed for the door. At the steps, she hesitated for a split second, her hands feeling for a handbag, keys, phone, anything… then she remembered. Her shoulders sagged and she trailed Izzy to his car.

She had nothing left to lose, except her life. Could she trust him with it?

Chapter 11

"Can we go to the shop first?" Mia asked, buckling the seatbelt and pulling her knees to her chest.

"Yeah, that's the plan." Izzy eyed her, a hint of concern crossing his face. "We can skip the music and... stars. We don't have to. What Deke said, I—"

"It's okay. I don't mind him. He's funny."

"You like funny?" A flicker of a smile.

Mia considered the question. Based on her choice of dating Mikko, the answer was no. How had she ended up with such a serious guy? "I haven't laughed like that in ages," she admitted. "Like I'd forgotten how to be silly. But here, it feels easier. Must be some kind of New Zealand magic." A shy smile broke out as she thought of herself pirouetting in his kitchen.

"Believe it or not, that was the first time I've seen Deke dancing. Maybe you're the funny one – the wild one who gets everyone riled up." Izzy shot her a meaningful look and started the engine, steering them onto the dark, quiet suburban road.

"Ha-ha." Her, the wild one? Yeah, right.

"No, seriously. I was close to joining you guys. My foot started tapping to the music. I had to hide it under the table. Two more minutes and I would have been doing some kind of godawful river dance to salsa music."

Mia laughed. "Surely you can do the basic white man dance of shifting your weight from one leg to the other? Could it really be worse than Deke?"

Izzy widened his eyes. "Oh, yes. Deke's shameless. Whatever he does, he's owning it. I'd be doing the white man weight shifting and looking like I'd rather be dead. Nothing worse than that."

"I'd love to see it," Mia teased. "I'd join you, I promise, and shift my weight in sync with you and look more uncomfortable."

Izzy shook his head. "Sorry, that's not possible. I'm the king of awkward social situations, in case you haven't noticed."

Mia blushed. He must have been talking about his family's visit. The intervention. Could she let him know how much she'd heard? Mia opened her mouth and quickly closed it again, lost in his beautiful profile, painted by the passing streetlights. His dark eyes caught the bright lights, reflecting them back like two stars in the night sky. With the chocolate brown tangle of curls and the never-ending beard, he should have been an absolute caveman. But no. He was still gorgeous. He couldn't hide it.

They stopped at traffic lights and Izzy turned to her, catching her staring. His gaze lingered on her, dipping to her lips, sending shivers down her spine. Mia broke the eye contact, scared her face would betray her thoughts.

"You're not that awkward," she mused, casting a sideways glance at him.

He could joke all he wanted, but he had a quiet strength about him she couldn't ignore, a presence that sucked the air out of her lungs. There was nothing awkward about him, not in the way she was used to. "I've been around so much awkward I measure with a different yardstick. You should see Mikko talking to the media. That's awkward. Make him speak in English and he sounds more robotic than A.I.!" Mia tried to laugh, but the way Izzy tensed made her swallow the sound.

"Mikko?" The way he pronounced the name made it sound like Ikea furniture. "Does he talk to the media a lot?"

Mia squirmed in her seat, staring at the traffic lights that seemed to take forever to change. Why had she brought up Mikko? She didn't want to think about the guy, not now. "He tries to avoid it," she explained. "That's why he wants me to come back and work for him, do it for him."

"But you're not sure?"

Izzy's knuckles tightened around the steering wheel. The light changed and he surged forward, accelerating to join the motorway. His whole body seemed like it worked hard to restrain something more volatile and explosive that lurked underneath. It both scared and attracted her.

"I'm not sure about his business or ... us. That's why I left."

"But you haven't told him yes or no, have you?"

"No, not yet."

Izzy's expression hardened as he sped down the curving road. How far was this shop? After a moment, he came up a ramp again, navigated two roundabouts and parked in front of a big supermarket, its green signage glowing in the night. "Here we are."

Izzy fished his wallet out of his back pocket, pulled out a Visa card and handed it to her. "If you keep it under 180 dollars, you won't need a pin code; just tap the card on the reader."

Mia stared at the card but made no attempt to touch it. "You don't have any cash?"

"No, sorry. But there's an ATM outside the shop, if you want me to get cash out." He looked out the window. "Can you also pick up some drinks? And maybe some antacid. I got heartburn from those jalapeños. There's a pharmacy there at the other end—"

"Maybe it's better if you come with me?" Mia smiled.

Izzy straightened in his seat, a small muscle on his neck twitching. The way he stared at the shop gave Mia pause. He'd told her he didn't enjoy shopping. Was he so uncomfortable he'd rather stay in the car?

Mia cleared her throat. "I didn't mean you have to come with me. I just thought it might be—"

Izzy unfastened his seatbelt in one swift motion and burst out of the car so fast she couldn't finish her sentence. Mia ran after him towards the halogen-lit interior glowing behind the sliding doors, an uneasy feeling in her chest.

The supermarket was nearly empty of people but stocked with all the necessities. As they reached the doors, Izzy slowed down, gesturing for Mia to go ahead of him, his face stony.

Sensing his growing distress, Mia rushed through the aisles, gathering her necessities as fast as possible. To her relief, she found a packet of cotton underwear and socks.

Seeing the shampoos, breakfast cereal and underwear stacked in the cart, she felt an odd mix of gratitude and thrilling terror. A man she didn't know was buying her things, looking after her. Was this how mail-order brides felt? She should have been relieved he expected nothing in return, but some dirty part of her brain rebelled, wishing to submit to him. Watching the muscles in his forearms twitch as he reached for a packet of antacids, she imagined him pinning her against the wall in his basement, taking what was his. Yep. She really needed a new pair of undies right about now.

She also needed a less dirty imagination, one that could handle those smouldering looks without jumping his bones and forcing him to reject her. Because he would, no doubt. He had 'restrained gentleman' written all over him, and as long as she was technically with Mikko... that's right. Her boyfriend and potential business partner waited in Finland, and had possibly discovered her SOS message in his spam folder. He would send her money, effectively removing any need for Izzy's help.

Mia observed Izzy's expression as she placed a bottle of liquid foundation in the cart. It was the most expensive of all the items, a name brand one in roughly the right shade with high sun protection. "I will pay you back."

Izzy nodded.

"Can I use your internet to check something later?" Mia asked as they pushed the cart to the nearest checkout.

"Sure. You can use my phone in the car. Are you done? Anything else?"

"No, this is good. Thank you so much." Mia's chest vibrated with warmth and she grabbed the side of the cart for support. Why did she feel like this? What was this wobbly messiness that had taken hold of her since she'd lost her possessions? Or, more accurately, since she'd met him. It was like her heart was trying to split at the seams, cracking every time she breathed, every time he looked at her. The choked up sensation in her throat reminded her of pending tears, a feeling she'd almost forgotten, one that had since been replaced by that hollow chest ache. But this one hovered higher, squeezing her windpipe, stinging somewhere closer to her eyes.

They returned to the car with Izzy carrying her new belongings, everything she currently had. The thought hit her as she opened the car door, taking the bag off him. She'd had a nice laptop and a fairly new phone, lacy underwear, beautiful tops and the most comfortable but stylish leather sandals. Had she appreciated them? She couldn't remember ever feeling like this, fingers stroking the rough texture of the brown paper bag, heart full of gratitude for the necessities it contained.

"Do you want to go home, or…?" Izzy eyed her from behind the wheel, chewing an antacid. He looked out the window, more relaxed now that they were out of the supermarket. "The sky is still clear. If we drive to Till's Landing—"

"Let's!" Mia hugged herself. She wanted to hold on to this feeling. If it was possible she may rediscover tears… She hadn't even realised how much she wanted that, but now that she felt them stirring somewhere deep inside, she felt like moments from striking gold. Tiredness had seeped into her muscles again, dragging her towards sleep, but she wasn't ready to give in. "Take me anywhere you want."

Chapter 12

Izzy swallowed the remnants of the antacid tablet, trying to ignore the volatile energy vibrating through him. Had she just said 'take me anywhere you want'? Did she not understand that she wasn't allowed to use language like that around him? He already worked full time to keep his dick from getting the wrong idea, to respect the fact she was involved with someone else. Had he been alone in the car, Izzy would have rolled down the window and stuck his head out into the cool night air – anything to sober up and stop inhaling her scent. Her wispy, blond hair glowed in the light of the streetlamps like she was some kind of mythical creature.

"May I use your phone now?" She asked, her voice wavering.

"Sure."

Izzy unlocked his phone and watched from the corner of his eye as she opened a browser window and navigated an orange website he'd never seen before. After a moment, she blew out a deep sigh.

"Bad news?"

"It's just… I left a message for Mikko through this newsletter site, because I couldn't get into my email, but he hasn't seen it, I think. There's no response. Nobody has edited the template I created."

"You created a newsletter template to contact your boyfriend?" Izzy forced himself to use the word 'boyfriend', hoping his body would get the message.

Mia shifted in her seat, dropping his phone on the middle console. "Yeah, I had to get creative. But clearly it wasn't the best idea."

"If you don't mind me asking, what did you ask him to do? Can he somehow get you a new passport or something?"

Mia shook her head, her mouth curving into a sad smile. "No. To be honest, he can't do much from Finland. I was just hoping he could wire me some money. I didn't really want to contact him. Not like this. I'm supposed to let him know when I'm ready to sign the contract and start my job. It's a bit awkward. I'm afraid I'll—"

"Feel obligated to take the job if you accept his help?" Izzy finished for her.

"Yes! I hate it." Mia gathered her knees against her body and dropped her chin against them.

"In that case, don't worry about it. I'll lend you whatever you need and you can make an unbiased decision."

Izzy held his breath, letting the suggestion hang in the air. For a moment, Mia sat in silence, staring out the window.

Izzy tried to focus on driving and not on how much he wanted her to say yes, how much he wanted to cut those ties to the man on the other side of the world who could probably offer her far more than he ever could. Even if rejecting the job didn't really make her single or available. But still...

"Okay. Thank you," she finally whispered, lifting her eyes to him. Izzy only allowed himself a brief glance at the picture perfect face framed by dreamy blond hair. Any longer, and he would have driven off the road.

"I love that house!" Mia pointed at the old fashioned villa behind a white picket fence. It was one of the nicer ones in a fairly rough neighbourhood. She sounded happier, lighter.

Izzy smiled at her enthusiasm, turning onto a quiet road that led towards the edge of town. He'd been gathering courage to ask her to pose as his girlfriend, but so far, hadn't found the right moment. The longer he waited, the weirder it would sound. The more he offered her money and help, the more it would sound like a transaction. Izzy ran a hand across his face, grimacing. It would be weird either way. He could tell she still felt unsure about him. Deke's comments hadn't helped.

He decided to wait until they were out of the car, so she didn't feel trapped with him and had the option of walking away. Although, where could she go? He wouldn't let her run off. It wasn't safe. How could he ask her without making her feel like she was obligated to help him? And why was he agonising about this so much? If she felt obligated and ended up helping him out, wasn't that a great outcome? Izzy felt like shouting.

"Are you okay?" Mia asked.

"Yeah." Izzy scratched his beard. "I just want to make it clear that accepting my help doesn't obligate you in any way. Do you understand me?"

He sucked in a sharp breath, glancing at Mia's huge eyes. They flickered in the flashing night lights, her lids dipping slowly, as if in a daze. She looked tired and overwhelmed, but nodded. "I understand."

Izzy parked at the side of the road, grabbed the picnic blanket from the car boot, and they headed to the quiet, dark reserve. There were hardly ever people around Till's Landing. Locals walked their dogs up and down the hill in the daytime, but at night, only thick humidity and silence hung in the air. They stopped under the last street light at the end of the cul-de-sac, staring into the pitch black ahead.

"It's a short walk, but pretty steep." Izzy glanced at Mia's flimsy sandals. "And there are no lights, which is kind of the point, but..."

Mia rubbed her arms, glancing at the dark hill. "Do you think it'll get a lot colder?"

Izzy's gut tightened. He mostly ran too hot himself, but hadn't considered Mia's outfit. Her micro shorts and flowery top didn't look like the right gear for this. "You might get cold."

She pursed her lips, looking up at him apologetically

through a fringe of dark lashes. He wondered if they were golden brown under the mascara, just like her eyebrows. "I don't have any other clothes."

Izzy ran his hand through his hair, scratching the back of his neck. "We should have gone shopping earlier to get you some clothes. Nothing's open at this hour. I'm sorry."

"No, it's fine. I wasn't expecting to get a new wardrobe tonight. I'm just thrilled I don't have to sleep in the women's shelter, or in jail."

Izzy's breath trapped in his windpipe. "Are you serious?"

"Yeah, that's what the receptionist told me at the police station. That's why I called you. I don't know anyone else in New Zealand. Not that I really know you, either, but..."

Her face contorted in apology, fingers rubbing her bare arms as she hugged herself against the cold. Izzy's heart climbed up his throat. "Wait here. I might have something in the car."

He ran back and searched the boot for anything useful. A hoodie! Perfect. It'd be several sizes too big, but maybe that was an advantage. In a spare gym bag, he also located a pair of clean socks and added those to his offerings.

The grateful look on Mia's face as it emerged from the neckline of the hoodie warmed him like a hug. The hoodie reached her mid-thigh, completely covering the tiny shorts he'd enjoyed earlier. He'd tried hard not to look at her that way, but he was only human, and this woman had the most tempting bottom he'd ever seen.

Mia let out an uneven sigh, slipping her arms in the sleeves and resuming the tight hug of her middle. She seemed to spend most of the time with her arms wrapped around herself in a tight little package – one he longed to unwrap. He'd unwind those arms and kiss her senseless, make her every muscle relax... Nope. She had a boyfriend. She also had a home country on the other side of the planet and he needed to pull his mind out of the gutter.

Izzy took out his phone and turned on the flashlight, leading the way up the hill. With every step, he doubted the idea a little more. Why had he brought her here? This was where he came to listen to music and wait for those elusive film ideas that might turn into something. There was nothing to see here, in the pitch dark, other than the stars. Although... Izzy looked up, past the black treetops at the sky. A layer of clouds had gathered, leaving only a patch of starry sky peeking through. As they climbed higher, he felt the wind picking up, pushing against their backs. This was the worst introduction to New Zealand he could possibly have thought of.

"Everything smells so different," Mia said, her voice full of wonder. "Like I'm eyes closed inside a bouquet of flowers. It's so fresh, but not cold."

Izzy's shoulders dropped and he let out a sigh, guiding her to the top of the hill overlooking farmland, which in the dark looked like a big, open plain. Izzy spread out the picnic blanket and they sat down. He wiggled the two pairs of studio headphones out of his bag, handing the slightly better ones to Mia. "Ready?"

"So, we just lie down and listen to music?" She sat with her knees inside the hoodie and the hood drawn over her head, her nervous laughter almost disappearing inside the pile of cotton.

Izzy browsed his phone for the right playlist, wondering if she'd like any of the songs. He felt his confidence waning. "We don't have to, if you're too cold."

"No, it's fine. I want to try." She shifted inside the hoodie. "My legs will get cold, but I'll just do it for a little while and then I can warm up again like this." She hugged herself tighter, turning into a dark lump someone could have mistaken for a rock. Izzy imagined hugging her small body against himself to keep her warm. His arms twitched at that thought and he focused on his phone, his thumb hovering above the play button for so long the screensaver appeared, feeding up dismissed notifications. The top one was a text message from Mac:

Barbecue at ours on Sunday lunchtime! We're all looking forward to meeting your girlfriend. Mum won't stop talking about it, but I promise we'll all behave :)

Izzy bristled. Sunday? He'd have to get out of that. Even if Mia agreed to play the part, Sunday was too soon. But then again, if he wanted this to work out, he had to ask her. It was getting colder, the wind raising the hairs on his skin. "Mia?" He asked, his voice rough, throat tight.

"Yeah?"

"I have something to ask you. And I know it will make me sound like a dick since I just told you I don't expect anything from you. I don't! I mean it. But..."

"What? It's okay, I'd love to do something for you, if I can."

The earnest hope in her voice gave Izzy chills. Or maybe it was the wind, now pushing at their faces like it couldn't decide which way to blow.

"The thing is, I've been kind of focused on work and these creative projects, filmmaking mostly, so I haven't had much of a social life or ... you know." His words hung in the darkness, thick and regretful.

Mia leaned closer, her soft voice rising just above the sound of wind, matching his sombre tone. "I heard your family talking about you. I mean the intervention. Sorry, I tried not to listen, and should have blocked my ears, but I... didn't."

He caught the faint light of his phone screen reflecting off her eyes. There was remorse, but no judgment.

Izzy grimaced, his mind desperately scrambling the worst parts of that conversation. What had she heard? What did she think of him? He rubbed his temples, tucking his fingers into his hair. Too much hair. Too much beard. He recalled her expression when she'd first laid eyes on him. That's what she'd seen – an absolute caveman with no social skills or social life, an impression that his ever-so-helpful family had promptly confirmed. God dammit. For the first time in five years a woman entered his life, albeit a temporary visitor, and the cards were thoroughly stacked against him.

"It's okay," he said quietly. "I'm not going to pretend I'm something that I'm not. But I have my reasons, you know... reasons I prefer my life the way it is. It works for me. I have goals, these nearly impossible ideas I want to see through and I'm willing to sacrifice other stuff to get there. Maybe I'm wasting my life—"

"No!" Mia's sleeve landed on his arm and her hand squeezed him through the fabric. "Please don't think I'm judging your life or anything you do. Your family sounded like they really care about you, but sometimes people don't understand. They look at their own lives and think what works for them must work for everyone else. It probably comes from a good place, but it's misguided."

Her words sent a bucket of warmth down his gut, relaxing his shoulders. He held still, hoping she wouldn't break contact. "You're right. They mean well and I hate seeing their worry... I feel like I just want to buy some time, you know? Put up a front to show them I'm okay and carry on, finish this film project. And once I'm there, I'll build up my life again, start going out and meeting people. Get a girlfriend..." Her hand slipped off his arm and he wished he could take back the words.

But her voice brought him back, soft and warm. "I get it. Sometimes you need to do things on your own schedule. It sucks when people think they know better and make you feel like you're failing. Mikko thought I should have said yes to this business proposal. It's a no-brainer, on paper, but I couldn't commit. I told him I needed time and he agreed that I could do this trip first, but I felt like he never really understood."

"How long have you guys been together?" Izzy asked.

"About three years."

Izzy couldn't help his volume jumping up. "Three years, and he offers you a *business* proposal?"

Mia shifted on the blanket, turning slightly away from him. "It's a great deal. In a way, it comes with more commitment than marriage or something like that. Like, multiple legal contracts and shares and all that." She sounded defensive.

"Sounds romantic." Izzy bit his lip on his snarky words. He had to stop antagonising this other guy. It wasn't right.

He couldn't see Mia's expression in the dark, but heard her huff in his general direction. "I know what it sounds like, but it's a good deal. He's very pragmatic. For him, it's the best thing he could offer."

"I'm sorry. I didn't mean to offend. He sounds like a smart guy."

"Very smart. He's been so patient with me, waiting for me to do this trip and make up my mind. I should be there right now, working for them. Every day I'm away, I'm costing them... And now I can't even contact him. He can't contact me. And the worst thing is..." she turned to the faint light of his phone, her expression conflicted. "I like it. I just want to hide here." She bit her bottom lip in an adorable way, her eyes flashing with guilt. "I get to pretend I'm someone else, someone who doesn't have to make decisions at all. Someone who's hanging out with a new friend in a foreign country with nothing to worry about."

Her smile nearly stole his breath away, but Izzy steeled his nerves, sensing an opening. "Well, if you like pretending, I've got a gig for you."

"Okay. What is it?"

Izzy swallowed at something that felt like a golf ball in his throat. "I'm going to a barbecue at my brother's on Sunday. Would you pretend to be my date?"

Mia stared at him from under the hood, her eyes sparkling. "A fake date? You want me to be your fake date?" Her voice rose in delight and her smile widened to show off a beautiful set of teeth.

"Yeah. I know it's a silly idea." Izzy fiddled with his phone. Maybe it was time to shut up and turn on the music.

"I love it!" Mia exclaimed. "But you know it always leads to falling in love, don't you? Like, according to every romantic comedy ever made."

Heat flushed Izzy's neck, making him snort with nervous laughter. "Yeah, I hadn't thought about that. You're right."

"I'm just teasing you," Mia softened her tone. "I'd love to play your girlfriend, if it helps with your family. It's no bother at all."

"Okay, because I'm not talking about putting on a show or

anything. I can tell them we met online and have only just met in person for the first time. Nobody would expect us to act all... you know?"

"Lovey-dovey?" She giggled, her eyes lighting up with mischief, and Izzy fought the urge to push her down on the blanket and show her she was playing with fire.

"Yeah. None of that. No matter how irresistible you find me," he said mock-reproachingly, narrowing his eyes at her.

"It'll be damn hard." She pulled a face, then laughed again, making Izzy's heart permanently lodge in his throat. He'd known her for half-a-day, and in that moment, could have sworn he was already half in love with her. This fake dating thing was a terrible idea.

"Put on your headphones. Here comes the first song."

He lay down on the blanket, focusing his eyes on the sky above. He could count the stars with one hand, most of the sky obscured by rapidly moving clouds. Mia snapped on her headphones and lay down next to him. Izzy pushed 'play' and the first song blasted through, sending a ripple of pleasure through his shivering body.

They lay still for the length of the song, watching the clouds travel, allowing them peeks of the few stars behind.

Izzy tried to relax against the cold ground and focus on the music instead of the energy between them. In the dark, with a cool breeze sweeping across, he could almost forget her, forget everything and let the music carry his imagination beyond the immediate reality. The song was one of his favourites, one with a powerful drive, sung in that impeccable style and emotion that even studio headphones couldn't ruin. Would Mia like it? It shouldn't have mattered at all whether she did, but his stomach disagreed, releasing a pack of winged creatures, pulling him out of the zone.

And that's when the first raindrops graced his skin, delivering a warning that came too little and too late. By the time they got up and removed their headphones, it was already raining.

"Okay, let's go!" Izzy stuffed the headphones in his bag while Mia rolled the blanket under her arm, and they ran down the hill, trying to follow the barely visible path leading back to the cul-de-sac and Izzy's car.

Once inside, Mia let out a long sigh, shivering against her seat. "That was fast!"

"Yeah, the weather is changeable here."

"Are you okay? You're in a T-shirt. Do you want this back?" She glanced at the hoodie and visibly relaxed when Izzy shook his head.

"No, all good." He started the car and turned up the heat before steering them back to where they'd come from. "Sorry about that."

She laughed. "About what? Did you make it rain?" She stared out the window, a dreamy look in her eyes. "I loved that song. Like, really loved it. What was it?"

"Minimum by Charlie Cunningham."

Mia nodded, looking like she was mentally filing it away.

"Can I hear it again?" she asked, pointing at the bag Izzy had stuffed between the seats.

"Yeah, sure." Izzy's heart fluttered at the thought, and he yanked the bag free and offered it to her.

Mia found the headphones and his phone, and he helped her unlock the screen and open Spotify. "Yeah, I see it here. What are these others? Can I listen to the whole playlist?" She flashed him an apologetic smile. "I mean, we can talk, but I'm quite tired and that song was amazing—"

"No, go ahead! Enjoy."

Feeling like he'd won the lottery, Izzy watched her push play and close her eyes, her head lolling against the headrest. She adored the song. He could see the pleasure and joy written on her delicate face, her lips soundlessly mouthing the words.

Izzy drove home, occasionally glancing at the phone in Mia's lap to see which song was playing. From her reactions, he could tell she loved each song as much as he did.

"Okay, we're here," he said softly after parking the car in his driveway, reluctant to break the spell.

Mia didn't hear him, so he touched her arm and she opened her eyes, her body straightening up. "Sorry. I was somewhere else. These songs... I've never heard of these bands. Where did you find them?"

"I just... search. I love finding new artists."

"I always thought, if you're not one of the big names, nobody will ever find you. Other than maybe your friends and family. Would these guys make enough money to live off their music?"

"They're not mainstream, but the good ones have a following. I love the democracy of indie music. Anyone can have a go."

"Me too!" Mia sighed, and her brow wrinkled. She handed the headphones and phone back to Izzy, grabbed her shopping bag and climbed out of the car.

The house was dark and quiet. Deke must have retreated into his bedroom. Mia found her guitar in the kitchen and brought it down to the basement with her shopping. Seeing her standing in the middle of the floor, holding all of her current possessions in one hand, rubbing her bleary eyes with the other, a surge of compassion coursed through Izzy.

"Take the bed. I'll sleep on the couch," he said, opening the bedroom door.

"Are you sure? I'm fine on the couch, if you have a sheet to throw over it and maybe a blanket... and a pillow. Any kind." She smiled apologetically for adding to the list.

Izzy shook his head. "No. I'd feel so terrible I wouldn't be able to sleep. You don't want that, do you?"

Mia stared back, her mouth hanging open, as Izzy strolled into his bedroom and ripped the sheets off his bed. He'd take the old ones and use them on the couch himself. They probably had a week's worth of life left in them. Thank goodness he'd done laundry not too long ago, and had a change of sheets for her.

Mia jumped in to help him pull the clean fitted sheet onto his double bed – a modest size he'd chosen on account of low expectations. Why waste valuable square footage on an extra-wide bed, just to keep half of it permanently empty and cold? Floor space depressed him far less.

"This is just like the fake dating thing," Mia said, a burst of giggles escaping her. "The one bed trope, you know?"

"One bed what?" Izzy paused, holding a pillow case.

"Never mind, it's silly. I've read too many romance novels, back when I still had time to read."

"Ah." Izzy blinked at her, not sure what to say. "Sorry, I haven't read that many."

He glanced through the bedroom doorway at his bookshelf, trying to think of something that qualified as romance. "So, what is this one bed thing? Is it about who gets to sleep in the bed or something?"

"It's when there's only one bed and they have to share... and, you know." She focused her energy on turning the duvet cover in her hands. "This doesn't have the holes?"

"Holes?" Izzy stepped closer to see what she was looking at. "There's a hole at the bottom where the duvet goes in." He lifted the hem to show her.

"No, I mean the small holes in the corners where you can stick your hands through and find the corners of the duvet."

"That's a brilliant idea! It would be so much easier to position the duvet inside..."

"It's not a new idea. Every duvet cover has holes ... in

Finland. Well, until today, I thought every duvet cover in the world had those holes."

Izzy shook his head. "Some inventions take their time getting down here. In fifty years, I'm sure we'll get some holes in our sheets, one way or another."

He helped Mia wiggle the duvet inside the cover, diving half inside it like he was used to doing, wondering about the absurdity of how he'd dealt with this issue his whole life. "So, are you saying you want to share the bed? It's not very big."

Mia's face turned deep pink. "No! I was joking about that... It seems to happen in so many books and movies, I suppose that's how they get the characters closer to each other and then 'bam', they fall in love." She rolled her eyes.

Seeing her so flustered thrilled Izzy more than he wanted to admit. He wanted to push her further, to see how she'd react. "So, you're playing my girlfriend at this barbecue tomorrow... we'd be tempting fate with that many romance novel plot devices, right? We'd risk falling madly in love and end up in the world's longest-distance relationship."

Mia's face fell, and her eyes widened with sobering clarity. "You're right. Good thing you have a couch."

"Yeah," Izzy agreed, gathered his own bedding off the floor and carried it to the said couch.

When he returned to the doorway, Mia had finished making up the bed. "Are you sure about this?" She asked, eyeing the bed longingly.

"Absolutely." Izzy swallowed a lump. She was so beautiful there, in her little shorts and flowery top, hair sticking out to the side, eyes reflecting the nightlight that glowed on his bedside table. "There are T-shirts in that top drawer, if you want something else to sleep in."

"Thank you. Do you mind if I just go to bed?" She gestured at the sheets, looking like her legs might give in any moment.

"No, go ahead! Good night!" Izzy grabbed the door handle. "I'll use the upstairs bathroom," he said before closing the door between them.

As he later settled on the couch, he couldn't stop thinking about those words, those jokes about falling in love, and the distance that stood between them. How could it ever work? He had to keep this woman at arm's length, otherwise she'd leave his heart in pieces. He'd been successfully avoiding heartache for years. If he ever wanted to finish his film, he had to stay the course.

Nothing could come of this charade of fake dating.

Chapter 13

Izzy found Mia in the kitchen, opening cupboards and peering into them. The cereal packet she'd chosen last night sat on the kitchen table. Bran with raisins, gag. Next to it, she had a carton of unsweetened almond milk. Double gag.

"What are you looking for? Bowls?" Izzy pointed at the tall pantry cupboard.

"Ah, thanks." Mia opened the pantry and got on her tippy toes. She wore one of his old T-shirts, one he'd ordered online, in the wrong size. It didn't look too tight on her, but hitched up as she reached for the bowl, revealing the pair of black undies she'd bought last night. She was a bit too skinny, but even in supermarket underwear, her bottom looked spectacular.

To Izzy's disappointment, she got her bowl, found herself a spoon and sat at the table.

"Is it okay if I borrow this T-shirt?" She asked, looking down at her front, which read 'Fix it in post' with an image so pixelated you couldn't tell what it was. "I felt like this message is for me, since I asked you to fix all those things in editing… Plus everything else in your drawer was gigantic."

"Keep it. It doesn't fit me. But I've had clients far worse than you." Izzy smirked, popping bread in the toaster and switching on the hot plate to fry an egg or two. Maybe he could persuade Mia to eat something with a bit of fat and flavour.

"What's with the bran and fake milk?" he asked.

Mia looked up from the bowl she'd just filled, surprised. She picked up the packet, turning in her hands. "I don't know. I thought it'd be healthy. Is this not good? Why didn't you say something in the shop?"

Izzy shrugged. "I don't know what you like. Maybe you'll love that stuff?"

Mia poured the watery-looking milk in the bowl and lowered her spoon in, eyes wide. She chewed on the first spoonful, turning to him with accusation in her eyes. "This tastes like wet cardboard! Why didn't you say anything?"

Izzy laughed, breaking two eggs on the sizzling pan. The toast popped up and he fetched two plates for them. He wasn't much of a cook, but he could beat wet cardboard. "I'm sorry. I didn't know if we… enjoyed the same things. You're from the other side of the world."

Mia rolled her eyes. "Okay, from now on, please assume I'm human with taste buds, like you, and guide me away from the disgusting things in your country."

Izzy laughed, grinding pepper onto the eggs and flipping

them over. “Hating the same things doesn’t mean we love the same things, though.”

“That’s okay. Just warn me about anything like... Oh, god, it has raisins in it!” Mia’s face twisted in disgust but she kept eating. “I was so tired last night, I didn’t pay much attention.”

Izzy raided the fridge for extra goodies, and quickly built the egg sandwiches with cheddar cheese, sliced ham, and the spicy chutney he thought worked with anything. “Here you go!”

Mia stared at the plate in wonder. “You did this for me?” Her huge eyes blinked and a strange expression crossed her face.

***

Mia dropped her spoon and gripped the edge of the table, fighting the wave of emotion in her chest. This was the third time she’d felt something bubbling inside her since landing in New Zealand; each sensation a little different from the last. Whatever it was about this bear of a man that her insides reacted to, it was only getting stronger. If she had tears pushing through because of breakfast, she was in trouble.

Biting into the egg sandwich only made things worse. The delicious taste exploded in her mouth, sending a ripple of pleasure through her body. “This is so good!”

In the kitchen’s corner, Izzy fired up an espresso machine

she hadn't even noticed. "You want a coffee with that?"

"What, like a flat white?" Mia asked, proud that she'd learned the name of the most popular cafe drink on this side of the world. "Can you do that?"

"Sure," he said and got to work.

In a couple of minutes, he set the heavenly-smelling drink in a scratched orange mug next to her sandwich. "That's not almond milk, though."

"Good. I'm rethinking my dietary choices," she replied, taking a sip.

In a few minutes, Izzy joined her at the table with his own identical breakfast. Well, minus the bran. Mia had a feeling the packet would end up at the back of the pantry for years to come. She'd chalk it up to experience, like the strawberry-scented baby shampoo she'd accidentally bought. She'd been in no state to go shopping last night.

"When is the barbecue?" She asked. "I'd love to wash my clothes before that."

Izzy wiped chutney off his beard. "It's tomorrow. We should go shopping today, get you some new clothes."

Last night's discomfort returned, churning in Mia's gut. "I don't feel great spending your money. Didn't you say I could borrow something from your brother's fiancé?"

Izzy twisted his mouth. "Yeah, but... Are we still on for that fake dating thing? You haven't changed your mind?"

He looked at her with such adorable worry that Mia's mouth tugged into a smile. "I'm happy to do it if you are?

You'd be lying to your family."

Izzy looked uncomfortable. "Yeah, I thought about that. I don't really enjoy lying. I'm not a natural, but if we stick with the truth for everything else, like the part about you getting robbed, it might be easier?"

Mia gave him a slow nod. "So, you're saying, the only fake part would be the relationship, like what happened before I arrived..."

"Which would have been just emails and video calls, anyway, right?" Izzy raised his brow.

Mia chuckled. "What else could it be? Private jets?"

"Exactly," Izzy gestured with his hands, like painting a picture of their fledgling relationship in the air between them. "We... met through work, like we did. And got talking, and realised we had a lot in common, enjoyed chatting after hours, and..."

Mia cocked her head. "Does that really happen? After a few work emails?"

Izzy shook his head, smiling. "Not after *your* work emails. That's where we have to veer from the truth, slightly. Can you imagine a version of yourself that would do that?" His earnest gaze pierced her, exposing what she didn't want to see.

"You don't think I could ever get... friendly like that?"

Izzy flashed her a pained grin. "You were pretty matter of fact. No personal questions or chit chat. Nothing. And that photo of you on the company website... Not even a hint of a smile! It's terrifying."

Mia stared at him, her mouth hanging. Was that how she came across? Hurt swirling in her gut, she pursed her lips and engaged in a staring contest. "What about your dramatic silhouette? It didn't even show your face!"

"Nobody wants to see my face. I'm an editor."

Mia huffed and drained her coffee. "Yeah, okay. So, it wasn't love at first sight with the staff photos... Can I say we had a video call and you started flirting with me?" She threw him a cheeky smile.

"You can say that, but no one'll believe you."

"What then?" Mia ran her fingers through her hair, trying to think of something. How did couples meet? How could a long-distance work relationship turn into something more? Did it have to? "What if just tell the truth, that we met here when I was robbed? What difference does it make?"

Izzy straightened in his chair, his eyes lighting up. "It means we haven't been going out for very long... I mean, I'd rather pretend we met a few days earlier, not on the day that I told them..." He swallowed his words, looking like he wanted to disappear along with them.

"You told them what? When?" Mia's stomach tightened.

"You know yesterday when they came around. I kind of told them I'd met someone, just to get them off my back." Izzy hung his head, his attention firmly on the empty coffee cup.

Mia tried to process the information. "You told them we're

dating before you even asked me?"

"No! Not me and you. Only that I had a girlfriend. I didn't know if you'd agree, if anyone would, and I thought, if you didn't, I'd make some excuse and eventually tell them we broke up. I wanted them to leave me alone."

He let out a deep sigh, and Mia nodded. "I get that."

"You're a perfect ten!"

The squawk of a voice cut through their conversation, startling Mia so much she swiped her coffee cup off the table. It clanked on the linoleum floor, splitting in half. "Oh, my God!"

Deke stood in the kitchen doorway, a grey parrot on his shoulder. "Sorry, didn't mean to scare you. I'm sure Casanova didn't mean it either," he added, giving the bird an affectionate side-eye.

"We agreed the bird stays in its cage," growled Izzy, picking up the broken cup.

"I'm so sorry," Mia scrambled down on the floor to help him, too late. Their heads banged together. "Ow!"

"Beautiful girl! Beautiful girl!" Casanova piped.

"Take the bird away," Izzy told Deke, who pouted.

"I wanted Mia to meet his highness, so she knows he lives here, too."

Mia looked up, rubbing her forehead. "Nice to meet you, Casanova."

"You're gorgeous!" The bird replied.

Mia scoffed out a laugh. "The name seems very fitting."

She turned to Izzy, who'd gotten up to dispose of the ceramic pieces. "I'm sorry about the cup. I'll get you a new one when… I get money."

"Don't worry about it." He returned to the table and Deke sat down next to him, letting the parrot hop off his shoulder. It flew a short distance, settling on the back of the only unoccupied chair.

"Oh, look, he took a seat." Mia smiled, staring into Casanova's beady, black eye. "You're a clever bird, aren't you?"

"He's brilliant!" Deke beamed, his eyes still puffy from sleep. "And he has great table manners, if only Izzy would let him join us."

They both turned to look at Izzy, who glared at the parrot whilst chewing the rest of his sandwich. "Anyone who shits on the floor is not welcome in my kitchen."

As if on cue, Casanova dropped a load, which splashed against the linoleum.

"Fine," Deke grumbled, crossing the room to find a wipe. He cleaned the floor, rinsed the wipe and held out his arm for Casanova, who climbed back onto his shoulder, squawking something about beautiful girls. "He's my wingman," Deke told Mia, his eyes glowing with pride.

Mia chuckled at the pun. "I thought you were looking for true love?"

Deke raised an eyebrow. "I am! He's not. Casanova has a girl in every harbour." With the bird poised on his shoulder, he marched out of the room, shooting a hurt look at Izzy on the way.

Mia couldn't hide her amusement. "So, you don't like birds?"

Izzy's face softened. "It's a clever bird and all, but Deke's not great at cleaning after it. He put on a show for your benefit, but most of the time, the shit stays on the floor until someone steps on it." He jerked a thumb at himself.

"Yeah, that's not great." Mia winced.

"Should we go shopping then?" He asked. "We can get you some clothes for the barbecue, and for the next few days."

Mia bit her lip, feeling awkward. "I feel really weird spending your money."

Izzy cast her a frustrated look. "What do you suggest, then?" He gathered their dishes into the sink and opened the tap.

Mia shot to her feet. "I'll do that!" She leapt to the sink and tried to shove him out of the way. "You're making me feel like... I don't know, but it's not good. I need to do something. Otherwise I'll never be able to pay you back."

Izzy didn't move an inch, but turned to give her a wary look. "Write it in your notebook if it makes you feel better, but you're in my house and I'm going to treat you like a guest."

"Guests do dishes! If you stay overnight, you help out! Or is it just in Finland?" Mia let out an exasperated sigh. "Why are you being weird?"

Izzy grunted and stepped away from the sink, letting Mia in. She looked around, searching for dishwashing liquid and a brush. There was nothing. "Okay, where do you keep... everything?"

Izzy flashed her an infuriating grin, opening the cupboard under the sink.

Mia grabbed the dishwashing liquid and searched the cupboard in confusion. "There's no brush."

"We use this." Izzy handed her a sponge.

Mia shrugged off her confusion and filled the sink. She'd wash the dishes with her palm if she had to.

"You know," Izzy said. "If you think about this whole thing from the fake relationship perspective, it's not that weird."

"What do you mean?"

He leaned on the counter and watched her every movement, making her nervous. "I mean, if we want to sell this fake relationship, we should live it..." He cleared his throat, finally looking away. "I don't mean physically, but things like me buying you what you need. If you were my girlfriend, and you'd just lost everything, you'd be okay with me buying you things, right? You contacted your boyfriend in Finland and asked for help. How would this be any different?"

Mia kept her eyes on the soapy plates, trying not to let them slip off her shaky hands. "Are you saying you want to pretend we're dating even when there's no one around?" Her voice felt thick and syrupy in her throat and she tried to cover it up with laugh.

Izzy took a tea towel and dried the dishes Mia had washed. "I'm saying it would make lying easier if we didn't have to lie about everything. We wouldn't have to worry about every little detail, if it's mostly true."

Mia felt hot all over. "How about we just sleep together?" she blurted. "Then we wouldn't have to lie at all if it's so hard for you." Her laugh fizzled out. She shouldn't have used the word 'hard', or let her gaze dip down to his crotch. Too late. She could barely tear her eyes off the bulge in his jeans. She heard his sharp intake of breath and there was an honest-to-god twitch behind the zipper.

Izzy's voice was a gravelly whisper that resonated through her whole body. "Not saying I wouldn't enjoy that, but obviously, it's not an option."

She swallowed against the thickness in her throat and forced a smile. "Obviously. It was a stupid joke."

He didn't return her smile. "But seriously, your boyfriend's offering you something... you should talk to him."

Mia let out a wobbly sigh, staring back at the man her body clearly preferred. "I will." How, she had no idea. She couldn't even contact bloody Mikko. There were no moves left to make, other than keep her mitts off this bearded guy.

The admission of their mutual attraction hung in the air, sending a constant pulse to her core. How would she survive this?

"Let's go shopping then, faux boyfriend?" She said brusquely, setting the last cup down. "I'll get changed into yesterday's clothes. They should be fine for one more trip."

Her heart thumping in her ears, she rushed down the stairs into the basement.

Chapter 14

Mia watched Izzy's jaw tighten as he negotiated his car between two station wagons at the far end of the parking lot. "I have to admit, I don't enjoy malls either."

He looked so embarrassed fidgeting with his keys that Mia wanted to hug him.

"Do you want to wait in the car?" She surveyed the full parking lot. Why hadn't she considered this? It was Saturday, the day of the universal shopping mall rush.

Izzy sighed, reaching for the door. "No. It'll get way too hot. I'll find a place to sit. It'll be fine."

He sounded like he was trying to convince himself, and Mia couldn't resist placing her hand on his forearm. Why could she not stop touching this man? Izzy glanced at her hand and his mouth pulled into a faint smile before he climbed out of the car.

She waited for him to take his backpack from the boot and they walked together to the main doors. Once inside, Izzy beelined to a set of couches set up in the middle of the aisle and hid behind a large Ficus. Giving her an apologetic smile, he dug his headphones out of his backpack and plugged them into his phone. Within seconds, Mia could see Spotify lighting up on his screen. She propped herself on the couch next to him, wondering how she could ask him about the money. She still had no cash and could do no shopping without his help – a fact that made her nauseous every time she thought about it.

Before she could think of the right words, Izzy slipped her a credit card. "Just tap it on the card reader. If it asks for a pin..." He lowered the headphones around his neck and leaned into her ear, whispering slowly. "Three four four one." His hot breath filled her ear, sending a tidal wave of heat straight to her core. He lingered for a couple of seconds, his beard scratching her cheek. Before she could stop herself, an audible gasp escaped her lips. She closed her mouth, trying to swallow the tail end of the sound.

From his flicker of a smile, she could tell he'd noticed. She was probably blushing and there was nothing she could do about that. Mia sighed, trying to breathe through the embarrassment. If anything, her inappropriate sounds and expressions had helped Izzy feel more comfortable. The earlier stiffness was now replaced by a gorgeous grin as he studied her face, head tilted. "Did you memorise that or do you need me to repeat? I'd be happy to."

"Oh, God no. If they ask for a pin, I just skip that shop and go to the next one." Mia blew out a sigh, fanning herself.

His face lighting up, Izzy slipped his hand around her waist. "Don't be silly. You need to know the code. I want you to buy what you need." He leaned in again, so close his lips brushed against her ear and repeated the code, even slower than before.

Mia shifted away, slapping him playfully on the thigh. The solid, muscular thigh that would hold her safe if she straddled it. Dear Lord. "Stop it! You're not allowed to tease me like that. I can't help how my body reacts to your voice, it's just... biology. What? Stop looking at me like that!" She let out a nervous laugh, shoving his shoulder this time to avoid the thigh, but it felt like shoving a concrete wall. There was definitely no safe way to touch this man. "I'm in a foreign country. I've lost everything! I'm so easily confused right now... and we're supposed to be *fake* dating. Fake."

Izzy raised his hands, regret washing across his face. "You're right. Sorry."

Mia stood up, smoothing her shirt and jean shorts, suddenly aware of how wrinkled and in need of a wash her clothes were. Clasping Izzy's credit card, she waved at him and headed down the corridor. Reaching a display of summer hats outside of the pharmacy, she couldn't resist casting one last look over her shoulder. Izzy had put his headphones back on, but a smug smile lingered on his lips. At least she'd achieved that. Seeing him semi-relaxed and happy made her heart expand in a way she wasn't expecting. She barely knew him, but that moment felt worth any embarrassment.

And now she had his credit card. Who gave away their pin code to a stranger like that? Wandering from shop to shop, browsing the racks and figuring out what she needed for the coming days, Mia's mind kept returning to Izzy. The way he looked at her, the way he smelled, that hot breath flooding her ear… she was in trouble.

Gathering her wayward thoughts, she fixed her eyes on the sign of H&M – the first global clothing chain she recognised. Mia sprang forward, working through a mental list she'd been compiling on the way to the mall. Shorts, T-shirts, another bra, socks, tennis shoes, backpack… She couldn't remember ever standing in a shop, *needing* nearly every item her gaze fell on. What a strange feeling. After twenty minutes, she'd collected the basics and tried some on for size. Afraid to stay away for too long, she made a quick call, opting for a limited colour palette of white and blue (how very Finnish!), with a mint green backpack. Everything had to go together. As she paid for the clothes, she carefully stored the receipt to update her notebook.

Mia found Izzy where she'd left him, staring at his phone screen with a deep crease between his eyes. "All done! Are you okay?" She asked.

Izzy looked up, his face melting into a smile. "I am now. Let's go!"

Mia followed him to the car, sensing his relief as they closed the doors, leaving the world outside.

"Where should we go next?" He asked, navigating out of

the parking lot.

Mia sunk into her seat, blowing out a breath. "Can we just go back to your place?"

Izzy flashed her an incredulous look. "Are you sure? You haven't seen anything yet."

"I'm feeling a bit... spent. I'd rather lie on your couch and listen to music." Mia stretched her arms overhead, producing a genuine yawn. She wasn't really that tired, but she could tell Izzy had reached his limit. She wanted him back in his safe place, relaxed and comfortable. "Besides, I'm stuck here. I'll have time for sightseeing later."

"Okay."

He didn't sound convinced, but she noticed the subtle softening in his posture. Mia studied his side profile, chewing on her lower lip. What on earth was hiding behind the huge, bushy beard? Who was he and what had made him this way? One minute, he oozed irresistible charisma, and the next he seemed so tense and uncomfortable that she desperately wanted to save him, defend him. Either way, she couldn't keep away.

Seeing him relax, she couldn't help adding fuel to the fire. "And if we stay in, we don't have to lie about it tomorrow."

Izzy's head whipped around. "What do you mean?"

"Well, if I'm supposed to play your girlfriend and I just arrived in the country... I'm sure we wouldn't have any time for sightseeing just yet."

"We wouldn't?" His brow knitted in confusion.

Was he pretending to not understand? Mia shoved him with her shoulder. "Come on! Your long-distance girlfriend comes to town. What do you do? Take her to a museum?"

Izzy's face pulled into a lazy grin and he run his shovel-sized hand over his beard. "Yeah, nah."

"Can't go sightseeing naked, right?" She lowered her voice into a husky whisper. "And do you think I would rush to the shops to buy more underwear? I'd just wear one of your shirts with nothing under—"

"Okay, stop it before I drive off the road." His voice was gruff.

Mia flashed him a wicked smile, watching the muscle in his forearm twitch as he squeezed the steering wheel. Sure, she'd flustered herself, but it was worth it. "Payback." She grinned.

His eyebrows raised in mock innocence. "Payback for what?"

"For all that whispering in my ear! You're using that... caveman alpha male energy for evil!" She waved her hand at him, pursing her lips in disapproval.

Izzy erupted in hooting laughter. "What energy?" He puffed up his chest. "Besides, that's not the same at all. I'm driving! I can easily get us both killed. You know I haven't had a girlfriend..." his voice trailed off as darkness fell over his eyes. "I mean, I haven't even had visitors. You're playing with fire."

Was she? Mia straightened her spine, drawing a calming

breath. Maybe she needed to bring the temperature down a notch. Sparring with him filled her with delight, but every joke inched her deeper into the danger zone.

Chapter 15

Izzy shifted to make room for the persistent hard-on he couldn't get rid of. It was all her fault. He'd had this problem ever since she'd arrived in his life in those tiny shorts, and now she'd made it much worse.

He pulled up on his driveway and unfastened his seatbelt. As he reached for the door latch, he heard another engine. Deke's yellow Ford Mustang puttered as he parked next to them, waving from behind the wheel.

Mia grabbed Izzy's arm. "Wait! What do we tell him?"

"Who? Deke?" He shrugged, making another attempt to open the door, but Mia's grasp on his arm tightened.

"Yes, Deke. Is he coming to the barbecue? Does he talk to your family? He'll blow our cover!"

Izzy blinked, watching his flatmate haul two shopping bags out of his car. He wore a sleeveless shirt and a pair of wrinkled linen shorts, probably fished from the bottom of his laundry basket. Deke stopped in the middle of the path, casting them a smile over his shoulder, then skipped up the steps and disappeared into the house. Mia was right. Deke and his family knew each other. Even if they hadn't invited him to the barbecue, he might talk to one of them. Mac often chatted to him when he visited. Deke had come along to a working bee at his parents' community garden.

"You're right. I told him you have a boyfriend. How do we undo that? "

Mia stared at Deke's car, deep in thought. "Maybe you meant that you're the boyfriend. I mean, he thought you were acting a bit... possessive."

Her voice didn't waver but her cheeks reddened, and she raised her hand to her neck, hiding from his view. Izzy smiled, fighting an overwhelming desire to steal that hand and force her to meet his gaze, to feel the fire that coursed through him when he saw beneath the surface. He secured his hands around the steering wheel. "Deke's not great with secrets. He acts on impulse with little forethought. If we tell him the truth, he might let it slip."

Mia nodded slowly. "Okay. Let's stick with the same story. We met online through work, got to know each other and... you know."

Her blush was adorable.

"You mean you fell in love with my mind and decided to travel around the globe to find out if you also liked my body?"

Just like he'd hoped, Mia swung a playful arm at him and he caught it. As she raised her other arm to free herself, he secured it with his left hand, holding her hostage. She fought to free herself, muscles tensed, breath coming in short bursts.

"Come on!" She hissed, cheeks flaming red, blue eyes boring into his. "You fell in love with me but weren't brave enough to travel to Finland, so you begged me to come here."

Feeling a stab in his heart, Izzy softened his grasp but didn't let her go. "Fair enough."

"Good! Now, let me go."

He released her wrists and she pulled away, gathering her bags and exiting the car so hastily he had no hope of opening the door for her.

***

Mia tried to draw in cool air, keeping her focus on the house as she rushed to the door. Her wrists still throbbed from Izzy's touch and her legs wobbled like jelly. The way his giant hands had held her, not giving an inch as she fought with all her strength... She should have been scared... Was she scared? He overpowered her by so much. He could do anything to her.

As she reached the front door, Izzy threw his arm across to stop her. "Did I hurt you?" His voice brimmed with genuine regret and he stepped back just enough to avoid touching her.

She didn't meet his eyes. She couldn't. "No." Her voice came out in a throaty whisper and her insides trembled. If she was honest, she couldn't feel anything other than the searing heat that flooded her the moment he'd grabbed hold of her. Her body still throbbed in anticipation, longing for more. She wanted to be overpowered by him, which sounded so stupid and archaic that she wanted to kick herself.

"Are you sure? I didn't mean to..." the desperation in his voice rose to a painful level.

Mia forced herself to look up and nearly lost her train of thought as she met his searching eyes. "Relax. You didn't hurt me. You... flustered me."

"Flustered?"

The heat crept up Mia's neck and she threw him an indignant eye roll. "Come on! You know you're attractive. And huge. You can't be playful like that... it's... it's... very flustering. I'm not that much of an ice queen."

Izzy shook his head, his expression dissolving into a smile. "You're not an ice queen at all. And if it makes you feel any better, I'm constantly... flustered... around you. But I promise I'll be more careful."

Mia fixed him with a sharp stare. "How? We're meant to step in there and pretend we're together."

"Fair point." Izzy raised his hands. "Maybe we're together, but not that cuddly or hot for each other? Some couples are like that."

"Would you be like that?"

He shook his head, hiding his smile behind his hand. "No. If you were mine, I'd be all over you."

Mia let out a shaky sigh, reaching for the doorknob. This wasn't helping, and they couldn't solve anything standing at the door. "Okay. Let's just... wing it?"

"Sweet," he murmured, moving so close his beard rubbed against her hair. "I'll just act like I would, if you were mine."

He rested his hand on her waist and they stepped in, finding Deke in the kitchen, placing sunflower seeds along the dining table for Casanova, who followed the food trail with great enthusiasm. Deke looked up, his eyebrows raising suggestively. "What took you guys so long?"

"Hot damn!" croaked Casanova.

Mia smiled, her waist burning from Izzy's touch. "You know how I said I have a boyfriend? It's... um, Izzy. We thought we should tell you the truth."

Deke laughed, allowing the parrot to climb onto his shoulder. "I knew it! Please don't hide in the car because of me. I don't mind PDA."

"Good to know." Izzy slid his hand further around her waist and tugged her closer.

Her face made contact with his solid chest, and she did her best to pretend the combination of solid muscle and musky, soapy man scent didn't fire up her entire nervous system.

"How's Casanova?" she asked, turning her attention to the bird, the only safe subject around.

"Fall out of heaven? Angel! Angel!" the bird crooned, navigating along Deke's arm, back onto the table.

"He's great. I think he missed you." Deke offered Mia the

bag of seeds.

She detached herself from Izzy's side and took over feeding the parrot.

Deke grabbed a wet wipe, glancing at Izzy. "Don't worry. I'll clean after him."

"It's fine. Coffee, anyone?" Izzy lunged to the espresso machine and started working on drinks. Casanova perked up, thrilled by the attention. "Beautiful girl! Hey there gorgeous!"

Mia took a seat at the table, fascinated by the creature. Now and then, the bird paused and cocked his head, as if to study her, looking like he knew exactly what was going on. Maybe he did. Mia dropped the seeds on the table, one by one, forming a shape of a heart Casanova ate his way through.

"What was that?" she asked when she couldn't make sense of something the bird said.

"You had me at hello," Deke interpreted. "He also knows 'Did it hurt when you fell from heaven?' but I can never make him say it at the right time. Like now, when I'm with a beautiful girl."

Izzy approached the table with the coffees. He cast Deke a warning look, taking a seat next to Mia. He sat so close that their shoulders made contact and an involuntary quiver swept across Mia's body. She could sense his self-assurance, which she'd obviously fuelled earlier. Why had she told him how flustered she felt? Now that he knew, he'd take every opportunity to push her off kilter. She wouldn't survive this.

"How long have you guys lived together?" she asked.

"Almost four years." Deke lifted four fingers. "I moved in with Izzy after—"

"Film school," Izzy interrupted, shooting him a guarded look. "It was a few months after film school. We both needed to save some money and this place was a steal. For a good reason. The rent's gone up since then but it's still okay. Obviously, Deke could afford something far better than this..."

"But I like the company," Deke finished. "Do you live alone or with someone?"

"Alone. I gave up my apartment in Helsinki before I left Finland and took my things to my sister's place. She has an extra bedroom and I'd love to live with her, but she's pregnant and I think they'll need the extra space when the baby comes, so I'll have to find another flat."

"In Helsinki?" Deke stared at her in confusion and she realised her mistake.

"No, I mean... I'm not sure where I'm going to live. Izzy being here... I'm still figuring it all out."

"You're welcome to stay here," Deke offered. "I wouldn't mind."

"Me neither," Izzy lowered his voice, shamelessly breathing those words into her ear again.

"That's great." Mia swallowed. The man was playing a dirty game. "I'll get a shipping container for my stuff, then."

"Perfect!" Izzy's voice vibrated through her, reaching receptors she didn't know she had. Is this what he'd say if they were really dating?

"Hot damn! Hot damn!" Casanova echoed.

"I'm so happy for you!" Deke beamed, taking a big sip of his coffee. "You look cute together. Like a play on opposites. Large and small. Dark and light. Who do you think is my other half?"

"A short girl with blue hair?" Mia suggested, studying his strange, orange perm.

Deke's laugh echoed in the kitchen. "I'd be up for that!" He raised his brow. "She'd be cute, though?"

Mia tilted her head. "Well, if you're literally looking for an opposite, then maybe not."

Deke's laugh morphed into a hiccup. He nudged Izzy across the table. "Your girlfriend thinks I'm cute! How do you like that?"

Mia felt her shoulder hike up as Izzy shrugged, still attached to her side. "That's okay. She thinks I'm hot."

Mia hid behind her coffee cup, searching for a new topic. Her gaze landed on the wall clock, already edging to 1.30pm. "Is anyone else hungry? I'm happy to cook something."

Izzy got up. "No, I'll do it."

Deke also stood up, hastily cleaning the wayward bird seeds off the table. "I'm heading out to do laundry. I'm going to a singles night at my aunt's church tonight." He gestured at his sleeveless Pokémon shirt with its sprinkling of stains.

Mia jumped up to help him with the clean-up, but Izzy took the wipe off her hands. "It's his bird, let him do the cleaning." He dropped the wipe in the sink, pulled her into his arms and buried his face in her hair, inhaling deeply.

Deke finished cleaning and winked at them. "All done. I'll leave you to it." He took Casanova and headed out the door.

As the door closed behind him, Mia turned to Izzy, almost scared to look at him. "Okay. We can stop pretending now, right?"

Izzy he took a step back, breaking the contact. "Yeah."

Mia bristled. Losing his touch felt like a cold breeze. "You must be tired of having me in your space all the time? I can go out, or downstairs..."

"Okay. I can bring the food down when I'm ready."

Mia gathered her shopping bags and hurried downstairs. Gosh. She needed a cold shower. It wasn't just the throbbing between her thighs. Something about the way Izzy talked, like he was *all in*, like she was *his*, both excited and scared her. It was fake, but he wasn't. This is how he was wired, the exact opposite of every aloof guy she'd ever dated back home. They insisted on 'seeing how it goes' and 'taking time to get to know each other'. She'd felt on trial, most of the time; living together to prove she was good enough, worthy of commitment. With Mikko, she hadn't even advanced to that stage. How this bearded giant acted made no sense, yet she craved it with her whole being. Mia swallowed the hard lump that had climbed higher in her throat, her constant companion since she'd met Izzy.

It's fake, she reminded herself, heaving her shopping bags onto the couch. They were fake dating. *Fake.*

Waiting for Izzy to cook, Mia took another shower and changed into fresh clothes. She washed her old ones in the sink and hung them in the bathroom, hoping they'd dry quickly.

As she stepped back into the lounge, she found Izzy sitting on the couch and a plate of sandwiches and a bottle of apple juice on the coffee table. She joined him, leaving a respectful gap between them. "These look amazing. Thank you!"

"No problem."

They ate in silence, keeping their distance. It made sense. Yet, the distance between them distracted Mia almost as much as his touch and words had before. She couldn't wait for tomorrow and the opportunity to be together, acting like a couple. Okay. She'd officially lost the plot. Thank goodness he couldn't read her mind.

"Should we watch a movie or something?" she asked. Was there a ten-hour trilogy she could suggest that would distract her enough to survive the night?

"I have to get some work done, but I can join you later."

He fetched a laptop and a pair of headphones off his desk and placed them in her lap.

"Great. Thank you. I might just listen to some music. Do you have those playlists...?"

She opened the lid and browsed the application icons,

searching for Spotify. She hoped he'd step in and guide her, but Izzy stood firmly behind the couch. "Yeah, search under applications," he said, retreating to his desk.

They spent the afternoon in their own little worlds, headphones on. After a while, Mia relaxed, almost forgetting he was there. Listening to the new music on Izzy's playlists stirred inspiration in her gut. Checking that Izzy had his headphones on, she began humming a melody and wrote some lyrics at the back of her debt notebook. Excitement took over, and she snuck her guitar out to try some chords. Time flew as she immersed herself in the act of creation.

At dinner time, Izzy ordered sushi, and they ate on the couch, an arm's length away from each other, keeping up friendly, albeit pause-filled, chatter. Mia used the opportunity to learn about Izzy's family. She tried to set aside her first impressions – the concerned voices she'd heard through the door during the intervention – and get to know the real people. In turn, she told him about her own family, her sister Kati she missed terribly and her parents who lived up north but were planning a long trip to see the baby once she was born. Compared to Izzy's, her family was far less involved in her life, yet she sensed their expectations. Maybe the only difference between them was that Izzy had the courage to defy those expectations, whereas she'd always met them. Until now.

Still, Izzy didn't seem resentful. Hearing him talk about his family in a warm, loving tone calmed her nerves about the Sunday lunch.

"There'll be lots of food," he warned her. "So get ready for that."

Mia pulled a face. "Ugh. I need to go for a run or something."

"Actually," Izzy nodded at the rack of weights in the corner. "I need to work out. I usually just warm up here, but we could go for a run?"

Mia smiled at the thought. "I'd never keep up with you. I don't even have running shoes."

"Ah, yeah." He looked around the room, as if he might spot running shoes in her size lying around somewhere.

"That's okay. You do your thing. I'll go for a walk or something." She lifted her hand, silencing his protests. "I'll just circle the block. I won't get lost."

Izzy bounced up from his seat. "That reminds me... I have an old phone somewhere..." he started opening and closing drawers and eventually dug through a large container on his desk, pulling out cables and hard drives. "Here!" He held up a scratched Samsung. "I'll charge this, and you'll have a temporary phone. We can get a local SIM card for it from the supermarket. Sorry, I should have thought of that last night."

"Thank you!" Mia joined him, watching in anticipation as he plugged the phone into a charger and a progress bar lit up on the screen. "It's working!"

Izzy leapt up to search another box. "In fact, I might even have a SIM card. My brother brought one over when I didn't text back in a week or two... a month..." he muttered, avoiding her gaze. "It was a bit of dig, to be honest. Like, here you go, you obviously don't have a working phone number."

"Wow." Mia accepted the plastic card, still in its wrapper. She opened the package and, with shaking fingers, negotiated the tiny SIM card inside the phone, which already showed 10% charge. "Can I turn it on?" She asked, and Izzy nodded.

"I can buy you more credit from my phone. It's the same carrier."

A few minutes later, she sat in her favourite armchair, holding a working phone. It was morning in Finland. Time to check the newsletter site to see if Mikko had replied. Her fingers trembling, Mia navigated to the message she'd left him. To her shock, there was a reply right under it, saved within the same draft.

If you see this, I've received your message. Not sure how to help you, but I await further instructions.

Mia stared at the abrupt words, trying to shake the sense of disappointment. What had she expected? She hadn't given him an address, email, or a phone number. Mikko's response was entirely logical, just like he was. Besides, she was fine.

Izzy appeared from his bedroom in a sleeveless shirt, joggers and running shoes and Mia swallowed air. Those arms. They looked like they should lift cars and wrestle lions, not click a mouse in an empty basement. The way he looked made no sense.

Ignoring the rhythmic whip of the skipping rope hitting the floor, Mia got to work, creating a new Gmail address, something she probably should have done yesterday, had she not been so distracted by… well, him.

"What's your address?" she asked Izzy, allowing herself one miniscule glance at the man who was now doing bench presses, muscles bulging. Dear God. This wasn't fair.

He gave her the address between sharp exhales and grunts, spelling out the road name. Mia wrote it down and sent Mikko an email from her new address, including all her new contact details. Now, the ball was in his court. If he wanted to help, he could send her money. Mia looked up her airline's contact details and emailed them from her new address, explaining the situation and asking for her flight details. If they took pity on her, they might at least try to call the phone number she'd provided and investigate the situation.

The online errands taken care of, Mia finally wrote an email to her sister.

Dear Kati! I'm in New Zealand and first of all, don't worry. I got robbed on arrival, but I found a friend who's helping. I have a place to stay and I'm well looked after. I'm not sure how I can get a new passport sorted before the flights, but I'll try. I don't want to miss the birth of the lil' human. I swear.

She paused, fingers hovering above the screen. There was so much more she wanted to say, but no way of putting it into words, at least not without raising alarm. Mia dropped the phone in her lap and exhaled, sinking into the chair.

It was still light outside. She could go for a walk – get some fresh air and escape the gun show (Izzy was still flexing his biceps, with the mix of iron, chalk and sweat lingering in her nose).

Checking that her new phone had enough charge, Mia grabbed her backpack and headed for the stairs. "I'm going for a walk. I have the phone."

Izzy dropped two massive weights, making the floor vibrate. She heard his parting words as she entered the dark stairway. Something about staying safe. Well, that's what she was trying to do.

Chapter 16

Izzy parked outside his brother's townhouse block and hurried around the car to hold the door for Mia. It had become a game he played, to see how long it would take before she accepted his help and stopped expelling herself out of the car seat like a jack in a box. This time, he caught her stepping onto the kerb, and offered his arm for balance. She eyed it with curiosity but grabbed the car door instead.

"Is it this house?" She asked, looking at the small block of new townhouses that housed Izzy's entire family – his brother and his fiancée, mum and dad, and their friends he knew by name. He'd prepared Mia for each of them, warmed by her interest and endless questions.

"Yep. We're going to Mac and Shasa's, but all the units have a similar layout. Shasa and her friend Marnie built it together and my parents jumped onboard. They used to live in that old brick house next door. That's where I grew up." Izzy pointed at the old house, which had undergone some work since he'd last seen it, no doubt to bring it up-to-date for the tenants. The white picket fence shone from a recent coat of paint and the windows looked different. Izzy stepped closer, blinking in disbelief. They'd all suffered the state of that house for decades, and now it had new windows?

"This looks like a lovely neighbourhood." Mia spun on her heels, taking in the street view. Her white dress glowed and she squinted in the midday sun. She'd done something to her hair, making it puff up in volume and lined her eyes with black, adding a touch of drama that made Izzy's heart squeeze.

"Are you ready?" He gestured at the townhouse block.

Mia lifted her new backpack onto her shoulder and turned to face the right building. Their eyes met and nervous excitement fizzed in the air as if someone had just uncorked a bottle of champagne.

Mia's reassuring smile transformed into a silly grin. "Wait, I need to load the fake girlfriend experience! Let me just find the right disc." She fiddled with the back of her head, beaming like a broken toy.

Izzy laughed, a sense of lightness washing over him. He knew she was goofing around to ease his anxiety. He tightened his hands into fists, crushing the overwhelming desire to kiss her. "Great! Make sure you load the 'head over heels' upgrade. I want them to see you're serious about me, not just kicking tyres." He'd done so well last night, keeping his distance when they weren't around other people. This was his reward. He could walk in with this incredible creature on his arm and introduce her as his. So what if it wasn't real? What really was?

Mia locked eyes with him. "Challenge accepted!"

He led her to Mac's door and knocked, listening to the lively chatter on the other side. Shasa opened the door in a mustard yellow dress. "Hey! Welcome! I'm so glad you made it. You must be Mia." She reached her hand past Izzy to Mia, who introduced herself.

Lilla, her 5-year-old daughter, appeared behind her. As Izzy stepped across the threshold, she retreated in terror, staring at his face. Izzy flinched, smoothing down his beard. He'd only met his brother's step daughter twice before, and both times, she'd seemed reserved, which Mac had assured him wasn't like her at all.

"Lilla, come say hi. Lilla? Come on!" Shasa chased after her, but gave up as she ran upstairs. She turned to Izzy and Mia. "I'm sorry, I don't know why she's acting like that."

Izzy grimaced. "I think it's me. She's been a bit scared of me since day one. I'm not sure why."

"Could be the beard?" Mia suggested, swirling her index finger around her own face, a cheeky smile twitching her mouth.

Shasa's eyes lit with agreement. "You might be right! She's not a fan of Santa, either."

"What's wrong with beards?" Izzy asked, his brow buckling.

The women exchanged a glance.

"Nothing," Mia said. "Maybe it just needs a trim, so it looks like there's a shape of a human under there?" Her smile turned into a chuckle.

Shasa joined in. "Oh, my God! If you can get him to do something about it, you'll get into the family hall of fame!"

Mia raised an eyebrow.

"A wall in mum and dad's house where they put everyone's achievements," Izzy explained.

"You mean like degrees and awards or something?"

Shasa giggled. "No, more like participation trophies, winning play-dough sculptures from the nineties, gold stars from teachers..."

"A 15-year-old sticky note that says 'well done'," Izzy added, shaking his head. "Mum and dad believe in celebrating success, big or small."

Mia clasped her hands in delight. "I love it! I definitely want on that wall!" She narrowed her eyes at Izzy, whispering with pure glee. "I'll shave you one night when you're asleep."

Izzy laughed along but felt a tug in his gut. What if she actually did? He'd forgotten what his chin looked like.

"Everyone else is in the backyard." Shasa led them through the ground floor, dodging occasional barbies along the thick carpet, and out a set of sliding doors, towards the delicious smells drifting from the barbecue.

Mac dropped the spatula next to the steak he'd just flipped. "Izzy! You're here! And you brought a..." he did a double take, staring at Mia. "She's real." He glanced at their parents, sitting in a garden swing at the far end of the deck, urging them to get up. "Mum, dad! Come meet Izzy's girlfriend! She's real!"

Shasa shoved him. "Of course she's real. Behave!"

As Mac introduced himself and their overly excited parents to Mia, Izzy felt a stab of hurt. Had they all thought he'd been lying?

***

Mia eyed the excited faces around her, wondering why it was such a surprise to everyone that Izzy had a girlfriend. Maybe he preferred the solitude of his basement, but he wasn't unattractive or socially inept. Definitely not. He wasn't even odd like Deke, who Mia could also imagine one day finding his match.

If Izzy spent time anywhere with other people, he must have noticed the females looking at him. She'd noticed the sideways glances at the mall, during the short walk down the corridor. This morning her stomach did a little flip when he'd pulled his overgrown, unruly curls into a man bun.

Shasa excused herself to check on her daughter, and Izzy followed Mac back inside to get everyone a round of drinks. "Wine or beer?" He asked Mia at the doorway.

She shrugged. "Wine. Anything you have."

Izzy's mum approached her with a shy smile. "Hi, Mia! I'm Sue, Isaiah's mum."

"Nice to meet you." Mia took the woman's small,

weathered hand and returned the smile.

Sue wore her naturally grey hair in a feathery bob and seemed to love soft greens, which dominated both her and her husband's wardrobes. She offered Mia a plate and gestured at the barbecue, along with the outdoor table heaving with salads. "Please, dig in! It's a bit of self-service here, I'm afraid. You're not a vegan, are you?"

Mia accepted the plate, wondering how she was going to digest food with her nerves vibrating like guitar strings. "No. This all looks amazing, thank you."

Sue took a step back to give her space, and Mia began dutifully filling her plate.

John inched a bit closer to them, his plate already full of salad and steak. "Mia, was it? It's lovely to meet you! I'm afraid Izzy hasn't told us much about you. To be honest, we all doubted whether he'd show up today. He's been by himself for quite a while now." He looked over his shoulder at his son, worry and regret rippling his forehead. "You can understand this was quite a surprise."

"A delightful surprise!" Sue added, eyes shining.

Mia stared at them in disbelief. Were they really talking about the same man she'd been unable to take her eyes off for the past three days?

"So, how did you meet? Tell us the tale!" John urged.

Mia took a calming breath. Was this how actors felt right before the first take? "Izzy and I worked together remotely. That's how we met."

Their eyes widened as they took in her words, combined with her foreign accent.

"Remotely? So... where are you from?" Sue's mouth hung open.

"Finland." Mia flashed them a brazen smile, only partially prepared for the collective gasp that erupted from the old couple. "I quit my job and travelled around the world to see him."

"Really?" Sue stammered. "That's unbelievable." She sounded like she literally didn't believe her.

Sue shot a loaded look at her husband, who kept nodding like a bobblehead, and eventually found his voice. "Isaiah doesn't go out much. Not since—"

Sue gave his arm a firm squeeze. "He goes out, sometimes. I'm afraid we aren't making him sound good. He's had some rough experiences, but he's such a kind-hearted man."

John smiled. "That's right. I always thought it's better to be a good man than a great man."

Mia nodded, ladling pasta on her plate. Izzy was all that, but it hardly needed to be stated with such vehemence. "Absolutely. And he's promised to show me around New Zealand, so he'll be getting out of the house a bit more."

Izzy's parents smiled, genuinely excited. Head over heels, Izzy had said. He'd been joking, but witnessing their doubts, she felt the urge to show his family what she really saw in him.

"I'm in awe of his skills and his creative talent, to be

honest," she said, picking up a chicken drumstick. "Have you seen the movie trailer he's working on? It's epic."

Izzy's parents masked their confusion behind polite smiles.

"He's... shown you the movie thing?" Sue asked. "We know little about it to be honest. Isaiah tends to keep these things under his hat. He's always been creative though. In primary school, he wrote the most imaginative stories."

"I think it's so inspiring!" Mia took a deep breath, her hand landing on her chest. "I love filmmaking and used to work at a production company where we used Izzy as an editor. He's brilliant."

Sue rearranged her shocked mouth into a smile. "Great that you have that in common. I've never really understood his... film passions. I wish I did." She shook her head in regret, her eyes glistening.

Over her shoulder, Mia caught Izzy's gaze. He stood in the doorway, holding a glass of white wine and a beer, frozen like a statue, wearing the oddest expression on his face. Mia flashed him a smile, and he resumed motion, carrying the wineglass to her.

"Your mum was just asking about how we met, and I gave her the short version," Mia told him, peering at him over the rim of the wine glass. Goodness it smelled nice, a concoction of citrus and flowers.

"What's the long version?" Sue asked, and John perked up next to her. "I'm sorry for being nosy."

They looked at each other with such warmth and knowing that Mia's chest ached. Despite being fairly clueless about their son's passions, they seemed to care so much and worry inordinately about doing or saying the wrong thing, far more than she remembered her own parents ever worrying. They simply told her what they thought, patted her on the back, and moved on. Not that she'd given them any reason to worry. She'd followed her life plan like she'd been programmed, from a degree to a steady career path, her drive only matched by that of her boyfriend's.

Goodness, she thought with alarm. This was the longest she'd ever gone without speaking to Mikko. In Finland, they'd practically lived together. They'd spoken almost daily until she'd stepped on that plane – the first thing she'd ever done that veered from the pre-programmed success path.

"Did she tell you about the robbery?" Izzy explained what Mia had experienced within her first hours in New Zealand. "I should have met her at the airport, obviously, but she insisted she wanted to make her own way to Hamilton."

"Yes! I knew he was busy with work and I really wanted to have a look around by myself. But then he ended up picking me up anyway," Mia finished, grateful for Izzy's quick thinking. Why hadn't they considered that part of the story? A boyfriend would have picked her up, obviously.

Sue cast a reproaching look at her son. "You should have insisted a bit harder, eh? Now, look what happened! She lost everything. What a nightmare! Such a horrible start to your visit."

"It hasn't been that bad." Mia took a sip of wine, her head spinning from trying to keep the tale from unravelling. "Izzy has looked after me really well. Yesterday, he took me shopping for clothes."

Mac appeared at Izzy's side, slapping him on the back. "Shopping! Way to go, Izzy! Where did you go?"

"Chartwell mall," Izzy said, shifting in discomfort.

They all turned to stare at him in awe.

"Chartwell mall?" Sue repeated, her hand tapping at her chest like she was fanning herself. "How was it?"

"Didn't you go last weekend?" her husband asked.

"No, I mean, how was the... experience?"

"Fine." Izzy snuck Mia a dark look. "I don't really enjoy shopping. I told you I usually order online."

"No shit!" Mac laughed. "Last time Izzy went to the mall they still accepted cheques."

Izzy grunted, taking a long swig from his beer. He wiped the froth off his beard, clearly uncomfortable. "Yeah, it's been a while."

"He also took me to... Countdown, was it? I needed to get some toiletries and things like that," Mia added, trying to be helpful. Judging by Izzy's posture, she was only making it worse.

Feeling awful for him, she slipped her arm around his waist and nuzzled her head against his mile-wide chest. "Honestly, he's been the perfect host. I don't like shopping either. I'd much rather order online... But sometimes you don't have time to wait for a delivery. Like when you get robbed."

She felt Izzy relax against her. He shifted his drink to his other hand and threw his arm around her. The firm squeeze of his hand flushed her with heat, and she fought to keep her breathing steady.

Shasa joined them, holding Lilla's hand. "Hi guys! Lilla would like to say hello."

They turned to face the little girl in a unicorn dress, multi-coloured hair clips holding her dark curls. She stared at Izzy, her eyes wide. Izzy crouched down to her eye level, offering her a wide smile. "Hello, Lilla. I really like your dress. I love unicorns."

"I love unicorns!" Lilla exclaimed, forgetting to hold her mother's hand. She pointed at the one on her dress. "This one has a rainbow horn."

"I can see that," Izzy mused. "It matches your rainbow hair clip." He pointed at the one dangling from a curl framing her face.

"Do you need a hair clip?" She asked, eyeing his beard.

Mia lowered down to join the conversation. "I reckon he does! He let his facial hair grow too long and it could do with some styling. Do you have a spare clip we could use?"

Lilla nodded in earnest and ran away.

"Cheers," Izzy cast her wary glance, which quickly melted into a smile. "You really don't like the beard, do you?"

Mia swallowed. "Actually, I kind of do, but it could do with a trim."

"Noted."

Lilla returned with a unicorn clip, offering it to them with both hands like a gift from the gods. "This is my best one."

Mia accepted the little item with due reverence. "Thank you. We'll take good care of it."

With amusement dancing on her lips, she worked the hair clip into Izzy's bushy beard while he rolled his eyes, holding remarkably still. Once it was attached, he rose to his feet, displaying the new beard accessory to everyone.

Lilla clapped her hands, her face lit up with joy.

"Look at that, beards aren't that scary after all." Shasa smiled in amazement. "They're just extra hair you can style."

"Is anyone else coming?" Izzy asked, looking around at the small gathering.

"No," Shasa replied. "I was going to invite Marnie and Jason, but you know, plans changed." Her eyes widened, and she turned to Izzy and Mia. "My friend Marnie just had her baby. He came four weeks early, quite a surprise. They're still in the hospital."

"How are they?" Sue asked, her eyes filling with longing.

"Marnie is well. The baby is still in NICU but doing well. He's breathing fine, but needs to learn how to suckle."

Mac cleared his throat. "Since we're not expecting anyone else and we're all here..." he glanced at Shasa, who grinned back, eyes sparkling. "We have an announcement."

Sue looked like she might have burst a vein from excitement. “Yes?”

“We’ve set the date!” Shasa took Mac’s hand. “And it’s soon. I’m sorry guys, we meant to give you more notice since we’ve been sitting on this for so long… and in the end we decided to go with that original plan of keeping it small.”

She and Mac exchanged a starry-eyed look. “We found a wedding planner, who can do it on a friendly budget,” Mac explained.

“She lives in a tiny house!” Shasa added. “That’s why she can keep her prices so reasonable… and she found us this incredible site and glamping gear, so it’s going to be an outdoor wedding. A small one, like forty people.”

“When is it?” Sue asked, taking out her phone, worry lines appearing on her forehead.

“In four weeks,” Mac replied with a sheepish grin.

Sue glanced at her husband, who stared back at her, equally dumbfounded. “But… that’s Christmas!”

“Almost, I know. But we couldn’t find a time everyone would be off work.” Shasa’s eyes burned with mild panic. “And we really didn’t want to lose the whole summer to the wedding planning. It’s so stressful… so we wanted to get married first and then enjoy the summer.” She threw a pleading look at her fiancé.

Mac jumped in. “The point is to get married, not to have a wedding, right?”

“So, under an open sky?” Sue’s mouth twitched, working

itself into a brave smile. "It sounds very... romantic, I suppose. Let's hope the weather plays ball."

"We'll have tents!" Shasa assured, rushing to top up the wineglass she'd drained. "It'll be relaxed, but also comfortable. Ocean is amazing... she's the wedding planner. Seriously, I'm in love with her. She's taking away all the agonising and said we should just turn up."

Mac scooped her into his arms. "I'm the one who said we should hire someone to deal with all this. Do I get any points?"

Shasa pursed her lips. "One point. That's my best offer."

"I give you five million points!" Lilla shouted, hugging his knees.

Mia chuckled. These guys were adorable.

Mac turned to Mia. "How long are you in the country? We'd love to have you at the wedding!"

Mia bit her lip, thinking about the flight ticket she probably couldn't use. "I'm not sure."

"No return ticket?" Mac grinned at his brother. "Then definitely bring your plus one!"

"That's a great idea!" Sue enthused. "I think it's time for dessert." She exchanged a look with Shasa and they snuck away.

"Great." Mia smiled, taking a long sip of wine to lubricate her throat, which suddenly felt like sandpaper. She'd agreed to a casual barbecue lunch, but a wedding full of aunties and uncles? Could they take this charade that far? It probably didn't matter. She'd get her documents sorted before then and leave the country.

"So, what sights are you planning to show her?" Mac asked Izzy, nodding at Mia. "If it seems like I'm changing the subject, it's because I am."

Izzy laughed but tensed. Mia straightened, worried she was getting too cosy against him, but he tightened his arm around her shoulder, anchoring her to his side. She relaxed back into him, her body revelling in the delicious closeness. Fake as it was, her body didn't care.

"I have some ideas," Izzy said. "But I want to surprise her, so..."

Mac raised an eyebrow. "Say no more."

Something about Izzy's tone made Mia shiver with anticipation. He'd probably said it to sidestep the question, but she couldn't help the way her heart leapt at the thought. Izzy had already done so much for her, more than she remembered Mikko doing in the last couple of years. He'd been so focused on the business. That had been his excuse for everything. She'd organised her own birthdays and sent him reminders to make sure he didn't forget or double book himself.

She'd been the lowest maintenance girlfriend in the world, never needing anything... whereas with Izzy, she'd arrived in his life like a living, breathing emergency, needing his help with everything, and he'd stepped up, making her simultaneously uncomfortable and grateful. Being able to give back by playing his adoring girlfriend didn't feel right.

It was like getting paid to eat chocolate. She was enjoying herself far too much, openly touching his amazing body, staring into those brown eyes. Chocolate, indeed.

Izzy had made an effort this the morning, pairing his worn cargo shorts with a button down shirt. The wrinkled, navy blue linen had probably never seen an iron, but it had impressed her that he even owned something with buttons. He'd stopped at the door before leaving and asked if he looked okay. That flash of concern in his eyes, followed by a hopeful smile as he tried to smooth the creases on his shirt. She'd wanted to hug him right there, kiss that hairy face and tell him how attractive he was, how incredible. Instead, she'd given him a lame thumbs up. Now, finally locked into his embrace, her insides brimmed with wobbly warmth and she felt a subtle sting behind her eyes. Tears? Now? She waited a moment, holding her breath as the prickling fell away, replaced by a wistfulness.

"I don't mind where we go," she said, looking up at the unicorn hair clip dangling from his beard. "But I think we have to do a trip to Wellington to get my travel documents organised. Otherwise I'll never be able to leave."

Izzy kissed the top of her head. "Maybe I won't take you."

Mac laughed, staring at them in awe. "Look at you two!"

John washed down the last mouthful of his food with beer and cleared his throat. "So, what's the plan after your visit? Are you looking at moving here, or...?" he cast Mia a nervous glance, then shot an even more nervous one in the direction of the house. Mia wondered if Sue would have approved of this line of questioning.

"I don't know," Mia said, sensing Izzy's anticipation as he shifted his weight from left to right, making her head bump against his ribcage. She reluctantly peeled herself away from his warmth. "We haven't really figured that out yet. My sister is having a baby soon, so I have to get back for that. But maybe I can come back later. Honestly, I don't even know if I could get a visa to stay much longer."

John gave Izzy a meaningful look. "Well, there're always ways around—"

"Dad." Mac's tone held a warning.

At that moment, Shasa and Sue returned with a huge bowl of something creamy.

"Ambrosia!" Lilla shouted. She'd wandered into the garden, but returned immediately at the sight of the dessert bowl, jumping up and down like a cartoon bunny. John finished their conversation with a curt nod and joined the dessert line.

Mia glanced at the plate she'd left on the table. She'd barely made a dent in her lunch, too busy side-hugging her fake boyfriend. What if Mikko saw her now? What would he think? All these people believed them, excited about a story of a relationship that didn't exist.

They sat down at the outdoor table, enjoying the dessert and another round of drinks. Once finished with her food, Mia took the first spoonful of ambrosia and moaned. "Oh.

My. God. Where has this been all my life?"

Izzy gave her a glassy look, running his hand across his beard. Mia let out an embarrassed laugh. "Sorry. I didn't mean to make love to my dessert," she said, her cheeks flaming. "It's just so good."

"I'm sure Izzy will make you some more later," Mac replied with a wink.

Mia felt Izzy's hand on her knee under the table, sliding to touch her inner thigh. "I definitely will," he said in a gruff voice.

Despite the molten heat spreading between her thighs, Mia shot him a sharp look, and he pulled his hand away, mumbling an apology. "I think that beer went straight to my head," he complained, focusing on his own dessert.

Mia's insides throbbed as her mind caught up with the situation. There was no reason to touch her under the table. His family couldn't see his hand. It wasn't for them. She could feel his desire bursting through every look and every touch like a heat wave. How could she leave this lunch and go home with him? Without the other people as a buffer, she'd have to rely on her own willpower. What if they both caved in? She'd betray Mikko and the promise she'd made. How could she live with herself?

If only she could tell what the future held. What if they didn't have a chance, even with the attraction she sensed? Her feelings might have been brought up by the traumatic events, a circumstantial crush that would fade as soon as she returned home to reality. No one could live a fairy tale, and this felt like the most magical one she'd ever experienced. It couldn't be real.

Mac slapped Izzy on the shoulder and picked up Lilla, helping her sneak another portion of dessert. Sue and John continued to quiz Shasa on the wedding, offering helpful suggestions, clearly desperate to be more involved.

Grateful that the conversation had shifted away from her and Izzy, Mia retreated to the porch swing, tugging Izzy's hand. He followed, raising his brow as she sat down and patted the cushion next to her. "Come on, we should sit together. It'll look weird if we don't," she whispered, and he lowered himself into the seat, allowing her to snuggle up to him. "That's better."

"Uh-huh." Izzy wrapped his arm around her, settling into the seat. The swing creaked under his weight, swaying lightly. "Does it also look weird if I don't kiss you?" The rumble of his voice sent a dangerous shiver through her.

Mia held her breath for a split second half-expecting him to go for it. No. Thank goodness. If they ever kissed, which sounded like a mistake she should carefully avoid, she didn't want it to happen in the presence of his family. She gently elbowed Izzy in the ribs. "No, I don't think anyone's expecting anything from us. They seem quite preoccupied." She raised her eyebrows, listening to the fragments of wedding conversation drifting across the deck. "How long have they been engaged?"

"A year, maybe." Izzy had filled her in on his brother's story earlier, explaining how Mac had fallen in love with the tenant whose rental home he'd been trying to buy and turn into luxury condos. The modest townhouse complex, the current location of their barbecue, now stood in its place, built by Shasa with Mac's help. "Mac lost a lot of money with that condo deal and he had to start over. He's been working for a 3D house printing company and they've been saving money for the wedding."

"I'm glad they've decided not to spend that much. That sounds smart."

"You're not one of those women who've always wanted a big, fairy tale wedding?" Izzy asked, a tentative smile playing on his lips.

Mia scoffed. "Seriously? I was considering a *business* proposal because I thought it was the closest thing to a proposal I'm ever going to get." The words tumbled out of her mouth and her hand flew up as if to stop them in their tracks, too late. She cringed. "I mean, I'm still considering it. It's a multi-million dollar start-up."

She sank deeper into the chair, grateful that Izzy couldn't properly see her face from this angle.

"I couldn't offer that to anyone." Izzy's voice tinged with regret. "But I still think it's not the same as a marriage proposal. It's okay to expect more."

Mia wanted to protest, but he was right. If she'd been truly content with Mikko's offer, she would have jumped on it straight away, not travelled around the world to postpone the inevitable. It wasn't supposed to feel like this. Had she really left her stressful job to take on an even more stressful one alongside a man she wasn't sure she could stomach for that many hours per day?

Before she'd quit her job, she and Mikko had gotten along well enough, spending most nights in his small apartment in Eira, close to the city centre. The historic building with its curved, wide staircases and Art Nouveau wall paintings had been one of the perks of dating Mikko. That and the fact that she'd stayed in tiptop shape, modelling the self-discipline and work ethic he valued above all else. She'd loved the building and her own toned body, possibly more than she'd loved him. But when you worked so many hours of the week, little things that brought joy, like tracing her fingers along the chalky wall as she ascended those stairs at the end of the day, meant a lot.

She'd learned Mikko's quirks and gotten pretty good at navigating them, avoiding the obvious conflicts. If she closed every cereal box immediately after use and frequented the gym, they were good. But going into business with him would change the dynamic again. She wouldn't have her own life and career to disappear into. She'd be there at his side, dealing with all the frustrations she'd only been hearing about second-hand as he complained about his day before bedtime.

Mikko could get moody. If something hadn't gone well,

he'd been grumpy all night, muttering to himself, to her, to his laptop, to the TV... She'd tried to understand, but what if it turned out the world wasn't against him but he was partly to blame? Mikko needed her in his corner, she'd learned that by now. If she couldn't support him one hundred percent, the best alternative was absolute silence. Could she manage that? Usually, he whinged about other people acting like muppets in a generic way, but those couple of times that he'd opened up about the details, she'd started to doubt his story, wondering how things might have looked from the other person's perspective.

If she worked with him, she'd hear the other side of those conflicts. Hell, she'd know the people he talked about! What if she couldn't keep up her silence-or-full-agreement support system? It wouldn't be written in her contract, but it might as well have been. Maybe that's why he was offering her such a sizeable piece of the business. He needed her on his side against the other founding members, and giving up some of his rightful shares created an obligation she could hardly refuse. Mia shook her head, unnerved by the thought. Mikko had his faults, but surely there wasn't anything that sinister behind his generous offer.

She placed her empty wineglass on the deck and curled up on the swing, pushing with her bare feet to make it sway. The scent of sweet, exotic flowers wafted in the air. The wine was making her head light and unbothered, fading everything else into the background. Whatever was waiting for her in

Finland could never reach her here.

Mia didn't notice Izzy's eyes on her until he spoke. "May I ask you something?"

She nodded, holding her breath.

Izzy lowered his voice. "Does he love you? Is that why he's offering... millions?"

Had he read her mind? Mia hugged her knees to her chest, smiling to herself. "I don't know. This whole experiment..." she lowered her voice. "This fake relationship makes me wonder about my supposedly real one, and the future. That's why I left Finland, to think this over, so it's exactly what I should be doing. I only wish it was easier." She let out an uneven laugh. "I'm used to writing down pros and cons and making decisions based on the available data. That's easy. But this... this is really hard."

"Your feelings give you data, it's just not that easy to read. You're brave to go on a trip like this. It sounds like you needed some time."

He angled himself towards her and gave her such an adoring, earnest look that Mia's insides lurched. Nobody had ever called her brave. She'd considered herself a coward for running away, for not knowing how to answer.

"Thank you," she whispered back. "It's been a rough couple of days, but I love this moment, right here. I don't even care that it's fake."

Izzy's eyes held a faraway look. "I live in imaginary worlds. I don't even care what's fake and what's not, only about how it makes me feel. A good story can touch you as deeply as anything that happens in real life. It's fiction, but is it fake?"

"I suppose not," Mia conceded, surprised at how he saw the world. She relaxed against him, letting the physical desire for his touch ebb and flow with easy camaraderie, like the two states couldn't decide which one got to be on top.

Why did this feel so natural? She'd only just met him. A couple of days earlier, she'd been sitting on the plane, intensely uncomfortable with the close proximity of a businessman whose shoulders encroached into her space. She'd pressed herself against the cold windowsill and pretended to sleep.

"If I'm still here, I'll go to the wedding with you. But we'll have to go shopping for another dress." She smoothed the white cotton of her hem, noting a couple of grease stains.

"You can have my credit card, *and* my car," he whispered into her hair, and she heard the smile in his husky voice.

Chapter 17

Izzy pulled onto the quiet road, with both his stomach and heart full. He'd felt nervous going in, worried that the whole experience would turn intolerable, that he'd blurt out the truth at some point, disappoint everyone and embarrass Mia. The latter would have been worse, he realised. She deserved to get out of this with her dignity intact.

"Let's drive around the lake," he suggested, taking a sharp right onto the road that circled Lake Rotoroa. "It's beautiful this time of day."

He drove slowly, letting Mia soak in the view of gently rippling water framed by six-foot tall flax, with fat geese and blue pukekos lazing around on the surrounding strip of grass.

Mia pointed at the houses climbing the hill on the far side of the lake, their pitched roofs glowing in afternoon sun. "It's almost like those postcards of Switzerland," she said. "Only without the mountains."

"Oh, we have mountains. I'll take you to Tongariro if

you'd like?"

She smiled, shaking her head. "I meant what I said. I don't really mind where we go or what we do."

Izzy tensed, the question hovering on his tongue. "Did you mean what you said about... me?"

Mia's eyelids batted as she turned to look at him, her mouth ajar. Thank goodness he was driving, and could pretend to focus on that. "I meant the part about my film," he added quickly, his brain frantically arranging memories of the last few hours.

Mia's face relaxed into a grin. "Yes! That clip you showed me blew me away, and I'd love to read the screenplay, if you're happy to share?"

"Absolutely. I'd love to hear your thoughts."

Mia bit her lip, looking out the window. "I also have another song I might need some feedback on. It came to me yesterday and it's not ready yet, but maybe you can show me what chords you'd use. I'm not a hundred percent sure."

"I'd love to!"

They drove in silence for a moment, slowly crawling past the joggers and baby prams circling the lakeside track.

Ten minutes later, Izzy pulled into his driveway, noting the absence of Deke's car. Good. He wanted Mia to himself, although he wasn't sure he could trust himself. His hand had already got away from him at the barbecue and he'd nearly touched her again on the way home, almost instinctively. The easy intimacy of fake dating must have rewired his brain.

Izzy secured his misbehaving hand on his knee and reached for the door handle. This time, Mia waited patiently for him to open her car door. Maybe she'd given up the fight, pinned it on cultural differences or something. Izzy smiled. It wasn't a New Zealand thing. It wasn't even something he habitually did with every female. Only her.

He led her into the house, checking for bird poo on the way as they popped into the kitchen, storing away the extra salad and meat his mum had insisted on packing with them. She probably worried that their relationship would stumble on his dreadful cooking, but Mum didn't know how much he'd practised in the last couple of years. The less he went out, the more he cooked in his own kitchen. He'd raised the bar, no longer happy with a cheese sandwich or instant coffee. Or maybe he was procrastinating. Whenever his creative work hit the wall, he learned a new recipe or invested in a coffee machine and taught himself to steam milk.

The distant sound of Casanova interrupted his thoughts, squawking his favourite line, 'You're gorrrgeous!'

Mia looked at him, mirth curving her lips. "Is that...?"

"Yeah. Deke's out, so Casa must be feeling lonely."

"Casa?"

Izzy winced. He didn't hate the bird, in fact he quite liked it, but that full name didn't sit in his mouth. Every time he heard it, he thought of Italian guys with unbuttoned shirts, representing all that made him feel a little icky about being a man. Not because he wasn't like that, but rather because he was. He wanted to take the woman standing in his kitchen, strip her naked, hoist her onto the kitchen table and drive into her with abandon. And the fact that he got there from a stupid parrot's name told him all he needed to know.

Izzy took a step away from Mia, cocking his head at the doorway. "I'll just check he's got food and drink, okay?"

Her eyes shone with excitement. "Can I come?"

Oh, goodness. He'd just been looking to create a bit of distance, to breathe away the hard-on that was draining the blood from his brain. "Sure. Deke won't mind." He gestured towards the hallway, and she followed him.

Deke's room was cluttered with clothes, comic books and an odd collection of cables on his desk but, to Izzy's relief, he spotted no dirty underwear or vintage pornography. Casanova's cage stood by the window, a large rectangular one with two hanging swings, several perches and colourful toys affixed to the bars. Casanova sat on the edge of his feeder, working on a shrivelled slice of orange. Izzy added some pellets into his bowl and cut up an apple he found on Deke's desk, replacing the old orange slices with fresh fruit.

"Beautiful girl!" Casanova exclaimed, sinking his beak into one of them.

"He looks so happy!" Mia gushed, leaning so close her nose was nearly touching the bars. "Hey, Casanova! You're a handsome fellow, aren't you?"

"How're *you* doing?" The parrot croaked.

"Oh, my God! Has he been watching *Friends*? That sounds

exactly like Joey!"

"It's one of Deke's favourite shows," Izzy admitted, his mouth twitching. He'd never seen anyone so excited about Deke's pet, especially a female visitor. This was probably the response Deke had been hoping for when, a couple of weeks ago, he'd finally brought a woman around, but he'd come on a little too strong and received an entirely different reaction. Izzy felt for the guy.

"I love him!" Mia sighed. "I wish I could keep a pet. I've never settled long enough to even consider it."

"Yeah, it's tricky if you're renting. Deke wanted to get a teacup pig, but our landlord is only okay with an aquarium or a 'tidy bird', as he said."

"You're very tidy, aren't you?" Mia cooed at Casanova.

"You're gorgeous!" He bellowed back.

Mia fanned herself, her grin turning silly. "Oh, man, you're smooth!"

Izzy chuckled. "If you were to settle down, what would you go for? A cat or a dog or something else?"

Mia pursed her lips. "I don't know. I used to think I wanted a little dog, like a miniature schnauzer or a pug, but now I'm thinking I want... what is he again?" She pointed at Casanova.

"African Grey parrot."

"Yes!" She grinned at the cage. "I'd get one just like you. A female one! And I'd bring her around for a playdate!"

"Beautiful girl!" Casanova chorused, clearly excited about

the idea.

Warmth flooded Izzy's chest and he looked away. If only it was that easy, if only she lived down the road and could turn up for a visit with her bird. He could feel himself falling for this girl, and everything about that sucked. She couldn't pop over from Finland for a playdate.

They were already doomed.

"That parrot cost more than my car," he said.

"What?" Mia's gaze flicked from him to the bird and back. "How could Deke afford that? I mean... he said he does volunteer work."

"His parents have money." Izzy wove his fingers through the bird cage, feeling exposed. "They pay part of our rent. In turn, I sort of watch over him." Izzy looked up, hoping for the right words to fall into his mouth. "Deke was born a bit different."

Mia's eyebrows lifted in curiosity. "How?"

Izzy expelled a huff. "He... um... he has learning difficulties and doesn't read social cues very well. He says what's on his mind without considering the consequences and people get offended. But I've kind of grown used to him."

"So, you're his guardian in a way?"

Izzy shook his head. "I'm just looking out for the guy."

Mia slid her teeth across her bottom lip, her eyes crinkling. "I really like him. I like how he doesn't seem to care what anyone else thinks. Like he's... free."

"Yeah. Sometimes, I look at him creating things and I feel

a bit jealous. Nothing stops him. There's no voice in his head shooting down ideas and making him feel like shit. Other people do that, though."

Mia smiled wistfully. "He seems happy."

"I think he is, for the most part."

She stared square into his eyes. "Are you?"

Izzy's breath hitched and he swallowed against the dry stickiness in his throat. "I'm happy here with you."

"How about a week ago?"

"I thought I was," he replied diplomatically. "But I was so focused on my goals that I would have never stopped to ask myself that. I don't know if it's a good question."

"Why?" She narrowed her eyes.

"Because... If you make happiness your goal, you'll never be happy enough. I'm happiest in that state of flow, working hard but not too hard, when ideas pour out and my hands barely keep up."

She nodded knowingly. "Like when you're working on the film?"

"Yeah. I'm stuck with that at the moment, but I know I can get it back."

Mia studied him for a moment, quietly ruminating on something. "I like your take on it. I think I was like that at my job; hyper focused on ticking off the next thing on my list, reaching the next goal. I'm happy about the breather though, and this moment here with you. This is perfect. You're my catalyst. Maybe Deke is, too. I can learn from you and find a way forward or something."

"When you go back to Finland?" The needy edge in his voice made him cringe.

She nodded absent-mindedly, her gaze on Casanova who'd finished eating and had climbed up his cage as if to join the conversation. "I have to go back, but I just don't know what I'll do when I get there."

Izzy sighed. The first woman to capture his attention in years and she wasn't available. He couldn't date her. He'd either win her over, hundred percent, marry her and reorganise his whole life to make this work, or he'd let her go. And he had only days to figure this out, which was the cruellest of jokes the universe could have played on him. What if he blew his only chance because he couldn't figure it out fast enough?

Satisfied that the parrot was happy, Izzy led Mia back to the kitchen.

"Do you want coffee or tea?" he asked, holding up two cups.

"Maybe tea. What do you have?" She opened the pantry and peered inside, quickly locating three packets. She must have memorised the order of their kitchen at some point.

Mia chose a bag of spicy chai and sat down at the table to wait for the jug to boil. "I can't believe it has only been a couple of days since I arrived. My head's spinning." She looked out the window and Izzy held his breath, captivated by her halo of blond hair bathing in the sunlight.

He joined her at the table. "Same here, and I'm not even in a foreign country, or recently robbed... I know it sounds lame in comparison, but that barbecue was a big deal. I haven't seen my parents that happy in ages."

Mia played with the sleeve of her new denim jacket. "Your parents talked about you like—"

"Like I'm a hermit?" Izzy fixed his loosened hairdo, wondering if tying it up had only made things worse.

Mia tilted her head, looking at him like a puzzle she couldn't quite put together but liked anyway. "Yeah. Why is that? You don't seem that... bad. I mean, when I first met you, I thought you were pretty laid back, but I would have never pitied you, or worried about you. I just thought you were brave and didn't care what anyone thought of your appearance, or how you lived your life. Your family... I can see they care about you, but they also talk about you like you've somehow failed? I don't get it."

Izzy shivered, those sweet, accurate words cutting deeper than she'd probably intended. This may all crash and burn, he thought, but he had to tell her the entire story, to see if she'd still look at him like that, with eyes full of open interest. "I know. It's just... I should have maybe told you before, but I didn't know how to bring it up. Something happened five years ago. My girlfriend Erin, she jumped off the bridge, the one close by. She had her challenges, and we should have seen it coming. I should have asked for help or done something, but I was young and too focused on what she thought of me. She was always hot and cold, hard to read. I didn't realise what was going on before it was too late.

Her parents are the nicest people and never blamed me, but I knew it was my fault. I was the last person to see her alive. We argued. I said I wanted to take a break... I was so tired of fighting. She said if we broke up, she'd..." Izzy filled her lungs, forcefully expanding them against the tightness in his chest. He stared out the window, his mind flowing down the path towards the river. "She used to threaten me with suicide and I was so stupid, I thought 'she just wants attention'. I know it's bullshit now. I've cut together hundreds of those suicide prevention videos and know exactly what to watch out for, but there's nothing I can do for her anymore."

Izzy's breath rattled, a wave of emotion coursing through him. He'd thought he'd put this behind him a long time ago, but seeing Mia's huge eyes peeled as she listened to his story, he travelled back in time, to that cold July night, standing on the bridge, staring down at the fast-moving, black water as the helicopter flew overhead, lowering so close to the water's surface that it created a whirlpool, hearing the weary voices of the police officers saying they might never find the body.

They sat in silence for a moment as dust particles swirled in the stream of sunlight. Finally, Mia jerked, like waking from a dream. "I don't even know what to say. I'm so sorry." She grasped his hands across the table, holding them like she was trying to pull him out of the water, keep him from drifting away. Nobody had looked at him like that in years, and every second of her gaze restored a little more of his faith, making him feel more like a man. Someone who could be trusted. Someone who wouldn't fail all over again.

"It's okay. It was a long time ago." Izzy tried to shake off the weird mood, standing up to prepare two cups of spicy tea with milk. Mia declined sugar, but he added honey.

As he returned to the table, he caught the shine in her eyes. "Do you… have tears in your eyes?" He couldn't help leaning in. "Didn't you say…"

She squeezed her eyes shut and rubbed them with her fingers, studying them in the window's light. "Half a drop, maybe." She turned to him, shock etched on her face. "You are going to make me cry! Honestly, I can feel it. I haven't been this close to tears in a long time, but these last couple of days… What are you doing to me?"

"Wow. That sounds like a horrible goal, to make a woman cry." Izzy's mouth pulled into an odd smile. "Unless it's what you want?"

She blinked at him, more moisture gathering on the surface of her corneas, shining like jewels. "I do!" She looked away, swallowing. "I didn't even know how much I wanted it. I got so used to breathing through that tight feeling in my chest. The stupid thing is that I've felt grateful for it, more than once, even proud I'm not the one weeping in the office when things go wrong. Women tend to cry when they're humiliated or criticised, and they lose respect. Being the one not crying makes you powerful, in control. I thought I wanted that. If you saw me at work... you wouldn't recognise me." She fiddled with her tea bag. "I told you they call me the ice queen. Mikko is so proud of it. He calls me his secret weapon."

Izzy's brow furrowed.

Mia lifted her chin, noticing his confusion. "You can't imagine it, right? You've only ever seen me completely out of my comfort zone, right after I lost everything. I still don't know how I'm going to get myself sorted. I'm entirely reliant on you. This isn't me. I don't rely on anyone. This is some through-the-wormhole version of me." She shook as she spoke, eyes burning.

Izzy placed his palms over her fidgeting fingers. "Do you like this version? Or would you rather go back through the wormhole?"

Mia stared back at him, startled. "What do you mean? Why does it matter if I like it? It's not me."

Izzy smiled, stroking his thumb over her hand. "Of course it's you. You just haven't seen this side of yourself in a while. What were you like as a kid?"

Mia shrugged, a faint smile passing her lips. "Full of ideas, always creating something. It's sad how things change, isn't it? You grow up and notice that it's not worth making things yourself. Those who do get paid a pittance. If you want to get ahead, you have to manage others, or you manage the people who manage them. That's success, right? Getting further and further away from doing anything ourselves."

Izzy shifted in his seat, releasing her hand. "I wouldn't

know about that, other than being paid a pittance." He belted out a sad laugh.

Mia's eyes flashed with alarm. "I'm sorry. I didn't mean it like that! I don't think it's right. Our contractor rates were abysmal. Now that I've seen how much food costs here, it makes no sense—"

"Don't worry about it." Izzy shook his head, smiling at her. "I've never tried to get ahead in the corporate world. It's not for me." He studied her for a moment. "And maybe it's not the only path for you, either? Can I hear your other song?"

Chapter 18

Mia hugged her guitar, afraid to look at Izzy as she stared at the lyrics she'd scribbled on the back of her notebook. Come on, nerves, she told the weird, buzzing feeling at the back of her head, settle down. It's only Izzy. He won't judge me.

Taking a deep breath, Mia played as much as she had of the song so far, her heartbeat kicking up a notch as she forced herself to sing out loud.

Izzy's eyes lit up like two matches as he stared at her fingers, and hummed along to the melody. Impatient, he grabbed his own guitar and started feeling for the right chords and trying new ones. Mia followed his lead, excited to discover his choices worked better, teasing out a haunting melody.

They worked through the song a couple of times, playing and singing together. Izzy discovered a secondary melody and they sang harmonies. The chorus gave Mia chills. "I can't believe how good you make it sound!" She gushed, holding onto her guitar as the last chord rang through it, vibrating through her ribcage.

Izzy shook his head, eyes sparkling. “It’s your song, I’m just playing it. And I love it.” He put down his guitar, turning to his computer. “Have you thought about recording it? We can do it here.”

Cold sweat prickled on Mia’s neck. “I’ve only just worked up the courage to play with you.” Her face broke into a conflicted smile. “It’s weird, since I’m not really a shy person. In my job, I dealt with all these difficult people, a lot of public speaking… It didn’t bother me at all, but playing my songs?” she grimaced, searching for words. “It’s like I’m fifteen again and performing at a piano recital at school. I’m terrified.”

Izzy chuckled. “That’s totally normal, I think. Creativity makes you vulnerable. You can’t be the ice queen, like you said. Not that I think you are. I can see the ice melting.”

Would it turn into tears, Mia wondered, sensing the familiar welling in her chest and behind her eyes, again a little bit closer, a little bit stronger. If she could somehow avoid getting in too deep, falling for a guy who lived on the other side of the planet, spending time in his presence could unlock her tears. She could take those home with her, and it was a good thing, right? Good for her music, good for her mental health. Except she’d be crying over him.

“Play another one,” Izzy urged, offering his own guitar.

An uneasy feeling stirred in Mia’s stomach, and she flashed him an apologetic smile. “Maybe another time.”

She wondered if that time would ever come. Soon, she’d

be on her way back to Finland. Who would she play her songs for? Who would show her how to choose the right chords? She'd miss him so much. She already knew that. The pain of that thought weaved itself into every beautiful idea, every touch and every moment they spent together, giving them a bittersweet taste.

Mia hung her head, barely understanding her own thoughts. She'd known him for three days. She couldn't feel this way.

"I'll miss this place," she whispered, staring out to his backyard.

Izzy followed her gaze, his eyes wide. "You've only just arrived. You've seen nothing yet."

"I don't mean New Zealand. I mean being here, with you. I'll miss this." The words floated out before she could stop them. She held her breath, letting her shoulders drop, watching his face like a roulette wheel, waiting for the inevitable.

He returned her gaze, square and honest. "Would you consider moving here?" He rubbed his forehead. "I mean, if you found a job or another good reason... in different circumstances." He flashed her a self-effacing grin.

Mia smiled back, regret piercing her heart. "I'd love to say I would, but honestly... my sister is having a baby any day now. I promised I'd be back before the baby comes, but she hasn't replied to my email. Maybe she's already in labour. Babies can come early."

Mia hugged the guitar, forcing herself to think about the unthinkable – going back. She had to get that temporary passport. Could she ask Izzy to chauffeur her to Wellington? According to Google maps, it was a 6.5-hour drive, one way.

"I was thinking I could take the bus to Wellington tomorrow? I have to get the passport thing sorted. I'll just need to borrow some money..."

Izzy smiled apologetically. "I'm sorry, I've already kind of... planned the trip."

"Really?" Mia stared back at him. "When?"

Izzy grinned. "Tomorrow morning. I have some work to finish, but I can do that tonight and then I'm free to go."

"That sounds amazing, but can you really just take off like that? Don't you have to deal with clients and emails and stuff?"

"I can earn my pittance another day." He winked at her. "Besides, I've already planned something on the way I don't want you to miss."

Mia nodded, her stomach fizzing with anticipation. "Well, I'll stay out of your way so you can get your work done." She headed for the stairs.

***

"Wait! I need coffee." Izzy followed Mia, thinking on his feet. Work was the last thing he wanted to do tonight, and he felt awful for leaving her at a loose end. "Can I make you a cup?" He asked, catching her at the kitchen doorway.

"Sure." Mia's lips twitched as she sat at the dining table

and browsed her phone. "But after that, go straight to work. Don't let me distract you. I can hang out with Deke and Casanova."

As if summoned by her words, Deke burst into the kitchen. "Good evening everyone!" he sang, rummaging the pantry for something. "What are you up to tonight?" He asked, opening a box of crackers and popping one in his mouth. "It's beautiful out there."

Izzy looked out the window, frowning at the golden sunshine. He had to make those changes to the suicide prevention video and send it away. "Yeah. I kind of need to get some work done..."

"You don't have to entertain me!" Mia waved her hand, accepting the coffee Izzy placed in her hand. "Or be my barista. But thank you."

"I'll take you surfing!" Deke announced.

"*You* can't even surf." Izzy grimaced. "And we don't have a wetsuit for Mia."

Mia shook her head, smiling. "Don't worry, I wouldn't go anyway. I'm terrified of sharks." She turned to Deke. "But I'd love to see the gardens. I looked up what I should do in Hamilton and apparently that's one thing you can't miss."

"Yeah, I suppose that's true," Izzy conceded, trying to accept the idea of Mia spending time with Deke. The gardens were within a walking distance, which eliminated the risks of driving.

"Do you want to go now?" Mia drained her cup in record

time. "I'll get my bag."

Deke shoved another cracker in his mouth. "Sure."

As Mia hurried downstairs, Izzy turned to Deke, lowering his voice. "Keep your hands off her, okay?"

Deke dropped his cracker, raising both hands in the air. "Chill! I know she's yours. I'm only being friendly."

Mia stepped through the kitchen doorway, carrying her minty green backpack, her blonde bob ruffled and her white tennis shoes neatly tied. "I'm ready!"

Deke pointed at his own Super Mario T-shirt and shook his furry mane in a theatrical manner. "Me too."

Following him to the door, Mia cast Izzy a hopeful smile that shot a beam of light straight into his heart. "See you later?"

Izzy's face responded before his brain caught up, splitting into a huge grin – probably coupled with a pair of pining eyes. The door closed and he ran his hands across his face, as if to erase the tell-tale signs. His fingers caught the hair clip in his beard he'd completely forgotten about. Perfect. He was an utter fool and there was no hiding how he felt. He'd wanted to stay with her, walk along the river and watch the sun dip on the horizon over the gardens. Nope. Life was not that kind.

Tonight he'd sit in his basement, tweaking animated suicide statistics, but tomorrow, Mia would be his.

Chapter 19

Mia skipped behind Deke's long, lanky legs as he powered along the footpath, passing more rundown rental houses with unkempt lawns. After a moment, they veered off the main road, onto a paved path that continued through tidier grass and leafy trees that somehow reminded her of summer in Finland, only more manicured. Birdsong was louder and more melodic, and the greens seemed brighter than anywhere else; nature on steroids.

The path wound down towards the riverbank, then ran alongside it, offering views of giant ferns and water that flowed in all shades of green. Definitely nothing like Finland. The closest bridge rose above them, a chunk of solid concrete, painted a garish blue. Deke slowed down, eyes fixed on its imposing stature. Something about his intense gaze made Mia think about Izzy's story. "Is that the bridge?" she asked. "The one Izzy's girlfriend—"

"Yeah. That's where Erin jumped."

The simple safety rail didn't look that high and Mia

shivered, imagining the desperate woman scaling it and plunging herself into the surging water.

"Did you know her?" she asked, stopping next to Deke who'd paused at the edge of the footpath.

"All of us met in film school. Izzy did post production, me and Erin did acting. We flatted on the North Shore, in Auckland. After graduation, Izzy was planning to move in with her. She didn't like me. She was so talented, but super sensitive." Deke shrugged. "I mean, she'd get offended over everything. And weepy. She could really turn on the waterworks."

"That's great for an actor, I suppose." Mia bristled at the forced perkiness of her own voice. This wasn't about her. She wasn't jealous of a dead woman's tears.

Deke hiked up a shoulder, a dark look in his eyes. "I know we're not meant to speak ill of the dead, but I didn't like her either. She expected too much... mind-reading. I like it when people are straight with me. If I have to guess, fuck it." He roared a laugh that nearly made Mia lose her footing.

She smiled back. "I know what you mean. I don't think you have to worry about that with me. I say what I mean. Finns are great at voicing the unpleasant. We don't do small talk. I wouldn't even know how to do that in Finnish."

Deke cocked his head, appreciation brightening his eyes. "I like the sound of that! Maybe I should move to Finland."

Mia chuckled. "Maybe you should."

They kept walking down the hill to the foot of the bridge,

then climbed up the steep rise onto the footpath. Up close, the railing looked even lower than she'd thought – she could have climbed it in seconds. A chill spreading down her spine, Mia picked up speed. As she reached the middle, Deke overtook her, jogging past. On the other side, he stopped so suddenly she narrowly avoided a collision.

"Phew." Deke caught his breath. "I don't like that feeling. Every time I walk across, I imagine jumping. I don't want to jump, but I can't stop thinking about it and it creeps me out!"

Mia stared at him, incredulous. "I thought I was the only one. Every time I'm somewhere up high, my mind plays those images. But maybe that's normal."

She cast one last glance over her shoulder and they hurried down a path along the river, surrounded by a medley of exotic plants flowering in white, purple and blue. The beauty of the gardens lifted her mood, chasing away the dark images. Deke felt like a breath of fresh air – a friend who she could be herself with. She needed a break from the feelings that stirred up around Izzy. Yet, she felt like something was missing, her hands involuntarily brushing her pockets. It wasn't just the lack of her old possessions, but an odd sense of emptiness that had followed her since leaving the house. Was it Izzy? Was she missing him?

They walked past a children's playground, complete with a carnival-themed stage, and continued over an arched stone bridge. Wisteria hung above their heads, filling her nostrils with its syrupy scent.

"It's so beautiful!" She sighed.

Deke gave her a funny look. "We're not there yet."

He led her past a pond, down some steps and through a narrow gate. "This is where it starts. Chinese, Japanese, Indian, American? You choose."

Mia shrugged, wandering towards the Japanese garden. The tidy order of the manicured hedges and raked sand soothed her nerves. The pond view that opened up on the other side of a pavilion was made for meditation. "This is so... calming." She took a deep breath, sitting on a bench. They were alone, surrounded by birdsong. The only thing she saw moving was one of the rocks... No, wait. "Is that a turtle?"

"Yeah," Deke said, sitting next to her. "They're my favourite. After African Greys, and teacup pigs, I think. They don't talk, so..."

Mia nodded. "Yeah, Casanova is unbeatable."

Deke beamed. "He's pretty special. Some people don't get it."

"You mean Izzy?"

He shook his head. "No. He acts grumpy, but he loves Casanova and looks after him all the time. He looks after me, too." His face shone with acceptance. "Izzy is my best friend."

They sat in silence, watching the turtle slowly slide off the rock, into the water. As Deke spoke again, in a clipped tone. "You don't live here. You're going back to Finland, right?"

He turned to stare at Mia and she bit back the soothing lies. Deke deserved the truth. "I have to go back. My sister is having a baby."

"But, you're coming back, right? You're coming back for Izzy?"

Mia tried to smile. "We've only just met. It's not like that—"

Deke frowned, staring out over the pond. "You said you'd be straight with me."

Mia swallowed a lump. She couldn't start deflecting with this guy. He wouldn't be able to read between the lines, and she could tell how much he cared about Izzy. Could she trust him with the truth? "You're right. If I'm completely honest, I really like him. The thought of going away and never seeing him again is... I try not to think about it, that's how much I hate it. But I don't know if we have a future."

Deke gave her a long, hard look. "I know I'm not great at reading all that stuff, but Izzy looks at you like he looks at the computer when he's working on that film... like he's seeing something nobody else can see. I've never seen him look at a woman like that."

"Not even Erin?" Mia asked, sucking in her lips. She had to stop fishing. This only made things harder, and her heart already fluttered in confusion.

"No. He never looked at her like that. They argued a lot. Izzy was louder back then. We all worked together. I love that about filmmaking. You know exactly what's expected of you and if everyone does their part, it comes together."

"I can't believe Izzy's doing all that work by himself. It looked incredible."

Deke bounced on his feet, throwing his hands out. "I know! If I had talent like that, I'd be shouting about it to the world. He keeps everything hidden in that basement. And I'm the weird one!" He collapsed back on the bench, hanging his head. "I audition for anything out there. I volunteer. I show up. And I keep asking women out. I thought I was doing the right thing, putting myself out there. If you don't even try, how can you get anything? But maybe I was wrong. I should just hide in the basement and the universe will drop a beautiful woman in my lap."

An uncomfortable laugh erupted from Mia's chest and she gripped the edge of the bench. "I don't think it's that simple. This all feels like a dream to me. Izzy is..." *Magnetic? Arresting? Unsettling?* She couldn't utter any of those words in public. "He's so passionate," she finally said. "But being dropped into someone's lap isn't a solid foundation for a relationship, is it? We're not even dating—" Mia clamped her lips, wishing she could suck the words back in. They'd been playing a couple in front of Deke. As much as she wanted to be honest with him, she couldn't do this.

"What?" A frown deepened on Deke's forehead as he sunk his fingers into his cloud of orange hair. "But, you guys are together, right? He's so possessive he threatened me with violence if I tried anything with you."

Mia ran her teeth across her lower lip, stifling a smile. She shouldn't have liked this side of Izzy, but the thought of him telling Deke to keep his distance thrilled her more than she wanted to admit. Not that she condoned violence, ever. She nodded. "Yeah, we're together. We're just trying to figure it out."

Somehow, it didn't feel like lying. The performance they'd given to his family had clearly messed with her head.

Deke dropped his shoulders, rewarding her with a relieved smile. "He planned something for you tomorrow, and I'm not supposed to tell you, but it's good. You'll like it. Just promise me one thing?"

"What?"

"Don't hurt him. He's... more fragile than he looks."

Mia's stomach lurched, but she returned his smile. "I won't." She really hoped she wasn't lying this time.

Chapter 20

Izzy set two plates on the breakfast table, energy vibrating under his skin. Mia would join him soon. He'd noticed she took little time to get ready. It might have been the lack of toiletries, but he suspected she did everything with the same speed and efficiency he'd sensed in their work emails. Nothing in them had particularly intrigued him, which made him wonder how much he missed by conducting his life via email. The true Mia, the one who'd burst into his life like ball lightning, was nothing like her emails. With her around, the creative dead end he'd wrestled had faded to the back of his mind. He felt better about it, almost peaceful. He'd discover the perfect ending for the story.

Izzy scratched his jaw, marvelling at how different it felt. He'd gotten up early to trim his beard. The operation would have probably required a hedge trimmer to begin with, and had caused him to stare into the mirror for a lot longer than he was proud of, wondering how he'd allowed himself to get like that. He'd filled the upstairs sink with facial hair and discovered two more pieces of red cabbage (seriously?), but eventually, his face had been transformed. It felt oddly light. He could only hope Mia considered it an improvement.

She stepped into the kitchen just as he hefted a pan of scrambled eggs on the table. Her hair stood up on the side and she carried the screenplay he'd given her before bedtime, along with the bloody debt notebook she brought everywhere. Her attention, however, was firmly on the phone she held in her other hand, and she took a moment to look up and notice him. As she did, her expression morphed in seconds, from worry to bewilderment. "Oh, my God! You look so... different," she added the last word on an inhale and it sounded like an airless gasp.

"Good, different?"

She cleared her throat and refilled her lungs. "Amazing, different." She stared at him for an unnervingly long time. "Who knew you had a face under that thing? Honestly, I kind of expected—"

"A triple chin? A spider nest?" *Probably best not to mention the cabbage.*

"Ew. I just meant... never mind." She fanned herself with the script and sat at the table, laughing, and then turned to marvel at the breakfast. "This looks so good. You're totally spoiling me!"

"I've pretty much used up all my tricks now. Fried, boiled, or scrambled. Don't expect me to poach anything." His amusement dropped as his eyes landed on Mia's phone, the screen still glowing bright on the table. “Did you hear from someone? You had that… deep frown just now.”

Mia gave him a meek smile. “Yeah. Mikko emailed me the flight details. I’d sent them to him before I left Finland, so he just forwarded the message to my new email. I tried to call him but he didn’t pick up. It’s Sunday night in Finland, so he might be out.” She didn’t sound too convinced. “Or he didn’t want to pick up. I can’t complain too much. I’ve been kind of avoiding him lately, even before I lost my phone.”

“Maybe you can try again tonight,” Izzy suggested, getting up to make coffees. It was easier to talk about her boyfriend if he wasn’t watching her, reading into every micro expression flitting over her face. It was none of his business anyway.

“When’s the flight?” he asked, his back to her, every muscle in his body tensing against his will.

“Wednesday evening,” she said in a small voice. “But it doesn’t matter. I might not get the travel documents in time. It said on the website that it can take up to two weeks. I’m sorry.”

A sigh of relief escaped Izzy’s chest. “No! Don’t worry about any of that,” he called over his shoulder, grateful that the loud hiss of the milk steamer covered the inappropriate brightness in his voice. Wednesday was only two nights away. Far too soon.

“I have to ask the airline if I can change my flights. I think I have flexible tickets, but there’s a fee…”

“I’ll lend you money for the fee. Just write it down in your little diary." Izzy threw a dirty look at the notebook and poured a beautiful flat white.

Mia accepted the coffee with her cheeks flushed. "I'm racking up quite a debt here. A BnB with all meals included, and these coffees are like five dollars each."

"You're not writing that down!" Izzy raised his hand to stop Mia from opening the notebook. He'd seen her scribbling in that thing, listing things like petrol costs whenever they drove somewhere. His first instinct had been to demand her to stop, but the act of bookkeeping seemed to calm her, and he didn't want to mess with that. He'd burn the book at the end or something. There was no way he'd accept money from her.

Pouring a coffee for himself, Izzy joined Mia at the table, risking a glance at the screenplay. Had she read it? Why had she brought it up here? He felt almost too nervous to ask, but he had to know.

Mia noticed his gaze and smiled. "I read it."

Izzy's heart lodged in his throat. "What? The whole thing?"

"Yeah. I couldn't stop." She yawned for good measure. "It was past three a.m. when I finished."

Izzy held his breath, waiting for more. Mia chewed her toast and sipped her coffee, the silence between them extending into what felt like hours but was probably thirty seconds.

"Okay, you're killing me!" Izzy finally blurted. "What did

you think?"

Mia's face spread into a cheeky grin, as if she'd done it on purpose. She looked him straight in the eye, her voice firm. "It's a fantastic story."

"What about the ending? I told you I'm not sure about that. I'm going to rewrite it, again. It needs to be satisfying, but also left open for the next episode, because it's meant to be a TV pilot."

"Really?" Mia's eyebrows shot up. "Sorry, I wasn't thinking of it as a series. Do you have to leave it open? You'd essentially keep this poor protagonist stuck in limbo forever. I thought you could end with him getting out? Unless you're one of those jerks who hates happy endings?" She cast him a mock horrified look.

Izzy laughed. "No. I think happy endings are a bit unrealistic, but I haven't lost hope completely."

"Even if real life sucks, it doesn't mean we need more misery in books and movies, right?"

Izzy tilted his head, studying the fascinating woman across the table. "You're speaking wisdom, oh wise one."

Mia's eyes sparkled. "Well, hear me out" She leaned closer and dropped her voice. "I think… it should be a book."

"A book?" Izzy blinked. "But, I'm a filmmaker…"

She tapped her fingers on the printout. "I mean, I don't mind reading a screenplay. I've produced plenty of scripts, but I always found that format a bit breathless to read, you know? I would have loved to read it as a book. There's so much to ignite your imagination. If you published it as a novel, you could actually share it with the world."

Izzy stared at her, forgetting to breathe. His body seized, his mind resisting, but Mia's gentle voice had already broken through, planting a seed of doubt. What if he was working in the wrong medium?

His gaze drifted to the stack of pages, stapled in the corner and crumpled from handling. She'd really read it and digested it. "Maybe you're right. I just haven't felt ready to share it with anyone."

"How long have you worked on it?"

Blood rushed to Izzy's cheeks. "Three… four years, maybe. I've had a lot of other work on, so sometimes nothing happened for months. About a year ago, I picked it up again and I'd just been learning about motion capture, so I decided to try and make a few minutes of it… that clip I showed you. Turns out it's a really slow process."

"I bet." Mia raised her brow, a subtle challenge in her eyes. "You're doing it all by yourself."

Izzy lifted his coffee cup to his lips, embarrassment tightening his stomach. Why was he doing everything himself? Initially, he'd planned a small production team, but over time, he'd lost his nerve and had found endless excuses not to pitch his project to anyone. When he'd discovered that it was technically possible to make the whole thing with a skeleton crew of himself and Deke, he'd pounced on the idea, relieved he didn't have to leave his basement.

"Thank you," he said, reaching for the script.

Mia blocked his hand with her own. "Can I keep this copy?"

She cast him a pleading look and he relented, distracted by the energy that passed between them at the slightest touch. "Yeah, okay. If you want."

He would have given her anything, and it scared him to his core. They ate in silence.

"So, where're we going today?" Mia asked, finishing her breakfast.

She stood up and cleared the table, gently pushing him out of the way as he tried to beat her to the sink.

Izzy fought back a little, enjoying the sensation of her hand on his arm. "You'll see."

Chapter 21

Mia stared in awe at the endless rolling hills behind the car window. "It's the Shire!"

They'd only been driving for an hour when Izzy turned to her with a secretive smile. "Close your eyes."

"Why?"

"Just do it."

She wanted to protest, but the song on the radio had lulled her into a state of relaxation. Mia let her eyes close. The playlist Izzy had curated for the drive had a dreamy, mellow feel. She felt the car take a right turn, then another one.

Eventually, they came to a stop. She cracked her eyelids, and found him smiling at her, holding a piece of white cloth with frayed edges. "What's that? Chloroform?"

Izzy's eyes widened. "What?"

"You're holding a rag next to my face."

He chuckled. "No. Believe it or not I actually prefer you conscious. It's a ... blindfold."

On a closer look, it seemed he'd cut up a pillowcase. Mia

stifled a laugh. "You don't trust me to keep my eyes closed?"

They'd stopped on a gravelled area surrounded by thick greenery. What was there to see?

Izzy held up the sad piece of fabric, pleading. "I want it to be a surprise."

Mia relented, and he helped her secure the blindfold.

"You might need a jacket," he added.

"Really?" It was so warm outside they'd blasted the air-con on its highest setting the entire drive, and Mia regretted not wearing a dress. Jeans had been a mistake.

She felt something warm land on her shoulders, probably the hoodie she'd borrowed earlier, and Izzy helped her out of the car. She held onto his arm, taking tiny steps, only detecting a bit of daylight through the fabric.

"Where are we going?" Mia asked, struggling to keep up. After a while, a shadow fell over them and she heard a beeping sound. The ground under her feet turned hard and solid and Izzy guided her through a doorway of some kind. The air became cooler, moisture gathering on her skin, and she heard an echoey dripping sound. She felt like she was inside a giant well.

"I'm scared," she whispered, her fingers tightening around his arm.

"Trust me." He said softly, leading her forward, along a slight downward slope.

Despite the full-body shiver, the floor under her feet felt solid, so she kept moving. The dripping sound intensified and the air turned even cooler. Mia relished the warmth of Izzy's hands on her shoulders as he guided her forward. She became a little bolder, taking bigger steps, trusting him to keep her from hitting anything.

The ground levelled and Izzy stopped her. "Wait here."

He disappeared for a moment and she heard a screeching sound. It must have been another door. His hands reappeared on her shoulders, guiding her into a space that sounded different. Softer, less echoey. Were they still going down? How was that possible? Was this another basement in the middle of nowhere? New Zealand's version of Alcatraz? Mia trembled, trying to think of an explanation that didn't sound homicidal.

"How much longer?" She asked, swallowing a lump of fear. She was letting a man she'd only just met lead her, blindfolded, deep underground. What was his fascination with basements, anyway? It was suspicious, right? Any sensible woman would have called the red flag and ripped off the blindfold. Yet here she was, walking like a lamb to the slaughter. If this turned out badly, no one would pity her. She'd get a Darwin Award for removing her low intelligence from the gene pool, or end up in the local news: *Remains of Gullible Tourist Found in Torture Chamber.*

"Almost there. You'll love this. Trust me."

Mia bristled. Closing her eyes in public had led to disaster. Yet something in Izzy's voice relaxed her, or held her in a trance. Either way, she kept walking.

After a moment, she detected a faint light, which soon dimmed, and heard a distant rumble of water, growing louder with each step. Finally, Izzy stopped her. "Okay, we're here."

In the watery grave where her body would never be found? Mia took a breath, almost too scared to open her eyes as Izzy untied the blindfold.

The first thing she saw was his face, lit by a small torch he held. Behind him, she saw the path they'd walked down – a narrow platform suspended across rocks, leading through a tunnel decorated by the strangest rock formations, like opaque icicles, their pearly glow highlighted by hidden spotlights. Stalactites! She'd never seen them in real life. They stood on a wider platform overlooking a huge cave that seemed to stretch in every direction.

"Look up." Izzy's voice rang with excitement.

"Stars? That can't be..." Mia stared at the tiny pinprick lights dotted in the darkness.

"No. They're glow worms. Since our stargazing didn't really work out, I had this idea."

"I can't believe it." The lump rose back into Mia's throat. "I didn't even know something like this existed. I couldn't imagine..."

Izzy laughed softly. "I really scared you, didn't I?" He brushed his thumb across her cheek, tugging a strand of hair behind her ear. "I thought the blindfold might be a bit much, but I couldn't resist."

Mia focused on her breathing, letting his touch melt her

fears, enjoying the otherworldly scene. She'd never seen anything like this. "It's incredible. How did we even get in here?"

"Deke works here as an occasional tour guide and he let us sneak in between the tours. We don't have heaps of time, but we can walk a bit further and I'll show you where they recorded the sounds for the Gollum scenes."

"Gollum? Like in the Lord of the Rings?"

"The very same one." He pointed at a narrow, pitch dark passage that seemed to lead deeper into the cave. Despite the hammering in her chest, Mia followed him inside the rock. Feeling her way through the dark tunnel, ducking to avoid hitting her head, she accidentally stumbled onto his foot. "Sorry."

Izzy grabbed her arm to hold her steady. "All good. Just hold on to me and stay close. Don't touch the rock."

"Why?" Mia whispered, holding perfectly still, inches from his chest.

"The glow worms are pretty sensitive. We shouldn't even breathe too close to them."

Mia could barely breathe at all. When Izzy released her arm and resumed navigating down the path, she quietly filled her lungs, trying to settle her racing pulse. They came to another larger cave with a wall covered in the tiny, glowing blue-green dots, so close to the bridge they could have touched them.

Izzy pointed his flashlight at a cluster closest to them,

revealing strings of tiny baubles hanging off the rock's surface.

"Oh my God!" Mia gasped, leaning in closer. "Those aren't worms. What are they?"

"Essentially, they're threads of spit," Izzy said. "The glow worms use these spit bubbles like a spiderweb, to catch other insects. Including other glow worms in fly form."

"It eats its own?" Mia grimaced. Nature was so weird.

"Yeah. And when it catches something, it drills a hole in its head and vomits acid into it, to make it easier to digest."

Mia's stomach heaved. "Jesus. Just when I thought it was so beautiful."

"Sorry." Izzy chuckled. "I probably shouldn't tell you that when they become flies they have sex for up to 72 hours and literally exhaust themselves to death." His eyes glinted with delight.

Mia pulled a face. "What a tantric way to go."

Izzy wiggled his eyebrows and pointed his flashlight down, over the railing, revealing an underground river that ran in the depths of the rock. "That's where they do the black water rafting."

"What? The glow worms?"

Izzy's laughter echoed in the cave. "No! Tourists."

Mia shivered. The thought of doing anything in depths of an underground river made her a little ill.

They walked on, gradually lowering deeper underground, until they arrived at the river. Another cave opened up above them, this one with a lower ceiling and more glow worms clustered as distinct colonies, like cities and towns seen from a plane landing at night. It was magical. Peaceful. Mia felt the final remnants of fear melt away, replaced by a sense of wonder.

"Music?" Izzy asked, pulling ear buds out of his pockets.

"Yes, please!"

He handed her one earbud, slipping the other one into his own ear. "Sorry, I left the big ones in the car, so we have to do this teenager style."

"That's perfect. I'm already wearing white sneakers that I'll get all wet and gross and Mum will be so mad!"

"I wish I had a stick of gum."

Mia grinned, producing the packet of Xylitol-sweetened little pillows from her pocket. She'd transferred the gum into her jeans pocket as she'd washed the shorts. Now she knew why. "All the way from Finland."

Izzy accepted one and chewed. "Wow, this stuff is like an explosion of toothpaste."

"Yeah, it's really good for your teeth. Gum is like a responsible, healthy thing in Finland. Kind of ruins the whole teenage rebellion vibe."

"That's okay. I'm 29."

"Hey! You're younger than me! I'm 31."

"Which makes me one of the coolest kids in school, right? Like the freshman dating the senior."

Mia swallowed hard. *Dating*. This didn't feel like fake

dating.

Izzy tapped on his phone. Within seconds, Eminem's 'Lose Yourself' blasted out of her earbud and she erupted in giggles, instantly back in 2002, trying to figure out what to do with her life, what to study, which chances to take...

Had she seized every opportunity? Had she tried hard enough? If she didn't take this chance with Mikko's start-up company, would she get another one? Would she go back to being a TV producer, working long hours on a modest salary, to sort out everyone's mess, saving for a one-room apartment on the outskirts of Helsinki? Mikko was offering her ownership, shares and potential fame as part of a team making history. He'd been so patient with her, waiting for her to travel around the world before she gave her answer, but it didn't mean she had to say yes. If the job was tied to a relationship with a man she wasn't sure she really loved, she couldn't take it. Maybe it was that simple.

Mia squeezed Izzy's hand, letting the strange combination of glowing lights, damp, earthy smell and the 20-year-old rap song flow through her. Izzy didn't have millions of dollars, but he had this nature's wonder in his backyard, and a truckload of passion and drive. Why did she have to measure everything in money?

As the song came to an end, Mia peered up at him. "Do you have a plan B? Like, if the film project doesn't work out?"

Thousands of tiny green lights reflected off his eyes. "How would it not work out? I can support myself with editing work, which means I get to keep going. If you work hard enough on something, it'll work out eventually." He let out a rueful chuckle. "That's what I tell myself anyway, even when I feel like I'm banging my head against the wall."

Mia blew out a sigh. "That makes sense. It's not a like a business that has to become profitable within a certain timeframe."

"I might be biased, but I think some of the best art is born when there's only an urge to create and no one's thinking about the finances yet. There's time for that later."

"I wish I had a portable skill like you do, something I could take with me anywhere to make money. Like some people travel around and teach English or code websites or something. What I used to do was all about the contacts and relationships, knowing the city and the local market. Outside of Helsinki, I'm basically unemployable."

"I'm sure there are a million other things you could do. What did you study?"

"Engineering." Mia huffed in amusement. "But I'm not that technical, so I steered towards management, being the scrum master, that kind of thing. Then I ended up working for the video production company because I craved something more creative. But it wasn't really, at least not in my role. I was just organising shoots and outsourcing this and that... babysitting people."

"Well, we get a lot of American productions here and they need heaps of babysitting, I've heard."

Mia laughed. "Ugh. That was like the worst part of the job! When grown up people can't keep appointments or get too drunk at business meetings... It's just sad."

"Maybe you need to try something new?" His voice broke, the playful edge of it gone. She could sense the meaning, and it sent a powerful surge through her.

Acting on an impulse, ignoring the warning bells, she placed her hands on his chest, inching closer until she felt his breath on her face. "Like a bearded New Zealand caveman?"

She felt his heartbeat under his shirt, thumping away like an anxious drum. She reached on her tippy toes until her lips touched his beard, desperate for him to close the distance. His heart pounded even faster under her palms and she inhaled the scent of soap and earth. She ached to feel his mouth on hers, her entire body vibrating with the possibility.

He whispered into her mouth. "You have no idea how much I want that, but I don't want to be the mistake you made on your travels. I need more, Mia. I need all of you." His voice thickened, full of restraint, his hands tightening around her arms. "If you were mine, I wouldn't just kiss you. I'd carry you out of here..." His gravelly voice sent tremors through her, pooling heat between her thighs. "I wouldn't even wait to get home. I'd lay you on the ferns outside... I can't even tell you what I want to do to you. We'd scare the birds." There was a smile in his voice and his lips brushed her cheek on their way to her ear, pouring in more words with his hot breath. "I want to keep you, Mia, but I can't take another man's woman. I can't choose the pleasure of being with you over the possibility of us together, for real."

His words stole the air from her lungs and every word from her mouth. She pressed her forehead against his chest and just stood there, leaning on him like on a wall, afraid to move. Another song started in her earbud, a classical piece with violin and piano she didn't recognise, so wistful and melancholic and perfectly in sync with her inner turmoil – or maybe it was creating the atmosphere inside her. She'd never experienced music like this, like an extension of herself, a trip to somewhere inside her own mind.

"What is this?" She asked.

She heard the bubbly warmth in his voice. "I thought you'd know. It's Sibelius. Opus 76:2 Etyde."

"Seriously?" Mia's eyes widened at the name of the Finnish national composer. She hadn't listened to classical music since her childhood and associated it with coffee and painkiller commercials, as well as those chilling music school matinees. Russian maestros who spoke in broken Finnish but played every instrument perfectly sitting in the front row, their faces contorted in pain at having to listen to the subpar renditions of their hallowed composers, counting mistakes to offer critique afterwards. They needn't have bothered. She'd already counted each time her fingers fumbled, each time she lagged behind on the tempo. Music had been unforgiving. Terrifying.

"It's such a beautiful piece. Nothing like Bach and

Beethoven. So moody and unassuming. Did you look it up for me?" Mia lifted her head off his chest, trying to see his eyes in the dim lighting.

"No. It's one of my favourites." He showed her the phone screen with a playlist titled 'Writing soundtrack vol.4'. "I had no idea why I liked it so much, but now I'm thinking it has something to do with Finland."

Mia smiled, reluctantly detaching herself from his chest. His hands still held her arms in their warm grip and she stood still, not ready to step away. "Maybe you're secretly Finnish! Do you like saunas?"

"I used to go to a gym that had a sauna. I liked it, especially if there was no one else yapping in there. Or... looking for a date."

"Yes! Sauna is for silence, or maybe sharing something really deep and personal... but not for idle chitchat. And definitely not for dating. That's sacrilege! A true Finn will keep a two-metre distance from strangers whenever possible."

"Sounds perfect. You know I'm pretty good at keeping away from other people. Other than you, really. I can't keep away from you."

He circled his thumbs on her bare arms, and Mia shivered, hugging herself. Despite Izzy's hoodie that she'd wrapped over her shoulders, the cold of the cave had begun to seep in, yet she didn't want to leave. These confessions came so much easier in the dark. Would she have taken that step and tried to kiss him in bright daylight? And would she have received the hot, startling honesty of his response? No. This wasn't daylight stuff.

Knowing where she stood, how much he liked her, buoyed her like a helium balloon, but it didn't make the reality any easier. She'd have to talk to Mikko. Somehow, she had to get him on a Zoom call and tell him she couldn't stay with him, even if she had to return to Finland. Even if there was no way she could make this longest-distance-in-the-world relationship work. The way she felt here with Izzy... He was daring her to see them as something real. All or nothing. It felt like a dream, yet part of her responded to the challenge, logic bowing to emotion more powerful than any sane argument. If she couldn't have this, she'd have nothing.

"Are you getting cold?" Izzy rubbed her arms, pulling her closer. "One more song, then we'll go?"

"Okay." Mia secured the slipping earbud back into her ear and Izzy pulled her against his chest, either to keep her warm or keep her from slipping off the rock. Or maybe just to keep her. He'd made it clear, she thought, as the layers of emotions swarmed through her, carried on the tunes of an acoustic, folksy song.

The only time I ever heard the voice of God
Was in the silence of the night
In the arms of the one I love
Staring at the ceiling up above
Like it contained the secrets of the stars

She wiggled the phone from his hand to check the name of the artist: Milk Carton Kids. The song fit the moment so perfectly that she shivered against his chest, almost afraid to hear the rest of it. The chorus seized her body, bringing on a wave of emotion looking for a way out.

And to love one another helplessly

So breathing feels like putting out a fire.

Mia tilted her head to see the glow worms. Their lights seemed to twinkle like actual stars. Izzy held onto her, his arms keeping her safe, his body heat fighting the damp cold of the cave. The song wound down, and they stood in place until its faintest echo was long gone.

Mia passed the earphones back to Izzy and he took her hand, leading them up the walking bridge. "Let's get out before the next tour."

They navigated through a dark tunnel, then through a heavy, wooden door and more walking bridges, past the Gollum's cave, until they arrived back at the first landing where Izzy had removed her blindfold. A loop track. Mia stared in awe at the stalactite formations and shiny pearl walls. The spotlights made them glow.

"It's formed out of crushed seashells, from when New Zealand was under water. When Deke first got the job, he practised his spiel on me." Izzy shot her a crooked smile and opened a heavy iron door, leading them into the entrance, the one that had sounded like a giant well. That's what it looked like, too, but with lights lining the spiral staircase that led back to the ground level like an inside-out Christmas tree. In the middle of the space stood a large rock, tall like a tombstone, a constant drip of water hitting the middle of it, running down a path it had carved over time. Izzy stepped in to wet his hands under the drip and then shook them over his shoulders. "This is how we thank Waitomo for letting us visit. It's a Māori custom."

Mia followed his example, feeling oddly reverent as the cool droplets hit her skin. "Thank you," she whispered to the rock, wondering if the cave had any idea how much she meant it.

The walk up felt lighter than she'd expected, and soon the outside air hit them like a sunshine bath, warm and vibrant. The birdsong sounded so much louder than before, and they both blinked in the bright daylight. The cave entrance had a touristy look about it, concrete shaped as fake rocks made for a showy doorway. Maybe it was good Izzy had led her in blindfolded, bypassing the manmade, taking her straight to the magical.

Mia glanced at Izzy. "I think I preferred the cave."

She spotted moisture in the corner of his eye as he turned to her. "Me, too. It's easier to talk in the dark."

"Why do you think that is?"

He frowned. "I don't know. Maybe it's because I'm not trying to read your face. It makes me more cautious."

"Yeah. The information we get through our eyes is almost… distracting. There's too much going on. But when you touch me—"

"It's simple," Izzy finished, covering her eyes with his hand. "Like this."

She held still and closed her eyes, hyper aware of every location where his skin made contact with hers. His other hand traced her face, tickling her jawline. She lived for those moments when he touched her, always waiting for the next one, her skin vibrating like it held a charge.

"You're right. That's simple. Can we just stay eyes closed from now on?"

His voice sounded light and happy. "I might need my eyes a little to drive us out of here."

"Yeah, okay. But as soon as we arrive in Wellington, I get to blindfold you! And then it's my turn to pick songs."

Izzy coughed, his voice sounding thick. "Um... Sure."

Mia blushed as her mind replayed the words. "I didn't mean... never mind." She took a step back, heat rushing to her cheeks.

Izzy pulled his hand away, letting the sunshine stream into her eyes. "Yeah, I know. We should get back on the road."

He led them along a path to the carpark. The warm, muggy air coated her skin with a film of sweat and she missed the cave even more.

On the way, they bumped into Deke with a group of tourists, including a mother pushing a pram. He raised his thumb for Izzy, who returned the gesture. "It's locked. Thanks, Deke."

"Thanks," Mia echoed, and they rushed past the group. She watched as Deke guided the people to the cave entrance, gesturing wildly as he explained something to the captive audience. She could hear their laughter, but couldn't make out the words.

"He must be a great tour guide," she mused.

Izzy nodded. "He's really good at dad jokes."

As they reached the car, Izzy's phone rang, startling them both.

"Excuse me," he muttered, pulling it out of his pocket.

Mia circled the car, giving him some space. She might as well check her own email since they were clearly back within mobile coverage. But before she got to it, she happened to look across the roof of the car and froze. The expression she caught on Izzy's face made her feel colder than the cave.

Chapter 22

Cold sweat trickled down Izzy's brow.

"Mia Forsman?" The female voice on the phone said with mild frustration. "I'm trying to get in touch with her. She reported her personal items as stolen and her passport was found as part of a recent raid. If you are in contact with her, please ask her to call the Auckland city police station as soon as possible."

Her sharp question woke Izzy. "Sure, yeah. She's right here with me. Hang on." He looped around the car and handed his phone to Mia, who stared at it in confusion.

"The police, about your passport," he whispered, and she took the phone.

Mia listened to the police officer, her face white, eyes startled. "Yes, this is Mia Forsman."

She rattled off her city of birth (he couldn't have repeated if he'd tried) and middle name (something like Katherine, but not quite).

"Yes, that sounds great. Thank you so much." She ended

the phone call and returned the phone, her face still registering the shock. "They found my passport at some drug den or something."

"Drug den?"

"She mentioned the National Drug Something Bureau and a raid. That's what it means, right?"

Izzy tried to smile. "Yeah, I guess. That's great news, isn't it?" His voice betrayed his lack of enthusiasm, and he hated himself for it. This was wonderful for Mia, a lot easier than driving to Wellington and applying for some temporary document that would possibly take weeks to organise. But those weeks had been his lifeline, a ray of hope that he'd get to keep her here, maybe long enough to win her heart.

This is not about you, fool.

"What about the other stuff?" he asked. "Was there anything else than the passport?"

She shrugged. "All sold on. Maybe they didn't find any takers for a Finnish passport, so it was the only thing left?"

"Too exotic?" Izzy guessed, lifting a brow. He opened the car door. "Back to Hamilton, then?"

Mia got in, fanning herself in the stuffy heat that had built up inside. Izzy hopped in and started the engine to get the air-con going.

"They said they'll courier the passport to Hamilton police station and will call this number." Mia shot him a glance. "I should have given her my new phone number!" She waved the old phone he'd lent her – one he hoped she'd keep.

"It doesn't matter. I'll just pass you the phone when they call."

Which meant she'd have to stay with him. Izzy scolded himself for the possessive thought as they joined the motorway, turning back towards Hamilton.

They drove in silence, Izzy staring at the road, Mia at her phone. A small crease had appeared between her eyes and remained there as she tapped the screen. Finally, she looked up, the words bursting out of her with urgency. "The airline came back with my flight details and said as long as I have my passport, I can fly out on Wednesday." She shook as she exhaled. "Wow. I never thought this would work out."

Izzy's stomach tightened. "What time on Wednesday?"

"Noon. Sorry. I won't make it to your brother's wedding. If I don't take this flight, I don't know... I can't. I can't stay."

He nodded. "I know." He hadn't asked her to stay, but hearing her apologise, so torn, shot another ray of hope into his heart. A dangerous ray.

"But we still have two days." She dropped her phone, offering him a look of wistful sadness. "If you need a fake girlfriend for anything else?"

Izzy pushed down the sour taste of disappointment creeping up his throat. "That's fine. I'll tell everyone you had a family emergency and had to fly back early or something."

"Yes! Tell them my sister's gone into labour. She's already eight months and kind of high risk, anyway." Mia screwed up her mouth in regret. "I probably shouldn't jinx her like that!" She tapped at her phone, then raised her chin, her smile sparkling. "She wrote back!"

"Your sister?"

"Yes! I emailed her earlier and told her what happened..." Mia dropped her gaze back on the screen, reading the email. "Oh, my God! The baby has turned around and dropped lower... whatever that means, so she could go into labour any day. Oi, little one, stay in there! Auntie's coming!"

She had a life to return to. She wasn't his to keep. Izzy smiled, trying to expel the sadness welling in his chest. "Let's do something fun, so you have some good memories of New Zealand."

"I already have plenty." She looked at him with such awe Izzy's throat threatened to close.

Two days, or rather two nights, was nothing, but he'd do his best. Maybe he could take it as an opportunity to practise social skills. He hadn't even realised how dreadfully rusty he'd become, especially with the opposite sex.

"Are you hungry?" He asked. "Can I take you out to dinner?"

"Like a... date?" Mia's eyebrows drew together while a flicker of longing crossed her face. Her inner battle matched his in frightening synchrony.

He chose his words carefully. "Like a... dining experience."

Chapter 23

Mia rubbed her formerly white shoes with a soapy rag, her mind warring over semantics. Did it matter what they called this dinner? If she could keep her hands off him, she'd be fine, but ever since he'd trimmed that facial hair, he'd become irresistible. Like right now as he stood at the kitchen doorway, waiting for her to get ready. She could barely tear her eyes off the perfect angles of his face.

She'd changed into her white dress, the nicest piece of clothing she currently owned, while Izzy had raised his game with a collared, button down shirt, this one freshly ironed. Its rolled-up sleeves seemed to deliberately advertise his bulging forearms. His eyes reflected the afternoon light like they'd stolen the sun and burned with equal brightness. Her fingers itched to run along that dark beard, touch those full lips and feel them all over her body... Oh, no. Her mind was as dirty as her shoes.

Mikko had agreed to a call later tonight, his Monday morning. She knew what she had to tell him and dreaded the conversation. If only she could stay in this bubble, far away from her real life.

During the drive back, her mind had woven a string of lyrics. She could feel a new song forming and wondered how many more would come if she let them. It felt so different to the creativity conjured during brainstorming meetings, where everyone stared at a whiteboard and every idea was mind mapped to serve a higher purpose. This creativity ran through her like a wild current, unpredictable and invigorating.

Mikko had warned her about getting distracted – millions of dollars awaited those who didn't succumb to self-indulgent time wasting. She'd agreed with him, looking down on artists who lived on government grants and produced whatever tickled their fancy. But travelling around this fascinating land, so far removed from her previous goals, she struggled to remember why it mattered so much. What was the real difference between time wasted and time well spent? They all died in the end, with or without millions of dollars, with or without business success. Or the love of someone who truly understood…

Mia glanced at Izzy. "I can't believe I have to fly again in two days." She got up to rinse the rag. Her shoes looked better – once the fabric dried, they might even pass for clean. "I don't think I'm ready for anything."

Izzy crossed the floor, standing right behind her, the heat and presence of his body overwhelming her senses. "Then…"

He swallowed the rest of the sentence.

Mia dropped the rag and turned to face him. “Then, what?”

A muscle in his neck twitched. “Never mind. You know how I feel, but this isn’t about me. I’m just a random guy you bumped into, who freaked you out by coming on too strong.” He laughed humourlessly. “It’s only because I’m so out of practice, you know?”

Was that what he thought? Mia’s heart squeezed. He’d been so brave, yet she hadn’t been honest with him in return.

“You’re not coming on too strong,” Mia whispered, heat engulfing her face. “Everything you told me… I feel the same. But you’re right. I don’t want to make a mistake. I want to make a choice.”

Mia swallowed, risking a look into his eyes. Would she make the right one?

Chapter 24

The sun had dipped below the buildings as they entered the city centre. Izzy parked on Victoria Street, snatching an available spot just as someone else pulled out, sighing with relief. He hadn't considered parking, which apparently had gotten worse in the last couple of years.

The chairs from the restaurants spilled out on the wide footpath and the lights hung under the eaves, warm orange against the blue of the night.

"Where are we going?" Mia asked as Izzy paused on the footpath, looking both ways.

"I thought we could take a walk and you choose."

"But I don't know any of these places."

Izzy scratched the side of his face, discomfort twisting his gut. "Well, that makes two of us."

Mia's jaw dropped as the realisation sunk in. Izzy tensed, bracing for her reaction. But within seconds, her face softened into a warm smile. "You came out here for me, even though you never leave your house."

"I know how it sounds," he grumbled. "I've never liked crowds, but it's not like a phobia. I go out with Mac about once a year to show him I haven't fused to my chair... I just don't feel like going out. It's not for me. And most of my friends live somewhere else, so it's easier to stay in touch online. Like my film school buddies... Hamilton doesn't have much of a film industry."

"I'm not judging you." She stopped in the middle of the footpath and grabbed his hand, forcing him to meet her gaze. "It's difficult to change your habits. How're you feeling right now? Do you want to go home and order something, because I don't mind. Seriously."

Izzy fought the part of him that wanted to accept the offer. "No. We're eating out." He peered over his shoulder at the myriad of hanging signs and specials boards. "Do you want me to check the restaurant ratings, or should we go old school and choose one that looks nice?"

"Old school!" Mia grinned and pulled him down the footpath.

One of the names caught her eye. "Iguana? We have restaurants called Iguana in Helsinki. I thought it was a local chain? This one looks different, though. It's probably just a coincidence."

"Should we try it, then? See if it's different?"

"Let's!" She led him into the classic open floor restaurant featuring solid wood tables and indoor plants. "No, this is nothing like the Tex-Mex place in Helsinki."

A cute waitress with a bouncy ponytail showed them to a corner table and ran through the specials. "Monday is pizza night!" she exclaimed, and they ordered a small pizza, bao buns and curly fries.

As the waitress collected the menus and left, Izzy's gaze flitted over her shoulder at the window and he shrank back in his seat. "Shit."

Mia followed his gaze and saw the group of people stepping into the restaurant. "You know them?"

Izzy blew a heavy breath, resigned to his fate. Apparently, he wasn't allowed to have one night out with the woman he liked without running into his dead girlfriend's father and his work colleagues.

As the waitress left their table to tend to the arrivals, Henry spotted Izzy. His eyebrows shot up and his mouth stretched into a half-shocked smile. Izzy lifted his hand, and the old man got up, slowly, holding onto the table. Okay, he couldn't let the man break a hip. Izzy closed the distance. "Don't get up."

"Isaiah! How lovely to see you out here! You know Claire and Carol, and this bright young thing here is Bibby, she's just joined the helpline..."

Izzy offered polite nods to the ladies, blinking a couple of times at the pair of boobs trying to escape Bibby's cleavage.

"This is Isaiah. You've all heard about him, and here he is! He makes those beautiful videos you've seen..." Henry's voice brimmed with pride. "Did you change your mind about pizza night, or…?"

Izzy scratched his neck. Pizza night! Of course. One of these days, he'd have to start paying attention to Henry's invitations, so that he could avoid these awkward encounters. "Um, not really. I actually forgot. I have a guest and decided to bring her out for dinner before she flies back to Finland."

"Finland? Wha… how?" Henry's gaze flicked at their table.

Mia raised her hand and smiled. Izzy's stomach tightened at the thought, but there was no way around it. "I'll bring her over to say hi," he promised and returned to Mia.

"What's up?" She asked, upbeat and curious.

"Henry wants me to introduce you. Is that okay?"

She shrugged and followed him to the other table. Izzy took a slight step to the side to create a bit of distance, and gestured at Mia. "This is Mia, a client of mine from Finland who's travelling around the world and decided to stop by."

Mia's smile looked a little startled, but she nodded in confirmation. "Yes. Izzy made some videos for the Finnish government. How cool is that?"

"Very cool," the ladies echoed, openly staring at her.

"This is Henry. I work with him on the suicide prevention videos." Izzy nodded at the old man, and Mia shook hands with him, then everyone else as they introduced themselves.

"I hope I haven't kept Izzy from his work." Mia smiled. "I think he was working on one of your videos yesterday."

Izzy scratched his beard, wondering if Henry had noticed the new, trimmed look. "Yes, it's all taken care of. Henry has the new version."

"I do," Henry confirmed. "Don't worry about that. Izzy is very reliable. Never misses a deadline, always finds a way to fix things, no matter how hard we make it for him. One in a million, this man."

Izzy pushed down a surge of emotion. What would Henry think if he knew what went through his mind when he looked at Mia? Could he see it? Izzy had a feeling these professional introductions didn't fool anyone.

"Well… our food just arrived." Izzy glanced at their table, relieved to see a bowl of fries already there.

Henry waved his hand. "Absolutely. I'll see you Friday morning, then."

Every Friday, for five years. It hardly needed mentioning anymore, but Izzy nodded and they returned to their table just as the rest of the food arrived. Mia's eyes lit up. "This looks amazing. Do you want to split everything?" She slid one of the bao buns onto his plate, and took a slice of pizza in exchange.

"That's not an even trade."

"You're like twice my size." She studied him, the tentative smile hovering on her lips. "Are you going to tell me what that was about?" Her eyes flicked to Henry's table.

"What do you mean?" He asked, buying time.

"Well, we've been fake dating for everyone else you know, but—"

"That's Erin's dad," he cut her off, his voice strained. "Erin was—"

"Your girlfriend," Mia finished. "Deke told me." Her eyes widened and she snuck a glance at the other table, her brow furrowed. "You work with your dead girlfriend's father?"

"Yes." Izzy took a long sip from his beer, hiding behind the glass.

"Doesn't that feel… weird?" Mia whispered. "I would find it really hard to move on if…" she seemed swallow the rest of the sentence, her eyes growing larger, voice even softer. "That's why you haven't, right? That's why you stay in your basement?"

Her words hit Izzy like a kick to the guts, but in slow motion, not catching him unprepared but muscles tight, anticipating the impact. He knew it, but nobody else had put it in words for him, not with such clarity. Her voice held no judgment or pity, only a simple, accurate statement.

Izzy gave her a sad smile. "It's hard since I really like the guy. I think he's doing amazing work and I want to help. And ever since they got the government contract, he's been paying well, too. That work pays my bills and I get to work on my film. I always thought it was a good trade-off, but now I don't know. I'm sorry…" Izzy grimaced. "I shouldn't have introduced you like that. What if Henry talks to my folks? They all think we're together." Izzy rubbed his hand over his face.

He felt Mia's hand on his arm, her thumb stroking his skin. "We can fix it, if you want."

Izzy peeked at her from behind his hand. "How?"

Mia gave him a small smile. "Well, I can tell he's already wondering if we might be more than work colleagues. We can just tell him we are."

Izzy hung his head, a thousand memories rushing through him. How could he do this to Henry? "I don't know," he grumbled under his breath. "The man's been like a father to me. If he sees me dating someone else... I don't know."

"Are you sure he'd be that upset?" Mia asked him softly. "He's sneaking looks at us... at me... and he's smiling. A lot. I think he's excited to see you out here with someone."

Izzy risked a glance at Henry, who indeed was looking straight at them, a silly grin on his face, eyes sparkling. Could Mia be right? He'd expected Henry to feel betrayed.

After Erin's death, Izzy hadn't even entertained the idea of dating someone else. He'd built a new life for himself – a safe and predictable life where he couldn't fail anyone. Over time, he'd gotten used to it. Just for the time being, he'd told himself, until he'd reached his creative goals. But looking at Henry, he felt the old pang of accusation in his chest. This was his baggage; baggage he'd inevitably drag with him to a new relationship. If he wanted to have any hope with Mia, he had to be honest. He'd lay himself bare and throw everything on the table. They had so little time. Taking it slow was not an option.

Izzy raised his eyes at Mia. "You know how Deke doesn't worry about what others think?"

"Yeah?"

"I sometimes really wish I was like that. I know he has challenges, but the idea of not feeling that... shame. The voice that reminds you that you're no good. It must be amazing."

"Why would you think you're no good?" She asked, eyes full of confusion.

Izzy sighed. Moisture gathered in his eyes and held them open, scared to blink and spill. "Because I failed her. I should have been there... I knew she was going to the bridge. She told me. I swear I didn't know she'd jump. I just thought she was angry with me and trying to be dramatic. But she waited for me there, she waited for me to come and stop her. And I didn't." The tears strangled his throat and he clamped his mouth shut, staring at the table. "I can't be counted on."

Mia took his hands in hers, squeezing hard. "He just said you're the most reliable guy ever. They count on you. I count on you. And right now, he's watching us and smiling. I think he wants you to be happy."

Izzy took a breath, the tightness in his throat slowly dissolving as Mia's words floated in the air, poking holes in the dark thought he'd carried for years. "That's the stupid thing about shame, I think. It just sits there, blaming you, holding you back. If you feel guilty, you want to fix it and make it better, and then you get to forgive yourself. But what do you do with shame?"

"If it was me, what would you tell me?"

"What do you mean?"

"If this all happened to me... if it was me and my boyfriend, what would you say to me?"

Izzy straightened in his chair, taken aback. "I don't think there's anything you can say to make it better."

"How about 'it's not your fault?'" Mia raised her brow. "Because, ultimately, it's not. Maybe you could have called for help. Maybe you could have stopped her. But you didn't throw her in the river. You didn't even want her to die. And clearly, it prompted you to learn a lot about the topic and if you were in the same situation now, you'd act differently, right?"

"Yeah, of course."

"Well... Considering all that, could you take it a bit easier on yourself?"

Izzy's mouth tugged into a sad smile. "You're pretty smart, aren't you?"

Mia laughed. "If I was, I'm sure my life wouldn't be such a mess right now."

Izzy felt a glimmer of hope, a lightness that almost lifted him off his chair. It was now or never. He had to take the first step. "Let's go. We have the fake dating thing down to an art now."

His whole body vibrating with fear and energy, he stood up and offered his hand to Mia, who followed him across the room. Henry put down his pizza slice and rinsed his mouth, smiling at them. He knew. The thought hit Izzy as he stopped at the table, gathering Mia against his chest, drawing courage from the warmth of her body. "Henry, I didn't do a very good job with our introductions earlier. I...

This is very new, but Mia and I are dating. We used to work together, but she's here because, well... we wanted to meet in the flesh..." Izzy pulled a face at the gory sound of 'flesh', losing his train of thought. Why couldn't he string together a normal sentence?

"Well, good on you." Henry coughed into his fist. "I appreciate you telling me."

Nobody else spoke. The awkward moment seemed to stretch into minutes until Izzy finally lifted his chin in greeting and steered them away again. Reaching their own table, he let out a long sigh, giddy and confused, but several pounds lighter. "Well, that was awkward."

Mia gave him a cheeky smile. "I think he needs to digest that a bit. Especially the 'meeting in the flesh' part. I think you gave the poor man nightmares."

An unexpected laugh erupted from Izzy's chest, shaking his entire body. He felt better than in a long time. And that was the moment his brain chose to remind him of the impending end.

How could he let her leave?

Chapter 25

Mia stared at the pixelated image of her boyfriend on the phone screen. Seeing Mikko there, talking to her in Finnish like nothing had happened, felt both odd and incredibly familiar, like she'd travelled back in time and magically erased everything that had happened in the last few days.

"Seriously, since that first story went live, we've had so many media enquiries I've had to turn some down. It's make-or-break. We need to get this ready for the next round of investors." Mikko halted his monologue, looking up at her like he'd forgotten she was there. "Have you looked at the link I sent?"

"I… um… no, sorry. I'll take a look soon."

"I invited you to the new Jira board. If you could—"

"That's great. I really need to talk to you about something." Mia cut him off, impatient. She'd locked herself in Izzy's bedroom, which felt like the wrong place for this phone call, but she needed the good internet and there weren't that many options around. She wondered if Izzy was listening, not that it made a difference. He wouldn't understand a word of Finnish.

"Sure, what's up?" Mikko asked, his smile confident. "Have you finally decided to join the most exciting start-up of the century?"

Mia could barely smile back. "I… actually wanted to talk about us. I don't think this will work out. You and I."

Mikko raised a brow, puzzled. "You and I? Working together you mean? Why wouldn't it? We've done heaps together."

Mia grimaced. Was it really this hard? "I mean as a couple. I don't think that's going to work. We're just not that well suited…"

Mikko huffed out an incredulous laugh. "Agreed. But what about the job? We need to get cracking as soon as you come back. We're behind schedule, as you probably know, but we've been patient with you. I told the guys you're worth the wait. Did you hear about Wolt? They sold for a hundred million. The shareholders are all multi-millionaires. I'm not saying that'll happen to us, but heck! Maybe I am. All I'm saying is you don't want to miss this train."

Mia stared at his white face and light brown number two buzz cut, feeling like she'd missed something. "I'm sorry… did you say that you agree we should break up?"

Mikko rolled his eyes. "What's there to break up? We used to sleep together, but then you wanted to travel around the world by yourself. The message I got was clear."

Mia blinked rapidly like trying to clear up the fuzzy picture that started to emerge. "What message? I told you I needed time..."

Mikko's brow knitted together, a tentative smile hovering on his lips. "I'm certain you said something about taking a break."

Mia held her breath, her jaw hanging. Finally, his behaviour made sense. "So, you thought we already broke up?"

"Yes, but I thought we're both adults and there's never any drama with you, so... You know me. I'm not a petty guy. I didn't want to kick you out of the company over that, especially since we work so well together. I need my ice queen to keep the crew under control!" He laughed at his own joke, but dropped the act as he noticed Mia's serious expression. "Don't tell me you've changed your mind! I don't have time to recruit." Mikko groaned, scratching his head.

Mia took a deep breath, trying to catch up with what was going on. Everything she'd thought had been wrong. She wasn't in a relationship. She'd been single this whole time, holding a candle for a guy who couldn't care less. Which obviously made things easier, but she couldn't help feeling hurt. Was she really so 'drama-free' that Mikko hadn't thought twice before moving on?

"I thought we were in a relationship," she said, her voice choking up in a very uncharacteristic way, a film of tears blurring her corneas.

"Are you... upset?" Mikko asked, his eyes wider than she'd

ever seen them. "What's going on?"

"Of course I'm upset!" she shouted. "I have trouble producing tears but I'm not a robot! You broke up with me and didn't even tell me."

"You're the one who flew across the world and didn't even ask me to come with you." His voice was laced with hurt, the first glimpse of something real, and it kicked her in the gut. In her hurry to leave the country, she hadn't really talked to him. But crossing national borders didn't automatically invalidate a relationship, did it?

"Did you want to come with me?" she asked.

"Well, it wasn't the best timing for me, with the business and all, but I would have appreciated the gesture." His voice sounded dark and far away, even though the connection was crispy clear. "But I moved on. I won't let relationship stuff get in the way of my goals. As I'm sure you won't either."

"What goals? I don't even know what I'm going to do..."

"As I said, we need a product manager, or chief evangelist, or whatever you want to call yourself. Pick a title. Help us prep for Slush."

"I don't know," she said quietly, discomfort twisting its way through her gut. "Wouldn't that be weird? If we're not together anymore."

"Only if it's weird for you. I think everyone's gotten used to the new normal over here." Mikko flashed her a deeply uncomfortable smile, and Mia automatically held her breath.

"What new normal?"

Mikko looked away, stretching his words out like they were escaping involuntarily as he tried to reel them back in. “The new normal where I’m dating one of the developers, Carlotte. She’s Portuguese.”

He added the nationality as if that explained everything. Maybe it did. Mia paused for a moment, waiting for the wave of emotion. What was she supposed to feel? Betrayal? Jealousy? Only a weak bout of nausea rippled through her, leaving a trail of emptiness. Relief. That’s what he’d been like. Her reliable, if a little boring, long-term boyfriend had only been waiting for her to leave the country so he could jump in the sack with someone else.

She’d always thought his one-note personality and laser focus meant he would never betray her, that he didn’t even notice other women. Their relationship may have lacked spark, but they’d been a team, encouraging each other to get ahead. Even if Mikko’s idea of success for her equalled a career in his company. One that was still on offer, as odd as that sounded.

“Great,” Mia finally replied, battling her mouth into a smile of sorts. “I’m happy you’ve found someone. Wouldn’t it be weird for her if your ex-girlfriend shows up at the office?” She shook her head. “Seriously, Mikko, it doesn’t sound like a good idea.”

Mikko huffed. “Think about it, okay? We’re recruiting, but it’s so hard to find anyone not useless.”

“I’ll think about it,” Mia promised, her stomach lurching

at the thought. "Gotta go now, it's pretty late here."

They ended the call, and she collapsed on Izzy's bed, hugging the phone to her chest, staring at the ceiling. What did this all mean? She had a job to get back to, but no boyfriend. She was free, and apparently full of tears that bubbled up just under the surface. They'd come out, she felt it. Believed it. Wanted it. With Izzy, she could feel the tears right there, like a layer of soot had been wiped off, leaving her soul bare and fragile in the bright New Zealand sun.

Mia gathered herself from the bed, trying to organise her thoughts. Did it really matter how things had turned out? The only thing that rattled her, made her sick to her stomach, was the impending flight home. If she didn't think about that, she had everything she'd ever wanted right here.

She had Izzy.

Her feet moving before her mind caught up, dressed only in her underwear and Izzy's T-shirt, Mia rushed out of the bedroom, looking for him. The basement was empty, so she climbed the stairs, poking her head in the kitchen – empty – and finally Deke's room, where she found his flatmate asleep in his bed. Where was Izzy?

Mia tiptoed through the dark upstairs rooms, explored the worn out lounge that smelled like a summer cottage after winter, and stepped through the double doors onto the empty deck. As she peered into the darkness lit only by the nearest street lamp, she noticed Izzy's car was missing from the driveway. She padded into the overgrown garden, wondering where he'd gone.

That's when headlights swept into the driveway. Izzy. She ran to the car and opened the driver's door before Izzy could step out, causing him to burst out laughing. "Is this payback?" He scooped a paper bag off the front seat and climbed out.

"No, I was just waiting for you." Butterflies, or maybe mature glow worms, danced in her stomach as she waited for him to look at her.

Izzy stood in front of her, suddenly quiet, his gaze resting on her face. "Why?"

"Because I wanted to kiss you," she whispered, biting down on her lip, unable to contain the thrill that surged through her, tugging her mouth into a grin.

"You talked to your… boyfriend?"

"Ex-boyfriend."

She could have sworn the air crackled between them. Izzy stared into her eyes, holding the paper bag. "So, you're single now?"

Mia felt heat working its way up her neck. "Turns out, I was single all this time. Mikko thought we broke up, and he's sleeping with someone else."

"What?" Izzy took half a step back, his arm frozen in mid-air. "Did he just forget to tell you?"

"I really don't know how… I said I needed a break. I think he took that to mean we should break up."

"So, no million-dollar opportunity?" Izzy studied her face,

concern wrinkling his brow. "Are you disappointed?"

Mia shook her head. "I don't want his hypothetical millions."

"So, how *are* you feeling?" The palpable concern in his eyes shot through her heart.

She looked at her toes. "Honestly, I feel like a fool. But I'm relieved at the same time. I'm sure you know why." Her voice nearly disappeared in her throat, heart beating out of control. He knew. They both knew.

Izzy dropped the paper bag and took hold of her head, entwining his fingers in her hair. "You said you wanted to kiss me?"

She nodded breathlessly, and his mouth crashed onto hers, claiming her for New Zealand, for this place on earth. She reached for his shoulders, shivering as she made contact with the now familiar solid muscle. He felt like a tree trunk, all width and height and solidness that held her in its steady grip. His hands slid to her lower back, sending a tingle down her spine. Mia raised on her toes to get closer. She wanted more of him. All of him.

"Finally," he rasped in her ear, then returned his tongue to where she needed it, owning her mouth, sending a powerful jolt into her core as his hands enclosed around her waist, tugging her closer.

Mia wasn't sure what she'd expected, but his no-holds-barred passion stole her breath and cleared her mind, replacing every thought with one consuming need. The night sky seemed blurry, the stars in the sky spinning.

Finding her balance, she tripped on the paper bag at his feet. "What's in here? Where did you go?"

"Just picked up some supplies." She tried to peek into the bag, but he folded it closed, securing it under his arm. "It's a surprise for tomorrow, to celebrate your last day—"

"Don't say it," Mia pleaded, running her fingers over the rough beard and lips she'd been dying to touch. The contrast of rough and soft. So real. He grabbed her wrist and kissed her fingers, then trailed his mouth along her bare arm until he found her mouth again. She parted her lips, allowing him to go deeper, and he responded with a fervour that created a hot, insistent throb in her core. She'd take the pain of separation later, if only she could have him now. There was no way she could step away. There had never been a way.

Izzy's hands lowered to cup her bottom, and she instinctively pressed against him, gasping at the hardness that met her lower belly. He was so much taller. He slipped a finger under the waistband of her underwear, grinning from ear to ear. "We should really go inside. The neighbours might enjoy the show, but I'm not ready to share."

Mia's face flushed with heat. "I didn't mean to run around in my underwear. It was... spur of the moment. I saw your car and I couldn't wait."

"I know the feeling," he growled.

Without warning, he secured the paper bag under his arm and scooped her up, somehow holding everything as he rushed to the door. Mia's protest melted into a squeaky laugh. She'd never been carried by another person, not since childhood, and it flooded her body with an odd sensation – weightless, helpless, and so dazed she could have sworn she was drunk or high, her senses overwhelmed by him, her legs dangling like a rag doll's. A rag doll carried by a gorilla.

They tumbled into the house, the sweet torture of anticipation building with every step. Izzy dropped the paper bag at the kitchen doorway and carried her all the way to the basement.

The soft glow of his floor lamp greeted them down in his lair. This was his hideout, his contained universe she'd crashed. She didn't belong here, yet she'd never felt so at home anywhere. Izzy lowered her, and she caught the shadow in his eyes. Would he push her away again?

He looked into her eyes. "If we do this, I don't... take it lightly. This is it. You're mine."

Mia's face burned. "I'm yours tonight," she whispered, a lump rising in her throat.

Izzy grabbed a handful of her T-shirt and tightened it inside his fist, pulling her closer. She'd never seen a look like that in a man's eyes, burning passion laced with pain, and it both scared and exhilarated her.

His voice carried a dark edge. "I need more time."

Mia swallowed. Glow worms had longer relationships than she could have with this man. "Izzy, if I could... I'd stay a week or two longer. Believe me, I would."

He nodded slowly, eyes full of pain, and slid his hands around her waist, pulling her against him. "I'd need more than that, though. A lot more."

She barely dared look into his eyes – deep, dark windows to a vast landscape, so open and candid that she almost bolted but his arms held her tight, melting her hesitancy, second by second. "How long would you keep me for?"

"Forever," came his rough answer, just before mouth landed on hers, chasing out all the other words.

Hot urgency zipped through her, settling between her legs. Throbbing heat engulfed her entire body, building up a hollow ache she could hardly tolerate. She needed him closer, with nothing in between. She slid her hands under his T-shirt, urging him to pull it off. Izzy complied, throwing the shirt over his shoulder, exposing an upper body that made her think of some Viking character, except darker, more dangerous. No one who spent their time hiding in a basement was allowed to look like that.

"You know you could make money just posing in your underwear, right?" She traced her finger down his impeccable abs.

Izzy laughed. "I lift weights when I'm bored or frustrated."

"Sexually frustrated?" She swallowed the last bit of saliva in her mouth.

He lifted a knowing eyebrow. "That, too."

Mia stared at the bulge in his jeans, hot and cold, suddenly hyper aware of her own less-than-toned body. Izzy crept closer, grabbing the hem of her T-shirt, eyes sparkling with mischief. Mia stuck her arms down at her sides, her courage wavering. “I don’t have a six pack.”

“Believe it or not, a six pack is not what I’m looking for in a woman.” He slipped his hand under the shirt, his touch unbearably light, eyes searching.

Mia yanked off her T-shirt and threw it on the floor. She’d already had a taste of him and she needed more. She needed everything.

Izzy’s gaze swept across her and his eyes glazed over. He sucked in a breath and his hands secured around her waist. Agonisingly slowly, he lowered his mouth onto hers, his rough beard rubbing against her chin. Desperate for more, she responded by tasting him, submitting to every move he made. A fire surged through her, escaping as a ragged whimper. She felt a shiver pass through both of them, his hardness throbbing against her stomach. His touch was anything but light, yet she could feel him holding back, handling her like a glass bowl, afraid to break her.

She led them on the nearby couch, pulling Izzy on top of her. He balanced his weight on his arm, careful not to crush her. He kissed her again, then lowered his mouth to her breasts, giving each nipple a delicious suckle before he pulled back to stare at her in awe. “You’re so perfect,” he grumbled, his voice thicker than ever before.

His hand traced the soft curve of her belly. “I’ll get into shape when back into my routine,” she whispered.

His giant hand paused on her waist, so tantalisingly close to where she needed him that her entire body tingled with anticipation. His eyes narrowed at her. "Are you apologising for this body? Because if you are, please stop." His lips lowered on her nipple and sucked it in, sending a hot surge of need between her thighs.

Mia shuddered from his reassuring words and the incredible sensation of his mouth as it trailed down her torso, his beard tickling her as he tasted her skin, moving with reverent enthusiasm. Hearing the sounds of his uninhibited arousal relaxed her and she spread her knees wider as he moved down from her bellybutton.

His fingers pried the waistband of her underwear.

"Do you have a condom?" she asked.

"Yeah, but..." He reluctantly pulled away. "Do they expire?"

Her eyes widened. "In... five years? I think they do."

"Then I need to run upstairs real quick."

He left her on the couch and disappeared up the stairs, shirtless, jeans hanging low on his hips. Mia's excitement erupted in laughter, and she hoped Deke was a sound sleeper. She rushed to the bathroom, quickly checking her face, hair, armpits (no unseemly smell) and bikini line (due for a shave, but oh well). Hearing Izzy's footsteps, she met him at the bedroom door.

"Second thoughts?" He asked, holding a strip of condoms, jeans riding so low that she could see his strained boxer shorts.

"I can't even form first thoughts." She unzipped his jeans and helped him out of them.

He flashed her a wicked smile, grabbing her behind the knees so that she fell on her back onto the bed, letting out a yelp. In seconds, he was on top of her, stealing kisses, his breath hot in her ear. "So, you've been thinking about it? It's not just me?"

"So many times. I wish I'd bought more panties. I have to change them all the time. It's not funny."

He growled in her ear. "Oh, no. You can't say stuff like that. I want to last."

"I don't care. We'll have a snack and do it again."

"I like the way you think." Izzy peeled off her underwear, smiling as his fingers brushed against the evidence. She saw his massive hard-on grow even bigger, stretching the boxers out of shape. When he finally took them off, she stifled a gasp. Seeing his huge, toned body in all its glory, hovering over her, she could only stare. No other reaction was appropriate, or possible. She drank him in and memorised the shapes of his muscles, the incredible power and beauty of those hard angles.

He stared back at her, his gaze dipping between her legs, open and hungry. "Can I taste you?"

"Yes." Mia swallowed and he placed a tentative kiss on her inner thigh, then another one, moving incrementally closer, his lips leaving behind tingling rings, like tiny fires along her skin. They grew and joined, building up into an inferno inside her, a pulsing in her core that echoed in her ears.

"So much yes," Mia gasped. She'd lost her grasp of English language. She couldn't even produce coherent thoughts in her native tongue. Oh... tongue.

"So much yes?" He repeated, a smile in his voice.

He trailed up her leg, his hot breath arriving at her centre.

She could hardly stand it. "Yes," she panted again. "Please."

Her muscles tensed as she turned into a throbbing bundle of need. His tongue worked with a skill and precision she hadn't expected, sending her mind into oblivion. Her toes flexed against the edge of the bed as wave after wave of overwhelming pleasure surged through her, tensing and relaxing her spine as she climbed higher and higher, unable to think anything at all.

"You taste incredible," he rasped.

The tension built in her core and she whimpered like an animal, her own voice foreign to her ears. "Stop, or I'll..." She heaved a sigh, trying to get up, but he laid her back down.

"Let it happen, Mia."

He dove back in, sliding two fingers inside as his mouth owned her, savoured her. She had no choice, other than to tilt her pelvis and surrender, sparkles exploding behind her eyelids as she came apart. Wave after wave pulsed through her, filling her with delicious, shivery pleasure but not bringing her back down. She was too charged.

"More," she gasped. "I need more. I need you."

She registered him pulling on the condom and glimpsed at the impressive size of him. If she'd been younger, and not swimming in a sea of endorphins, she might have felt scared. But not now. She sat up on the edge of the bed and reached for his length, hard like marble, urging him closer. He climbed on her, gently teasing the slick, swollen flesh.

"You ready?" He panted and she moaned from sheer anticipation, never having wanted anything so shamelessly.

He sunk into her, pushing the air out of her lungs and groaning in a way that made her insides flip. She wanted to see him lose control, stop holding back and take everything. "Harder," she whispered, raising her hips to meet him.

Hunger darkened his eyes. He sat up and scooped her onto his lap so she straddled him. He blinked, soft and unfocused, eyes glazed with lust and... something more. Something deeper. "I don't want this to be over." His hands tightened around her hips and she felt blood pumping into him as he pulsed inside her, holding back.

She weaved her arms around his neck, tasting his neck, inhaling him. "It's not over. This is only the beginning."

"Promise me."

She pulled back to look at him and the raw emotion behind his eyes shot straight into her heart. "I promise," she whispered, closing her mouth on his, tasting him like he'd tasted her, with a relentless appetite.

He hardened a little inside her, making her tremble from pleasure. She couldn't resist the tempting friction and bucked against him.

Pushing him on his back, she settled on top of him, enjoying the view of that mile-wide chest. Watching his glassy eyes flutter, she rolled her hips, savouring the way he filled her. He gripped her buttocks, trying to slow her down. But she wouldn't stop, moving faster and faster, forcing him to surrender.

"Mia. Mia." Izzy's body tensed and she lowered herself on him, relishing the moment of his release, rocking until her own arousal reached a new peak. The luscious sensation coursed through her, as powerful as the first one but soft and satisfying, a full unravelling that left her twitching against his chest, wanting nothing.

After a few minutes of catching her breath, she rolled off him, careful of the condom. Izzy turned to his side, resting his hand over her waist, his eyes misty but with a lazy smile on his lips. "I can't let you fly away, I'm sorry. I'm just going to lock you in here." He nuzzled his hairy chin into her neck, his beard tickling her skin, rocking shivers down her spine, straight into her heart.

Mia snuggled into him, letting the sentiment lull her into a sweet, false security. If only. She'd gladly be his prisoner, but then again, that's not who he was. The man she was falling for wouldn't capture her against her will. He'd let her go, and the thought of that moment terrified her. "I want you to lock me up," she said, turning around to look him in the eye. "Would you, for real? I don't want to think about

Wednesday."

"I wish." He blew out a heavy exhale. "But tomorrow is Tuesday. There's no Wednesday, not in my world. There's only Tuesday. And we'll have an amazing one, I promise."

Chapter 26

Izzy woke to the sound of birds, and the neighbour's lawnmower. He never left the window open – Mia must have done that last night. She filled his basement with life, forcing him to open up to the world outside and he wasn't sure how he felt about that. He wanted her, but the rest of the world could very well stay where it was and out of his hair.

His eyes roamed across the sleeping woman, as he rolled over to face her. She was so fair that her hair and skin glowed against the navy blue sheets like the moon in the sky. A creature of north. He'd captured a woman who didn't belong in this land, and he wanted to lock the doors and trap her forever. But he couldn't keep her any more than he could bottle sunshine. She'd have to return to her life and when she did, the memory of last night, as vivid as it was in his mind right now, would eventually fade, pushed aside by other things. Izzy knew the weight of responsibility. It could trap you for years.

His phone screen lit up, and he grabbed it off the

nightstand. The message in his inbox informed him Mia's passport was ready for picking up. They'd have to do that on the way. He'd planned a trip for the last day, hoping to distract them both from the upcoming farewells.

Mia stirred and Izzy lay back on the bed, locking her under his arm. She was still here, still with him, and he desperately wanted to stop time. If he had any hope of Mia ever returning to him, he had to keep his possessive urges under control and focus on creating beautiful memories together. Like the ones they'd made last night.

The moments of passion flashed behind his eyes and he smiled to himself. He hadn't been with many women, and it had been such a long time those experiences had probably expired along with his condoms. Nobody came close to this woman. For such a tiny thing with an innocent fairy face, she brimmed with fire. Just thinking of the noises she'd made had him instantly hard, and he snuggled closer, unable to stop himself.

Mia responded with a moan, arching her back to offer her perfect, round butt cheeks to him. Izzy didn't need more encouragement. He nuzzled between her thighs, groaning as he encountered signs of her arousal. Mia turned around, her huge eyes blinking at him. "I had a dream about the cave."

"Really? What happened?"

A blush rose to her cheeks. "We had sex against those rocks. What were they called?"

"You mean I fucked you against the invaluable, incredibly

fragile stalactite that's formed over millions of years?"

Her face was now crimson. "That's probably the naughtiest dream I've ever had."

"I agree," he said, his hands hungrily peeling off the sheet and exploring her body, desperate to memorise every inch of her. "Now tell me exactly what I was doing so that I can recreate the scene. Where was my hand? Here?" He slipped his fingers between her cheeks, searching for that slickness that lit a fire in his gut. He loved the thought of owning her dreams, being the one to make her come even when they were asleep. This was too good. There had to be a catch. Surely, the sky was about to fall on him at any moment, to restore the balance in the universe.

"Yes. There. Don't stop." She writhed against him. "Izzy. Isaiah. Can I call you that? I really like how it sounds."

Izzy pulled a face. "It makes me feel like I'm at school and being scolded, but sure. You can scold me any time."

"I would, but I have no complaints," she panted in his ear.

"So you enjoyed last night?" He couldn't help asking, his fingers working lazy circles between her legs.

When she opened her eyes at him, he saw the need, but also a film of tears, out of place, like a mist of rain on a sunny day. "I've never felt like that. Ever."

"Me neither," Izzy confessed. "I'm not sure how I'll survive on my own anymore. I had my routines and I thought I was okay, but now the thought of going back to just this life, in this basement, without you..."

Her fingers closed over his hard-on. "Don't go down that road. We can't. It'll ruin the last day."

She was right. Izzy took a breath, focusing on the delicious sensation of her hand, and soon he could think of nothing else. She grabbed a condom off the night stand and rolled it over him, then pulled him on top of her, urging him to take her. He gave in, driving into her, relishing every moan from her lips. She wrapped her legs around him, smiled and bit her lower lip, nudging him to roll over. Once on top, she moved with abandon, her breath coming in gasps as she rocked against him. He'd never seen anything more beautiful. Izzy held on, watching her without blinking until her body trembled and eyelids fluttered, her body swept into a powerful release. Izzy tried to hold back, but as her inner walls tightened around him and a low moan rose from her throat, he gave up the fight.

No. He'd never come back from this. If she left, she'd travel away with his heart. He was in deep trouble.

Her head dropped against his chest and he kissed her hair, feeling safe, satisfied, terrified. He had to stop thinking about tomorrow. Whatever happened, Mia deserved better than his insecurities for her last twenty-four hours.

Chapter 27

Mia navigated the river path, sniffing the sweet scent of jasmine, so thick in the air it could drug a lesser person. She was the lesser person, high on the flowery smell that seemed to penetrate everything around them. Izzy's wide frame moved ahead of her, carrying a large backpack, a guitar case and a chilly bin.

Her fingers brushed the backpack swinging on her shoulder, feeling for the passport in the side pocket. They'd driven by the police station to pick it up. Reuniting with the old I.D. felt odd, like carrying a piece of herself that she desperately needed and didn't necessarily want. She no longer needed Izzy's help. Mikko had sent her a money order, which she'd picked up after the passport. She'd tried to pay Izzy back for everything, but he'd stonewalled her, creating the most awkward encounter of her life. Mia had dropped the subject and decided to hide the money somewhere in his house.

"Can we just forget this for one day?" He'd asked her, driving towards the river.

She expected they were headed for a picnic by the river, although he'd asked her to pack an overnight bag, which she didn't quite understand. It didn't matter. She'd happily sleep under the stars if she could be with him.

They passed a dog walker, an older woman who smiled at them, pointing up. "Did you notice the eucalyptus? Beautiful smell."

Izzy nodded and gave her a faint smile.

"I can smell something sweet," Mia replied. "I don't think it's eucalyptus."

The woman's smile widened. "Yes, this is jasmine!" She informed them and described where exactly the eucalyptus trees were located.

"Do you know her?" Mia asked Izzy after the woman had moved on.

"No."

"Really? But she just talked to you like she knew you."

Izzy shrugged. "It happens."

Mia shook her head, smiling to herself. "Not in Helsinki it doesn't."

But as they continued down the path, she spotted the docks. An old guy with a deep tan wearing a linen shirt waved at them. He stood by a pickup truck pulling a boat on a trailer. For a moment, Mia thought he might be another overly friendly stranger, but Izzy beelined to the guy, his hand raised in greeting.

"Peter!"

"Izzy. How are you? Deacon told me you have someone special staying with you?" He turned to Mia with a self-assured smile. "You must be the someone special?"

"Mia." She shook the hand he offered.

"Peter Huntley."

"Deke's dad," Izzy explained, and Mia's eyebrows shot up as she tried to connect the dots. At a glance, he looked nothing like Deke, but then again, hardly anyone did.

"Lovely to meet you!" The old man exposed a perfect set of pearly whites that looked dentist-made. "I have to get going, but I trust you'll take good care of our old gal?" Mia's eyes searched the boat's shiny, wooden hull and located the name Rosalind in flowing cursive. It must have been a lovingly restored original.

"I will." Izzy accepted a key on a cork keychain.

"We're going on a boat?" Mia asked, her heartbeat kicking up a notch. She would have happily sat on the riverbank with Izzy, but this was seriously amazing. Maybe the act of sailing on the river would take her mind off the burning question of tomorrow.

"Yes," Izzy beamed at her. "I mean, if you want? I'm not going to force you or anything."

"You're not forcing me, but you really like surprises, don't you?"

Tension flickered behind his eyes. "Don't you like them?"

Mia cocked her head, considering the question. "I thought I didn't, but lately, I've really enjoyed them. What can I say?"

His smile brightened with relief. "I love seeing that look on your face. I'm seriously addicted to it." His tender hand brushed her cheek and she felt a rush of heat, suddenly aware of the old guy looking at them.

Peter winked, hopped in his car and expertly reversed the trailer so it was facing the ramp. Izzy heaved their bags onboard while Peter fiddled with straps and levers attaching the boat to the trailer. Izzy helped Mia board the boat and joined her, taking the wheel. Peter reversed down the ramp. Once they were afloat, Izzy started the engine and steered away from the ramp. And just like that, they were on their way, navigating downstream.

Izzy found two life jackets under the seat and Mia selected the smaller one for herself. The cockpit was just big enough for two people and had only partial cover, but the boat had a lovely feel to it, the lacquered wooden dashboard and old school steering wheel exuding vintage charm.

Jungle-like greenery hung off the river banks, climbing so high she could barely see the occasional houses perched on top.

"It looks like the Amazon rain forest," Mia blew a deep sigh.

The river was its own private world, occasional bridges the only reminder of the city that sprawled on both sides.

Izzy glanced at her, smiling at her expression. "I love it here. You can't hear the traffic, but you see this whole other side of town. The birds and secret swimming spots and the rich people's backyards." He flashed her an impertinent smile.

"It's gorgeous." Mia filled her lungs with the fresh air flapping at her dress and sat on the two-seater in the cockpit, letting Izzy drive. "Where are we going?"

"I thought we could just go downstream for a bit and find a nice spot to hang out, then come back up?"

"Sounds perfect." Mia closed her eyes, listening to the burbling of the water, mixed with the soft puttering of the engine. Then a thought hit her. "Why did I bring an overnight bag, though?"

Izzy's grin turned sheepish. "Um... there's a double bed down there." He pointed at the floor.

"Really? How do you get in there?"

"Just back up a little and you'll see the stairs."

Mia investigated the small space behind her, and discovered the entrance leading underneath the deck. "Can I take a look?"

"Sure. Take the bags with you. You can store them in the cupboards." Izzy pointed at the two backpacks and the guitar case which they'd crammed between the seats in the cockpit.

Mia took the bags, leaving the guitar, and negotiated her way down the steep, narrow steps. The space underneath was larger than she'd expected, and surprisingly cosy, with shiny wood detailing and jungle-patterned green cushions perfectly matching the river scene outside. Other than the rather hot, stuffy air, it felt cosier than any space she'd come across on her travels. Could she just stay here and never travel anywhere ever again? People lived in boats, right?

Stashing the bags in an empty cupboard, Mia climbed back up. "How much does a boat like this cost?"

Izzy kept his attention on the river, steering them between a green and red buoys. "Are you thinking of buying one?"

Mia perched herself on the seat by his side, hanging her arms over the railing. "Just dreaming."

"A hundred thousand, maybe."

"I'll keep dreaming." She huffed a sad laugh. "It's so cosy down there, I could easily live on a boat like this."

Izzy's face brightened in delight. "So you're okay to spend the night? I've only done it once, but it was the best sleep I ever had."

Mia grinned at him. "Yes! I'm not that keen on sleep, though. I can sleep on the plane."

Izzy narrowed his eyes. "No talk about tomorrow!"

She sighed. "I'm trying! It's just so hard. If there's something you're not supposed to think about, it's all you can think about, right?"

"Yeah. That's how the human mind works. Let me moor up somewhere and I promise I'll do my best to distract you." He winked, and a shiver ran down Mia's spine, her gaze zeroing in on the curve of his bicep stretching the thin T-shirt material. The veins on his forearms twitched as he handled the steering wheel. Yes. He could definitely distract her.

She'd never really cared about the male form, blissfully

uninterested in what Mikko wore and how his arms looked. Ogling the opposite sex felt embarrassing. But Mikko was skinny and pasty white, and she suspected he'd never cast a smouldering look at anyone in his life. The way Izzy's gaze roamed her body, his pupils dilating like a shadow grew from within, hit her like a heat wave, switching off her rational brain. And he hadn't even touched her yet. The previous night's events flipped like a slide show behind her eyes, making her legs shake. Could she ever get enough of him?

After a while, Izzy steered them closer to the riverbank, towards an off-channel area where the water pooled into small swirls before joining the main stream.

Mia noticed something in the middle of the greenery. "What is that?" It appeared someone had built a dock to access the bay.

"Must be someone's private access," Izzy said. "But it looks old. Might not be in use anymore. Should we moor the boat there?"

"Can we?"

Izzy studied the dashboard. "It's pretty deep around here. We should be able to."

Getting closer, they saw the true state of it. A tree had fallen on the part that attached the dock to the riverbank, leaving an isolated platform one could only access from the river side. Izzy dropped the anchor and they listened to the clank of the metal chain unfurling. Within moments, the boat slowed and they crept towards the dock. It was a beautiful spot, sheltered from nearly every direction by the green ferns and trees growing over the water, hanging their leaves just above the surface.

As they got within reach, Izzy jumped on it, tying a cable around one of the supporting poles. The structure didn't wobble beneath him and Mia relaxed a little. As the boat gently bumped against the dock, Izzy helped her onto it. She relished the sensation of something solid underneath her feet and happily peeled off her bulky life jacket.

The sun had dipped behind the trees, casting its glow on the opposite riverbank, making the windows of sparsely spaced, luxurious houses flash like diamonds.

"I like this place. Can we stay overnight?" Mia sat on the edge of the dock, swinging her legs just above the water's surface. "Or do you want to keep going?"

Izzy sat next to her, his bare feet dipping into the stream. "I don't care where we go. This is perfect."

It was. Mia closed her eyes, inhaling the fresh air that carried scents of plants, flowers and whatever lived in the water. "Should we get some blankets and pillows or something, and just hang out here? It's a nice boat, but the cabin is pretty hot."

"Yeah. It'll cool down at night."

Izzy climbed back on the boat and soon returned with blankets, pillows and the chilly bin, and they set up a picnic on the dock. Mia's eyes widened at the mouth-watering spread of pastries, strawberries, cherries and melon slices.

She picked up a strawberry and Izzy held up a can of whipped cream.

"Open wide," he said, and squeezed cream straight into her laughing mouth.

After pastries, egg sandwiches and two cups of Pinot Gris, Mia felt full and mellow, her head lolling on her shoulders.

Izzy lay on the blanket with his guitar, his head propped on a pillow, strumming a song she didn't recognise. There was so much more she needed to learn about this man, but right now, she felt the kind of kinship that hardly needed words. "Can you play that song from the cave?"

"Secrets of the stars? No, that needs two guitars. You'd have to play with me."

"We should have brought both! Although I'm not great at playing by the ear like you. I need chords and even then I struggle." A sad smile pulled at her lips. "I'm not a proper musician."

"What's a proper musician? You don't need a perfect ear or a higher degree. As long as you have ideas and find your own sound."

"You think so?"

"There are plenty of people who've built a music career on a gimmick of some kind, or a very unique sound, or lyrics... You just have to build your audience."

"What about your filmmaking? Are you building an audience?"

Izzy sat up, looking away. "No. You're right. I don't practise what I preach. Ignore me."

She took the guitar off him. "I can't ignore you. I think you're right, you just need to take your own advice and put that story out there."

Izzy threw her a lopsided smile. "If you record one of your songs."

She met his gaze, unflinching. "Deal." What had she just agreed to? Mia swallowed. The air vibrated around her, like she'd been captured inside an alternate reality. One where she shamelessly explored her creativity.

Izzy dug inside his backpack and produced a portable speaker, connecting it to his phone. "Should we listen to something?"

"What if someone hears us?"

Mia glanced over her shoulder. The shore seemed deserted. During their picnic, night had fallen and she struggled to see into the shadows. The day's warmth lingered in the air, although she could feel the beginning of the evening chill on her bare arms. The sky had turned a gradient of light turquoise and deep blue and a crescent moon hung above their heads like a discarded nail clipping. As the first beats of strings rose from the speaker, a different kind of chill vibrated through her. "What is this?"

"Shostakovich."

"It makes me want to dance." Mia swayed to the music.

"It's a waltz." Izzy stood up, extending his hand. "Dance with me?"

"The awkward white-man dance?" She chuckled, but took his hand. "We're going to waltz right into the river."

"Maybe, but we'll do it with style." Izzy hooked a hand around her waist and moved to the music, taking steps so small that they hardly moved from the one spot in the middle of the dock.

Mia relaxed against him, trusting him to keep her safe. The jazzy waltz flowed through her, making her heart ache with its beauty and wonder. He raised her hand and she did a cautious pirouette, her white dress billowing around her. As he pulled her back to his chest, she caught his scent and her stomach wobbled. Was it possible to smell pheromones? Inhaling him, she sensed the explosive strength under that dark skin, the way he could take her, the way he held her both gently and with desperate force, afraid to let go.

After last night, she'd briefly thought about staying away from him until it was time to fly back, to not complicate things further. But the decision had evaporated the moment she'd woken up, the powerful dream still lingering in her mind. Her entire body responded to his desire, her insides turning into liquid. She had no hope of doing anything but this man until the evil forces of reality ripped them apart. Yet, every moment of intimacy increased her sense of dread. She was lending him pieces of herself, pieces she might never see again.

Izzy's hand slid down from her waist, pulling her against his hard-on, stealing all strength from her legs.

"We're outside in public," she whispered. "Sort of."

"It's getting dark. There's no one around."

"What if someone comes?"

His rough voice brimmed with mischief. "Let's make sure we come first."

She stared into his eyes, opaque with need. Her body guiding her, she raised onto her toes to reach for his mouth. He met her half-way, his beard scratching her skin as his warm lips owned hers, his tongue lapping into her mouth. She sensed his hunger and urgency, but also his restraint, like he was fighting hard to keep from getting in too deep, but they already were, she knew it.

Detaching herself from the moment, Mia took Izzy's hand and pulled them to sitting, their legs hanging over the edge of the dock. "You don't have to keep things light, or distract me. Be honest with me."

He pulled a face. "We have so little time. I'm afraid to ruin it."

"Tomorrow is not the end of the world. It's not the end of us. Or is it?"

Izzy's eyes flashed with defiance. "No talking about tomorrow, remember?"

Mia twined her fingers through his. "I know I said that, but I don't think it's going to work. Not for me."

"What's the alternative?"

Pain seared through her heart, stinging behind her eyes. "I don't know. I guess we have to... talk about it? Because I feel we have something here, but it's too early to tell, isn't it?"

"Is it?" His voice thickened with emotion, making her shiver.

"I mean, even if we feel something, we can't really trust it yet. What if it's just a chemical reaction?"

"Isn't everything?"

"What?

"Um... digestion? A car starting? Rust eating metal... all chemical reactions. Doesn't make the process unreliable."

"You know falling in love fades, right? It doesn't last."

"But a relationship might."

"Maybe." She felt her heartbeat in her ears, heavy and fast.

Izzy's voice resonated so low she could feel it in her stomach. "Are you saying you're falling in love?"

"Are you saying you want a relationship?"

He squeezed her fingers. "I want you in my life, every day and night, forever. That's what I want. I don't expect to get what I want, but Mia... if there's any way you could see us having a future, please tell me. It'll kill me when you go away, but at least I'll know where I stand."

His words arrested her with their weight. Izzy was all or nothing. She'd known this from the start and it shouldn't have surprised her. But she had to be honest with him. "I don't know how it's possible to fall in love in... five days? Nobody can fall in love in five days, right? I don't know what's happening to me, but I want to stay with you. I want to miss the flight and hide in your basement. But my sister..."

Mia glanced at her phone, lying on the picnic blanket, which didn't show any messages. "I promised I'd be there, but maybe I could come back? I just have to work and save some money. It's so expensive."

"Can I buy you a ticket?"

Mia's eyes widened. "How? You don't have any money."

"That's not exactly true. I've been saving up for a new production studio."

Dread squeezed her gut. "I can't let you spend that money on me! I'll just work for a bit. It won't take that long. I'll happily live on canned tuna and noodles if I know I get to see you again."

"But you wouldn't just come for a visit, right? It's way too expensive to fly back and forth. We can't have a long distance relationship."

He was right. Finland and New Zealand were as far apart as two countries could be. With nearly thirty hours of flying one way, popping in to see someone was like popping into an Australian cafe for takeaway drinks.

Mia closed her eyes, the inevitable thought fighting its way out of her mouth. "Then one of us would have to move. Or we'd have to choose a third country in-between and live there?"

She noticed the hesitation behind his quick smile. He wouldn't leave New Zealand. Why had she even mentioned that? He'd only recently left his basement, and here she was, suggesting for him to move on the other side of the planet.

Delusional. "No. I'll come back," she corrected. "I want to see Deke and Casanova again. And your family."

"What about your family? What would your parents think?"

They'd be devastated, Mia thought, but offered a reassuring smile. "Can we think about it later? The important thing is that I'll come back. It might take a while, but I will. I wouldn't ask you to wait for me. I'll take my chances. If I find you with someone else, I'll just… I don't know."

He cast her a rueful look. "I just went five years without dating. You don't think I can wait a few weeks?"

Their vague plan had a lot of holes in it, but the words strengthened her faith. This wasn't the end. It couldn't be. And if it wasn't the end, it had to be the beginning. Mia reached for Izzy's jaw, shivering as her fingers traced the thick beard. He was so gorgeous it was unfair, like those teeny tiny appetisers that tasted incredible but were always gone too soon. A taster of something she desperately wanted but couldn't have.

"Would you leave me pictures?" He asked, his voice unmistakably throaty.

Straddling Izzy, both of them perched on the edge of the dock, Mia tasted his mouth, savouring the saltiness of his tongue. "I think I want you inside me while I think about it."

"That can be arranged." Izzy deepened the kiss, his fingers behind her neck, tightening their grip as his tongue swept in. Pleasure fired through her, concentrating on the bundle of nerves between her thighs, her insides aching for him. He negotiated his hand between them, unzipped his shorts and produced a condom from his pocket. Were they really doing this?

Mia rolled her hips and wiggled out of her underwear, teetering on the edge of the dock. She straddled him, allowing him to fill every inch of her. All coherent thoughts escaped as she rocked against his body, her knees digging into the picnic blanket. The skirt of her dress flared around them, hiding the action that showed on their faces. It was the naughtiest thing she'd ever done, and waves of excitement cascaded through her, pumping more blood down to her core. Oh, God.

"Slow down," he growled, squeezing the soft flesh of her bottom, pulsing inside her. "We have time."

She couldn't slow down. Her arms tightened around his neck, and she whimpered into his ear, chasing the peak of pleasure. "I can't stop. Please."

He responded to every sound with his low growl, rocking his hips to meet hers, leaning back to let her lay on top.

"Mia." His voice, rougher than gravel, thicker than syrup, vibrated through her, sending shivers down her spine. Every signal landed where she needed it, intensifying the sensation until she could no longer stand it. This was it. The highlight of her trip. The thought floated through her brain as the charge built in her core, finally exploding into waves of ecstasy. She saw the stars in the sky above, closed her eyes and still saw them bursting inside her eyelids. How was it possible to feel this much?

He pulsated inside her. Seeing him lose control, glassy-eyed and mouth open, satisfied her soul. In that moment, he wasn't holding back or protecting himself. He followed her lead, giving her everything she asked for, matching every confession, every vulnerability with even more. Right here, with him, she could be herself. She had nothing left to hide.

"I want to play you a new song." The words spilled as she scooted off his lap and reached for the guitar. "It's not finished, but I thought of some lyrics on the way here—"

In her excitement, she missed the edge of the dock. For a second that stretched the fabric of time, she plummeted, her stomach hollowing out as panic seized her. Then she felt his hand, an opposing force that grasped her dress and yanked her back onto the dock. "It's okay. I've got you." He tightened his arms around her and hauled her back to safety.

Mia shuddered. There was that rag doll feeling again, with a rush of adrenaline. Izzy held her for a moment, waiting for her racing heart to settle. In the dark, she'd forgotten how close to the edge they'd been. The stars shone brightly, reflecting on the water, the air still soft and warm like a foggy hug.

"You caught me," she whispered.

"I did."

She heard the elation in his voice and thought about the dark river. The same river.

Mia dropped her head against his chest. She felt his heart beat in sync with her own. "If I'd fallen—"

"I would have gone after you." He hugged her tighter. "The current's not that strong around here. I would have caught you."

"I know." She believed him, but she could only hope he believed his own words. If only he could see himself through her eyes.

Mia picked up the guitar and felt for the right chords, trying to remember the words that her mind her been rearranging on the way there. It was about him. She couldn't even pretend this song was about anything else. He'd filled her heart and as her fingers found the right strings, the words poured out.

Run, run, run
Run like the river, run
Turn your head towards the places
You would never go

Mia sang louder than she'd meant to, overwhelmed by the emotion. There was value in things like this, birthing something new, offering everything you had, not just skills cultivated for the CV. The song reached its chorus, and she switched to humming, trying the melody a couple of different ways.

"This is where I got stuck." she glanced at Izzy under her

lashes. "Any ideas?"

"May I?" He gestured at the guitar and Mia handed it over.

Izzy played the same chords, singing a lower tune. She joined him with the main melody and shivered at the beautiful harmonies, two voices that rose and fell, creating a sound that was far more than either could be on their own. She'd written this song for him, but it wasn't her creation. It didn't work without him.

She didn't notice the tear until it fell onto her hand, the moonlight reflecting off the perfect, salty pearl. "Look." She lifted it to Izzy.

He's face split into the widest smile. "You're crying."

Mia sniffed, wiping more tears from her eyes. Real tears. Lots of them. "Ye… ah."

"Are you sad?"

Mia shook her head. "I think I'm crying because it's so beautiful. So perfect."

Izzy set aside the guitar and kissed her wet cheek. "You know the chemical composition of your tears is different based on the reason you cry? I remember a study where they analysed tears of sadness, anger, cutting onions… probably tears of happiness, too. And they could tell the difference." He kissed her cheek again. "I was wondering if I could taste the difference."

Mia smiled through the film of salty liquid, marvelling at how different the world looked, all blurry and shimmery. "You did it," she whispered. "You made me cry. I thought I was broken—"

"You're not." He hooked his arms around her. "You were never broken. You got a little lost, and now you found your way back."

His soft voice cracked her heart wide open and more tears erupted, taking over her body as they poured out. This was so different from that tight feeling in her chest, that lump in her throat. These tears flowed like the river, washing away years of dust and cobwebs from her soul.

Izzy offered her the sleeve of his T-shirt, and she dabbed at her eyes with it, smiling at the gesture, hoping she wouldn't soak it in snot. He was too good to her. Even if it couldn't last. Even if it was a chemical reaction. As her sobs subsided, she wiped the last drops from her eyes and blew out a long sigh. Her whole body felt lighter, like she could float away on the wind.

"I never want to get lost again," she said, jerking from the subsiding tears, little aftershocks following an earthquake.

"I won't let you," he whispered into her hair.

Chapter 28

Izzy emerged from the boat's cabin, blinking at the bright morning sun. The river had burst into life with birdsong and a group of people on kayaks floated past them, disappearing downstream. In daylight, the water looked so harmless, reflecting the sun in shades of olive and emerald. But he knew what it was capable of, and thanked God for that moment of clarity and fast reflexes. He'd saved her from falling in, and from here on in, he'd come through. He wouldn't fail again. He wouldn't fail Mia.

Izzy lifted the anchor and untied the boat, letting Mia sleep below. Her flight was leaving at noon, which didn't give them a lot of time to get back to Hamilton, pack up and drive to Auckland. Especially if he wanted to record that song, and he had to try. The sound of it had haunted him in his sleep, the words he couldn't quite remember, the chorus that made him shiver. She had a gift, this woman, and she didn't even know it.

Izzy steered away, out to the middle of the river, pushing

upstream. He wondered what the scenery looked like to Mia. She compared it to the Amazon, which he found funny. But everything around here must have looked so different to Finland. What was it like over there? Izzy hadn't even considered travelling, other than maybe to L.A. one day, once he had his short film ready. It had been a hazy dream, one he'd only thought of in that vague way young people talked about retirement, as if all of that would one day happen to someone else. If he was completely honest, the thought of approaching those production companies scared him stiff, and he'd been happy to push it out of his mind, focusing on the painstakingly slow process of creating his vision, frame by frame. After years of saving, he had the money to upgrade his equipment and carry on with the task. Mia had even helped him figure out the ending. Thanks to her, he could actually reach this goal. But was it worth it?

"Wow, we're going fast!" Mia appeared behind him, hugging his waist.

She poked her head under his arm, looking up at him with sleep-bleary eyes, her blond bob mussed.

"We don't have a lot of time." He wished he could make the words untrue.

Mia's body tensed against his. "Oh, right. The last day."

She squeezed her arms around him, breathing into his T-shirt. Her head, nuzzled under his chin, smelled of strawberries. Izzy wished he'd washed in the river. Even the nitrate-rich water would have been better than no shower at all.

"How are we getting the boat out of the water?" she asked.

"Deke's meeting us at the ramp, bringing his dad's car."

"Oh, great. I get to say goodbye. I'll miss that guy. And Casanova."

Izzy shut his eyes for a second, trying to expel the image of goodbyes. In ten minutes, they arrived at the boat ramp, met by a broadly grinning Deke in his favourite rainbow-coloured tie-dye shirt.

"Deke!" Mia shouted above the puttering engine. "I love your shirt!"

His grin widened to cartoonish. "I love your dress."

Mia's hand brushed at the white cotton, her face brightening. Izzy slipped his hand around her waist. "*I* love your dress," he added quietly. Why hadn't he told her that? He wanted to be the one to make her face look like that. The regret of all the opportunities he'd missed and would miss blackening his thoughts, Izzy jumped out of the boat and helped to manoeuvre it back on the trailer.

"I can't believe you're leaving already." Deke enclosed Mia in a tight hug, which in Izzy's opinion lasted at least five seconds too long as they both whispered something he couldn't hear.

"I can't believe it either." Mia's voice choked up. She swiped a tear from the corner of her eye, casting Izzy a grateful smile.

"You have to come back." Deke gave them both a

meaningful look.

Mia nodded, meeting his gaze. More tears spilled out. Last night must have opened the floodgates, Izzy thought, his chest filled with pride and wonder. He'd never thought there was anything wrong with her, he simply couldn't accept the premise, yet he sensed the significance those tears held for her. Whatever life she'd lived before, it didn't matter to him. The real Mia was the one here with him, smiling through her tears, barefoot in a white cotton dress like a bohemian bride, her hair ruffled by the gentle wind.

Deke climbed back into the car. "Sorry, I have to take the car back." He started the engine, lifting his hand in a showy wave. "Don't look so sad. Love always wins!" he shouted before driving off.

Izzy and Mia walked down the river path towards Izzy's house, watching as the sun climbed above the opposite riverbank, bathing them in light.

Mia seemed quiet, her eyes fixed on the flowing water as they climbed up the path that eventually swerved away from the river, towards Bader.

"Let's take the scenic route," he suggested, wanting to avoid the abandoned car carcasses lined up in front of the state housing.

He led them to a path weaving through a small forest, its floor covered with tiny flowers, like white stars twinkling against the dark green canvas.

Mia breathed deeply, her face splitting into a wondrous

smile. "How does this country smell so good? Is it perfumed?"

Izzy chuckled, hoping the flowery smell covered the sweaty odour he'd definitely worked up on the way. He hadn't paid much attention to the greenery around his house, but now the flowery carpet filled him with gratitude. Good job, late New Zealand spring. Maybe the flowers would weigh in his favour when she returned to the ice and snow.

Once they arrived at his house, it was already past eight a.m. Knowing they'd have to be on the road by nine, Izzy made eggs on toast and coffees, while Mia packed her few belongings. She presented back in the kitchen only fifteen minutes later, having showered and changed, carrying her small backpack and guitar.

"I feel weird boarding a long-haul flight with so little stuff." She lowered her bags on the floor and her eyes lit up when she noticed the breakfast. "Thank you!"

As they ate, the clicking of the wall clock grew louder. Why did it have to march on?

Izzy hesitated, the question burning in his mind. "We should really get on the road now, to be safe. But I'd love to record that song. I understand if—"

"Let's." Mia lifted her eyes and he saw the flame.

They left the dishes on the table and rushed downstairs. Mia took Izzy's guitar, running through the chords while Izzy set up the microphone in the corner he used for audio recording. It wasn't exactly a recording booth, but the strategically positioned audio panels along the wall softened the sound and the basement was fairly quiet. Mia took out her phone and brought up the latest version of the lyrics. "Do you mind if I keep this phone?" She asked him. "I can send it back once I get home."

"Keep it."

With the microphone connected to his computer, Izzy tested the sound, turning to Mia. "You ready?"

She tipped her chin, her eyes burning like never before. The morning sun streamed in through the window, too bright and distracting. Izzy fought an urge to pull the curtains. The light he'd happily kept out now reminded him of Mia. Her hair, her bright eyes and burning passion. That directness that forced him to meet her there, eye to eye, with no pretence. She'd woken him from hibernation. How could she leave him here? He couldn't go back to sleep.

Izzy started recording, indicating for Mia to start. The fierce concentration on her face, she played, gradually surrendering to the song. He knew she'd written it to him, like a letter he could neither ignore nor dwell on. It made him too sad, but it had to be recorded. This song deserved to be heard, and he'd do his best to produce it. He'd spent years mixing audio tracks. He would figure it out, for her.

Mia played the song again, her confidence growing on the second round. Izzy gave her gentle notes, encouraging her to slow down and enjoy the moments. And she did, until there was no time left.

While Izzy filled a couple of water bottles, Mia poked

her head into Deke's room. Izzy heard Casanova calling her a beautiful girl and smiled to himself. That parrot was smoother than he'd ever be.

They packed her things in Izzy's car and he sped along the suburban roads towards the motorway.

"Let me choose the music, okay?" Mia said, taking his phone and quickly connecting it to the car stereo. After a moment, a melancholic male voice filled the car, crooning something in a language he didn't understand.

"Finnish?"

"Icelandic." She grinned at him. "I just love this song."

She curated the playlist for the rest of the trip, and they talked about music, New Zealand and Finland, carefully avoiding the topic of the impending farewell. Mia checked her messages. "My sister was having contractions already, but sounds like it may have been false labour."

"Hope you make it back in time." Izzy said. He had to accept his fate. If he pressed too hard now, he'd lose her.

He glanced at Mia, suddenly reminded of how she'd looked when he'd first picked her up. She no longer had her guard up. Instead of hugging her knees, she had her feet up on top of the glove compartment, her head flopping against his shoulder.

She had an edge to her, a fierceness that may have looked like lack of emotion, especially without the tears, but he'd seen the fire that dwelled inside, matching the one in his chest. How many people missed that about her? Would anyone in Finland understand what they had when she returned to their lives?

As the traffic slowed approaching Auckland, Izzy felt the familiar chill down his spine. Whatever Mia expected from their goodbyes, he probably couldn't deliver. Why hadn't he prepared her for this? He'd been so high on their time together, just the two of them hiding from the world. He wanted to think it was love, it had to be love... He thought when the time came, he'd find the courage to tell her. But how? He could hardly work up the courage to walk into a large building with... what? People wheeling luggage? What was wrong with him? Izzy wanted to slap himself.

"When was the last time you went to the airport?" Mia's tone was casual, but she dropped her feet on the floor and straightened her spine. She could see right through him.

"Never." he swallowed a sizeable lump.

"Really? Not even to pick someone up?"

Izzy shifted in his seat, knuckles twitching on the steering wheel. "I... people know I don't enjoy that kind of thing, so they never ask."

He felt sick to his stomach. Everyone had worked hard to make him comfortable, allowing him to avoid the most basic experiences in life. He'd been happy with his own imagination, creating a story that included a frightening transport hub in the afterlife, yet he'd never visited Auckland airport.

The traffic crawled to a halt just before the South Western

motorway ramp. They had little time. If she didn't make it onto that flight, what would happen? Part of him wanted that more than anything, but would it be a victory? She'd feel guilty for failing her sister and probably lose a lot of money on flight tickets. When she inevitably flew away later, she might never come back. Izzy tapped the steering wheel, the tightness in his chest intensifying by the minute.

Finally, they made it onto the ramp and the congestion eased. Izzy wove between the three lanes, trying to win back lost time. He wouldn't fail her. He wouldn't try to keep her against her will. No. He'd set her free and she'd return to him. Sending the desperate prayer out to the universe, he turned onto the airport road and floored the pedal on the open stretch of motorway.

Mia looked at her phone. "Calm down. We'll make it."

Izzy wanted to respond, but the tightness had spread to his throat. He couldn't tell what was strangling him, the thought of the airport with all its people and noise, or the thought of her getting on that plane. Either way, panic accelerated his pulse and he knew he'd already failed.

Chapter 29

Mia stared at the International Departures terminal, looming like a giant's mouth, aglow with fluorescent light and digital screens, waiting to suck her into its guts. This was the moment she'd feared. Her conversation with Izzy had become more and more tense as they approached Auckland. When the first airport signs appeared, he'd clammed up altogether, staring out the window, squeezing the steering wheel like a stress toy. Whatever she'd imagined, she hadn't accounted for this change in him.

Thinking back to their first visit to the shopping mall, Mia recognised the way his spine stiffened and his manner became short, almost robotic. He seemed absent, like he was channelling his energy into an internal struggle she had no part in. Except, this seemed worse.

She slowed down at the entrance, grabbing his hand. "Izzy. I can see you're not feeling well. What is it?"

He looked pale, averting her eyes. "I'm not good at this. I'm sorry."

"Good at what? Airports? Goodbyes?"

"Any of it," he grumbled. "I told you, I don't come here. I don't do this."

Sensing he was about to hyperventilate, she placed a hand on his chest. "Don't think about it. Just focus on breathing. In and out. That's all."

They stood for a moment, a constant stream of people passing them in every direction. To her relief, Izzy's breathing deepened and he met her gaze, face contorted in regret. What had she thought of, bringing him here? She'd seen him hiding in the dark corner of the mall, headphones in his ears. Headphones!

"Let's listen to something," she suggested, digging for her phone. "Do you have your headphones?"

Izzy started, pulling his earbuds out of his pocket. "Thank you for reminding me! I meant to give these to you, for the trip."

"Thank you! Do you have your phone? I don't have Spotify. Please play something. For me." She stared him in the eye for as long as he held her gaze. *Izzy, stay with me.*

Izzy took out his phone, plugged in the earbuds and handed one of them to Mia. She instantly recognised the song from the cave, the one about the stars. He smiled back, albeit distractedly.

"Do you want to say goodbye here?" she asked. As much as she wanted to keep him with her, what was the point of prolonging the agony? Without any luggage, she hardly needed help to get on this flight.

Izzy's eyes flashed with determination. "No, I'll come with you. Make sure you're okay." He glanced at the sliding doors, constantly opening and closing next to them.

"You don't have to go inside. I'll call you if anything happens," she said softly, placing a hand on his heart. The pounding under the surface took her by surprise.

"No. I do." He stepped out of her reach, marching through the doors.

Mia rushed after him, holding onto her earbud as the cord snapped tight. The airport version of Izzy was freaking her out. She wanted to help him, but how?

They ventured down the hall, instantly surrounded by the echoey bustle of footsteps and conversation, punctuated by loudspeaker announcements. Airports were the opposite of caves. Bright, loud and distracting, full of people, connected to everywhere in the world.

After finding Mia's first flight on the board, they stood in line for the check-in counter, wedged between a family with toddlers and two businessmen, the music in her ear constantly penetrated by the airport noises.

Reaching the counter, Mia removed the earbud and presented her ticket and passport. She felt naked without her luggage and launched into an explanation of what had happened. The lady nodded with mild sympathy, clicking her mouse, eyes on the screen. "So, you won't be checking in anything?"

"I just told you—"

"Here's your boarding pass. You should get to the gate as soon as possible. The priority passengers are already boarding."

Mia mumbled her thankyous and turned to Izzy, alarm squeezing her windpipe. "They won't let you through security without a boarding pass... do you want to say goodbye here?"

Izzy glared at the airline counter, pulling her further away from the swarming group of people. "I'll see you as far as I can. Where do we go?"

They followed the instructions towards security, finally stopping just before the conveyor belts and metal detectors. Mia turned her back at end of the queue, placing her hands on Izzy's chest, desperate for one last moment with him. She could sense him slipping away, retreating somewhere deep inside his mind as he blinked at the bright lights and the blur of people moving past.

"Izzy?" She whispered. "This is it."

She couldn't reach behind his stony facade, eyes hard and impenetrable. The connection she remembered only hours before had disappeared.

His voice sounded like it was coming through a tunnel. "This is not how I... I'm sorry."

"No. It's not your fault."

She should have never brought him here. They should have said goodbye in Hamilton, on the river. Izzy thrived in solitude. In darkness and silence. She could understand that. She couldn't force him into a life that didn't fit him. She'd break him. "Izzy, you don't have to say anything. We both know that long distance doesn't work. Finland is over ten thousand miles away. I looked it up." She pinched her eyes shut, pain shooting through her heart. "You belong here and you have your goals, the amazing things you're doing. Keep going. Promise me. We'll keep our memories and one day, once I have enough money, I'll come to see you again, but I don't expect you to wait for me. It's not fair." Her eyes blurred with tears. They came so easily now. Would she lose that when she lost him?

"Don't." Izzy spoke, barely moving his lips, his jaw tight, eyes two flickering shadows. "Please..." He grabbed the headphones which hung from his pocket, coiled them, placed them into her hand, his eyes pleading, breath shallow. He looked like he was about to faint.

Mia shook her head, a surge a desperation gripping her. She'd done this to him. She'd forced him here and caused him this pain. "Look at you. You don't even go to the supermarket. You can't be in a relationship with someone from the other side of the planet. That involves travel. There's no way around it." She sucked in her lips, tasting the tears that had travelled all the way down her face. "You need to find someone local. I want it to be me, but I don't know... stars would have to align."

"They already did." He spoke slowly, each word forced out

with great effort.

Mia shivered. This couldn't be the end. It was too cruel. If they'd met because of divine intervention, where was that intervention now? Mia glanced up, half-expecting the ceiling to fall, to stop her from boarding the plane. Why wasn't anything happening?

Mia Forsman. Mia Forsman. This is the final boarding call...

The sound of her own name on the loudspeakers gave her a jolt. "I'm sorry," she whispered, placing a hasty kiss on his lips and rushing to the nearest security gate.

Not looking back, she threw her backpack on the tray and walked briskly through the gate, then ran through the duty-free shops towards her gate. She made it just as they were closing the entrance and presented her boarding pass with apologies, out of breath. The airline staff took pity on her, letting her onto the jet bridge. She could feel everyone's eyes on her as she stumbled her way down the aisle, blinking back tears. Crying in public felt like such a foreign experience. This definitely wasn't her.

Once seated, her head pressed against the tiny window, she wept for good. The tears of sadness, unfairness, shame... why had she run off like that? She was supposed to be a brilliant communicator. What had happened to her? She'd planned this farewell in her mind, imagining words she longed to hear, words she was dying to say back to him. She'd promised herself she'd graciously release him of any obligations but promise to return. She'd released him alright. She'd downright told him it was over.

Was it? Or had she just let the enormity of the distance that stood between them, and his visible discomfort, erode the faith she'd had only hours earlier?

Mia stared out the window at the stretch of tarmac ahead, trying to remember the way she'd felt in his arms, on the dock, and in his house. It already felt far away, like a mirage flickering in the distance. If she couldn't sustain that feeling for one day, how could she sustain it for weeks or months? If she bought a ticket and came back, would he be waiting? She'd basically told him to find someone else. Someone local.

The plane jerked forward, rolling to the start of the runway. Mia fastened her seatbelt and dug up her phone. Maybe she could still send him a message, fix this somehow. After browsing her list of two contacts – Kati and Mikko, she realised her mistake. She didn't have Izzy's number. They'd been together the whole time, and she'd treated the phone as a temporary thing she'd only used to connect with people in Finland. In all honesty, she'd barely touched it in the last couple of days, too busy touching him. The only thing she found was a list of expenses she'd converted from the physical notebook into a digital one, showing a total of 345 dollars. It seemed too low. Their time together must have cost him more than that. But that's what she officially owed him, and she'd already hidden the money in his house, with interest. On paper, she owed him nothing, yet she'd felt indebted to him in ways she could hardly explain.

As she stared at the phone, a flight attendant came round to tell her to switch it into flight mode. Mia complied.

Well, that was that. She couldn't reach him at all until she arrived in Doha and hopefully found WIFI. Staring at the screen, her eyes landed on an icon she didn't remember seeing before. Spotify. Had it always been there? Mia launched the app and it displayed a selection of songs she remembered from the car trip. Was it Izzy's account? Mia navigated to 'settings' and stared at his username, dumbfounded. She had access to Izzy's premium account, along with several downloaded playlists. It had to be a mistake. Maybe Izzy had forgotten to sign out on his old phone before handing it over.

Then she remembered the headphones he'd practically forced on her. Was this the reason? Her fingers trembling, she opened the playlists. The first one up was called *Mia*. He'd made her a playlist! Like two teenagers sharing headphones, he'd made her a mix tape. The silly thought shot through her heart, producing more tears, along with an involuntary smile.

Letting the tears run, enjoying their salty taste and the way they expanded her chest, she slipped on the earbuds and pushed play.

Chapter 30

"You're gorrrrgeous!" crooned Casanova, interrupting Izzy's downward spiral for the tenth time.

He didn't have the energy to tell Deke off for letting the bird fly free. He'd already counted three shit-bombs on the kitchen floor, and there was probably some stuff on his toast, but what difference did it make? He already felt like shit.

"I know it sucks right now, but it's not the end of the world, is it?" Deke ladled cereal into his mouth.

Since Mia had left, his cooking had gone downhill, fast. Izzy had tossed between beans on toast or Cheerios for dinner, landing on the prior because the cheery brand name irked him so much. It didn't bother Deke, who was on his third bowl. Izzy cringed. He should have cooked for them. Losing the love of his life wasn't a good enough reason to stop caring about everyone else. He could ignore himself, stop shaving and return to his basement, but he still had to watch over Deke, and the parrot was his problem by proxy. That's all that was left in his life. Responsibility.

"It's not the end of the world," he admitted with a grunt. "She might come back one day, who knows. Although she told me to find someone local."

"She probably didn't mean it. When she looked at you, she looked like one of those heart-eye emojis. I can't always tell with that subtle fuckery females do, but she was easy to read." He swallowed a mouthful and grinned. "Also, she told me."

Izzy dropped his toast. "She told you what?"

"When she said goodbye at the river, she whispered to me..." Deke flashed a cheeky grin, enjoying the suspense.

"What?" Izzy growled, his patience wearing thin.

"Okay, if you must know, she told me to look after you until she comes back, because... she, and I quote, is head over heels in love with you."

Izzy's heart glowed as he stared at his friend, trying to figure out if he was as full of shit as his bird. He wanted this to be true, so badly. "She didn't say that to me. Why would she tell you?" His voice came out laced with hurt, but he hardly cared. Mia had stripped off the protective layers of his heart, exposing him to sunlight, hurt, everything he'd tried to avoid. Everything hurt. Everything.

"Sometimes it's easier to talk to a friend than a... lover." Deke's eyes bulged in a comical way and he tipped his bowl to drink the leftover milk.

Izzy pushed his plate aside, his heart doing funny things. If she really loved him, they'd find a way to be together, right? That's how it was supposed to work. "I was like a zombie at the airport," he said quietly, staring at the uneaten, cold beans. "I didn't say anything I was supposed to. I didn't tell her how I felt. I just… froze."

Deke tilted his head, his bouncy orange hair defying gravity. "A panic attack?"

"I don't know. I felt like my heart was going to explode."

"Yeah, that's probably what it was. Remember that one time you came home from Countdown and we googled those symptoms? Airports are a lot like supermarkets, only worse."

Izzy looked up, surprised by his friend's insight. "Yeah, it was similar. Physically. What's wrong with me?" He crumbled under his breath, raking his fingers through his hair.

"We're all fucked up in strange, wonderful ways. It doesn't matter."

"But even if she liked me before, when she saw me acting like that… she's right, I can't be with someone who lives on the other side of the planet. I can't even handle Auckland airport. It's never going to work."

He couldn't even apologise. She was somewhere in the atmosphere, unreachable. He could only hope she emailed him on arrival. They hadn't really discussed staying in touch via video calls or emails. That all fell into the 'long distance relationship' category, which had been firmly off the table. It had made sense at the time, when he'd been with her. Even the words 'long distance' had made him sick, but what was the alternative? Now she was gone and he had nothing.

Deke curled his finger at Casanova, who climbed on his

hand and made his way up to his shoulder. "If she really loves you, she will accept you for who you are, right?"

Izzy huffed at the statement he'd made to Deke many times before, comforting him after yet another woman turned him down.

"Nobody will love her more than I do. It's not possible." The words poured out like fog from a bug bomb, filling the room. He hung his head over the disgusting meal, now ready for the compost bin.

"Whoa! Dude. You're so love sick right now it's painful to watch. You need to go there and talk to her."

Izzy lifted his head, coming eye-to-eye with Casanova. The bird cocked his head, peering at him with a beady, black eye. "How're *you* doing?"

"Not well," Izzy admitted. "Thanks for asking."

Was Deke right? Did he really need to go to Finland? Even if he could get there without his brain exploding, how would he find her? He didn't speak Finnish. He didn't have any local contacts. He didn't know any of her friends or family. Mia had mentioned something about giving up her flat when she left for her travels. Where would she stay on her return? She'd quit her job and turned down whatever her ex-boyfriend had been offering, so she'd be looking for work. Would she stay in Helsinki or move somewhere else?

They'd talked about their families, but he hadn't paid attention to place names and had no idea where Mia's parents or even her sister lived. If Finland was the size of

New Zealand, he could easily spend months scouring the land trying to find her. The only email he had for her was the work email for her old job. He could contact the company and ask for her current contact details. They might at least have Mia's local phone number.

Izzy stood up and scooped his meal into the compost bin. "You're right."

Everything about this terrified him, but he'd figure it out.

Chapter 31

Helsinki-Vantaa airport welcomed Mia with a sea of people who all looked like her cousins. She trailed through the crowd of blond hair and deep-set eyes, trying to reset her brain to being back home. Back with her own kind.

Her brain resisted so much that she couldn't even remember where to catch the bus to town. The lady behind the info desk answered her question without a hint of a smile, staring at her computer screen. Mia followed the instructions out the door, towards the right bus stop. People moved out of her way, each avoiding eye contact. Had Helsinki always been this hostile?

A blast of freezing December air hit her face, the chill instantly penetrating her light clothing, digging through to her bones. She'd bought a scarf in duty free to lessen the blow, but she was essentially dressed for New Zealand summer. She adjusted the guitar bag on her shoulder, grateful for the way it shielded her back from the wind.

Thankfully, the bus arrived, taking her downtown, close

enough to her sister's address. It was the only place she could go. Her parents lived a three-hour drive way, and she needed somewhere to crash.

Mia scrambled out of the bus, onto the snow-covered footpath. At four pm the sun had already disappeared behind the tall buildings, having likely spent all day hiding behind a thick layer of clouds. The streetlights glowed their artificial orange light and pedestrians trotted along in their parkas and winter boots. Mia glanced at her white tennis shoes, already wet from the melting snow. She'd emailed her sister to let her know she'd arrived. Kati was having contractions again. Maybe this was real labour. Her message had been so short Mia imagined she'd dictated it to her husband in-between unbearable pain and had assured them she would make her own way from the airport.

Giving up her flat before travelling may not have been the best choice, but it had been the only way she could afford the trip. Now the cold reality hit her, along with the icy wind. She no longer had a home.

Mia tightened her woefully inadequate denim jacket around her chest and rearranged the scarf around her neck. Without much luggage, she could move fast, weaving through the foot traffic, rushing past the early 19th century apartment buildings with their arched doorways and gated entrances leading to exclusive inner courtyards. This was the rather fancy part of Helsinki, the part where you didn't have to see the boxy, seventies architecture, and one where she couldn't afford to live.

She located the building entrance and buzzed the intercom, her finger so numb she couldn't feel the metal button against her skin. After a moment, the speaker crackled to life and someone buzzed her in. The dry, stale air in the stairwell brought back memories of Mikko's apartment. She hadn't messaged him yet, but noticed two meetings in her online calendar under the new email she'd opened in New Zealand.

Kati opened the door on the first ring. Mia leapt to her arms, startled by the size of her belly. Of course it was huge.

"Oh, my God! Do you need to lie down or something?" Mia followed her to the beautifully decorated lounge.

"No. All good," Kati panted. "Sorry, I have to focus."

Her husband, Tommi, appeared from the kitchen with a bowl of noodles. He set it on the coffee table and escorted his wife back to the couch. "She's doing the hypnobirthing thing," he explained Mia. "They said it's better if you don't try to have conversations or really pay attention to other people."

"No problem." Mia smiled. "I can look after myself. Don't mind me."

A phone screen on the table had a timer running. Kati glanced at it. "Still five minutes apart," she whispered, glancing at the noodles. "No oranges?"

Tommi ran back to the kitchen, a harried look in his eyes. In his corduroy pants and long hair, he looked every bit the sculptor Mia remembered. She'd always thought it both cool and unsettling that her sister had fallen in love with an artist. Starving artist, they'd joked, one Kati had been supporting with her teacher's salary. But now, walking around their three-bedroom apartment, Mia sensed a shift. Most of the old student flat furniture had been upgraded, and Tommi's sculptures adorned every surface. The delicate figures would surely be destroyed by the baby that was making its way into the world right now.

Kati doubled over, grunting like an animal as Tommi rubbed her lower back.

Mia sat on the other side. "What can I do? How can I help?"

Tommi flashed her an apologetic look. "Sorry. She needs to focus. Maybe it's best you settle in and we catch up later?"

"I'll be in the guest room." Mia stood up, confused, and wandered down the hallway. She was exhausted and freezing. Not having to talk to anyone felt like a gift.

The guest room hadn't gone through much of an update, other than a new bed spread. Tommi must have gotten a big commission, she thought with relief. She'd been worried about them, always just scraping by. Kati insisted she didn't mind. They loved each other, and that was enough. Mia sat on the bed, sighing at the familiar sight of light, wooden floors and the cream-coloured Ikea chair.

Outside, the streets were covered in a dusting of fresh snow. Finland was so dark, yet so pale and white, everything around her aspiring to brightness, reflecting even the tiniest hint of light. Anything to combat the overwhelming dark of the winter. Gone was the richness of scents and saturation of colour. The soft, humid air was replaced by the dryness of central heating that tickled her nose.

Mia took off her cold, wet shoes and socks, found another (used but dry) pair in her backpack and snuck under the covers. Curled up on the single bed, she listened to the low voices carrying from the living room. She heard Tommi's footsteps against the parquet as he paced the floor, probably eager to leave for the hospital. First babies took ages, right, Mia thought, closing her eyes.

Images of New Zealand danced inside her eyelids, dark and intense like a feverish dream that couldn't have been real. She'd cried the whole way here, and now felt empty and bone-tired, but oddly soothed. There was no ache or pressure in her chest. The tears had washed it all away. She felt the overwhelming sadness of her loss, the separation... but they'd only just met. It would likely go away. He'd given her the gift of tears, and now those tears would help her get over him. Hopefully. Even if she planned to go back – a stubborn part of her heart insisted – she couldn't function in this mental state. She couldn't go to work crying, or even thinking of Izzy. Somehow, she had to slip into her old life, into a work mode, like a shirt she'd grown out of.

Fighting sleep that tried to drag her under, Mia grabbed her phone and searched for Kati's WIFI. Doha hadn't been kind to her. With only a few New Zealand dollars and no credit card, she couldn't buy herself into any of the better lounges with internet access, and the free one kept kicking her off. Thank goodness she remembered Kati's password. Asking for something like that from a woman in labour would probably earn her a noodle bowl to the neck. As the phone connected, she checked her email. No new messages. Did Izzy even have her email address? He'd been there when she'd created the new account, but she hadn't emailed him from it.

A cold sensation travelled up her spine. Was it possible Izzy didn't have her contact details? They'd spent every moment together, but then, getting closer to the airport, conversation had dried up and she'd only worried about his wellbeing.

Fingers trembling, Mia googled Izzy's business name and clicked her way to his contact page. There it was! Digital communication had given her such a headache over the last week that it felt like a miracle to be able to email anyone, especially someone she desperately wanted to connect with.

Creating a new message, Mia stalled, her fingers hovering over the keyboard. What could she say to him? Everything she wanted to communicate involved touch. Words would never suffice.

Izzy,

I just arrived. My sister is in labour, and it sounds like it will take all night. I really hope it goes well. God, it feels so strange to write to you! So inadequate. I feel horrible about the way I ran off at the airport. I'm not good with goodbyes and that just sucked. Not because you did anything wrong. Please know that. I know it was hard for you and you still came with me. It means so much that I'm crying just thinking about it. I'm crying all the time now, and it's all thanks to you. It's both good and bad, in a messy, equal measure. I don't think I could take being apart from you without crying. My chest would explode. So it's good. But if it weren't for you, I wouldn't be crying. I'd just be getting on with my life in Helsinki. Now I don't know what to do. I have to pull myself together and get to work, to make some money. It's the only way forward, but it means I have to forget you a little bit, to be able to function.

Please wait for me.

Mia

Mia took a breath, dread spreading through her chest to her fingertips. She'd told him to move on and find someone local. She couldn't really write to him now and demand he stayed loyal to her while she sorted out her life. Her heart aching, Mia deleted the last line and pressed send, too tired to think.

She dropped the phone on the bed and dozed off. Sometime later, Tommi woke her up to let her know they were going to the hospital and would keep her updated. She turned over in bed, mumbling 'Good luck' before falling back to sleep.

Chapter 32

I have to forget you a little bit.

What did that even mean?

Izzy lifted his weights back on the rack, sweat dripping from his forehead. Punishing his body helped, for a moment, but he couldn't switch off his brain, or pretend things were back to normal. That message had been sitting in his inbox this morning, after a fitful night. He had to talk to her. There had to be a way forward that didn't mean forgetting each other.

Not that he could ever do that. She'd gone through his life like a hurricane, blowing everything out of place. He felt as if the front door was permanently open, bringing in a breeze he could feel on his skin, even though he'd checked dozens of times that all the windows and doors were closed. He couldn't keep the world outside and the work that usually saved him, sucking him into its imaginary world, failed to hold his attention.

He'd fiddled around with the files, making meaningless changes to the 3D models he'd commissioned earlier, but instead of being sucked into the project and losing track of time, frustration built until he had to get off the computer and pump some iron. The progress was too slow, his plan too vague. Even if he could put that film together, who said he could sell it to anyone, anywhere? Instead of the film, he'd poured his time into Mia's song, recording the harmonies and mixing it. Hearing her voice brought back memories and pain, but it was the only piece of her that he had left and he couldn't stay away.

Mia had restarted his internal clock, and it ticked louder than ever before, reminding him that weeks, months and years could potentially be wasted. Life was going to slip through his hands. She was right. He should have written a book first, or at least published his screenplay for feedback before going ahead with creating anything on the computer. The technical challenge of it had lured him in and distracted him from the gaping hole in his plan. If he wasn't part of the world, his creation was unlikely to find its place in it either.

Blowing out a heavy breath, muscles in his arms and legs twitching from the post-workout exhaustion, Izzy dragged himself into the shower. Above the sound of running water, he didn't hear the footsteps and knocks until someone banged on the bathroom door. "Izzy? Are you there?"

"Mac?"

"Yeah, it's me. I'll wait."

What else was he going to do? Join him? Izzy frowned, wondering what his brother wanted. He didn't usually barge all the way into his bedroom without a warning.

Izzy stepped out of the bathroom, a towel flapping against his thighs.

Mac looked up from a book he was reading, his eyes wide. "Dude, you training for something?"

"No."

"Ah. You look like you're auditioning for a Rocky remake."

"Now *that* I would audition for." Izzy gave him a wry smile, sitting on the bed next to him.

Mac narrowed his eyes. "You do that in front of other people, you know?"

"Yeah. I'm turning into a social butterfly," Izzy sneered, a hint of pain breaking through his voice. "What are you doing here?"

"Deke called."

Of course.

"I'm fine," Izzy lied, sinking his fingers into his wet hair, elbows against knees. "She had to go... and I'm getting used to it, I guess."

"Is she coming back?"

"I think she's trying to, but she has to work for a while, to make some money." He tried to breathe out the heaviness, but it wouldn't budge. "It's fine. It'll give us time to figure out what we both want."

"You don't know what you want?" Mac's voice rose in confusion.

Izzy cast him an unimpressed look. "Of course I do. I want

her, but she doesn't want a long distance relationship."

"Then close the distance, bro."

"Me?"

"Yes, you! She came to see you. Now it's your turn."

Izzy rubbed a hand over his face. "I had a fucking panic attack just visiting the airport." His voice got stuck in his throat and he cleared it. "I'd never even been to the fucking airport! I'm just—"

"That's not true."

"What?"

"You were four or five when we flew to Christchurch. You were so excited you peed yourself. We had to go super early because you wanted to watch the planes take off before boarding."

"Huh?" Izzy lifted his head, taking in his brother's cheeky grin.

A faint memory floated from somewhere, of pressing his hands and nose against a giant window, listening to the hum of engines as they accelerated along the runway. Mac was three years older and sometimes dropped these childhood memories of things he couldn't quite remember himself.

"I wish I had that enthusiasm now," Izzy sighed, getting up to find a T-shirt. It was getting cold. That breeze again. Where the hell was it coming from?

"Do a practice run," Mac suggested. "I know Mum and Dad think you're this fragile flower that can't handle anything and have to be protected from the outside world, it's not true. You're not an agoraphobe—"

"A what?"

Mac lifted a finger. "Ha! I looked it up. It's a person with an irrational fear of open spaces and crowds and that sort of thing. But you're not. You're just out of practice. You've been here for too long, like an old lighthouse keeper, but you're not broken. You can move, you've just forgotten how. I know I should have dragged you out of here a bit more, but I don't have magic lady parts so..."

Izzy flinched. He appreciated Mac's pep talk, but he knew he wasn't just out of practice. He had some things to work through. But it didn't mean others had to coddle him. "Just for the record, I don't need anyone protecting me from the outside world. Mum or Dad or you..."

"That's what I told them!" Mac threw himself on the unmade bed, arms behind his head. "Where's that breeze coming from?"

Izzy crossed the floor, pulling up his shorts. "You feel it? I've been trying to figure that out..."

Mac stuck a finger in his mouth and lifted it in the air.

"Ah, the world's most inaccurate and disgusting wind meter," Izzy commented, stepping out of the bedroom.

Mac got to his feet, following his finger to the living area. "Is there a window behind the bookcase?"

"No... Oh, wait!" Izzy stuck his head through the crack between the bookcase and the wall. "I forgot! There is a window but you can't even open it from the inside."

“Maybe someone opened it from the outside.” Mac wiggled his hand through the gap. “I can almost reach the latch. If my arm was skinnier...”

Mia. She’d opened up his house from the outside. Why? Izzy trailed Mac out the sliding doors leading to the backyard, picking his way through the long grass around the corner. And there it was, an open window, sticking out of the wall like an advent calendar on first of December. Mac reached out to close it.

“Don’t!” Izzy raised his hand. “I think I prefer the breeze. It’s been a bit... stuffy in there.” He picked the T-shirt fabric that attempted to stick against his chest. Post workout sweats were still pushing through.

Or maybe it was the image Mac had planted in his brain of himself at the airport, watching those planes take off, getting on one with hundreds of people and heading to the other side of the world. Him. The guy who’d quit the gym and ordered groceries online. He was pathetic. Except if he did it. If he flew to Finland. No one in his family had made it further than Australia. They wouldn’t dare pity the man who flew to the other side of the world. He’d no longer be the delicate flower they had to protect from the world... or whatever Mac had said. Christ Almighty that sounded bad.

Izzy stepped back inside the basement, surveying his cosy den. It had served him well, but it was time to break free. He no longer cared how much it hurt. He hurt already, how much worse could it get?

He stared at his computer screens and the ergonomic chair he'd spent most of his time in during the last five years. It all looked the same, yet everything was different. Wait. Something *was* different. His camera bag, usually hidden away under the desk, sat next to his computer screen, half-open. Had someone moved it? Izzy reached into the bag, pulling out his camera. At least it was still here. He flicked it on and his knees buckled. Mia. Naked Mia filled the viewfinder screen, smiling at him, her cheeks flushed, face half-hiding behind ruffled hair. Drops of water glistened on her skin and she held a towel in her hand. She'd taken the photo right here, exactly where he was standing, and left it for him to find.

"What do you have there?"

Mac approached him and Izzy jumped, hiding the little LCD screen. "Um... nothing."

"Sure, nothing." His bother grinned.

Izzy dropped the camera into its bag. He'd have to hide the memory card, to not risk anyone else seeing his photo. It had already etched itself into his mind, probably going straight into long-term memory. He'd go back to it, he already knew it, like a junkie... even if it didn't make him feel better, only sadder.

"Why're you so jumpy?" Mac took a step closer, trying peer into the camera bag. Izzy yanked it out of his reach, sending a pile of twenty-dollar notes flying. They must have been hiding underneath. Mia's debt – he knew it instantly.

He'd refused the money, but she'd left it behind anyway. What part of 'no, thank you' did she not understand?

"Do you not have a wallet?" his brother grumbled, crouching to pick up the wayward notes, handing them back to him.

"It's not my money." Izzy crossed his arms.

Mac stared at him, jaw hanging. "Who else keeps money on your desk?"

Izzy sighed, balled up the notes and stuffed them into a pencil holder. Mac glared at him under his brow. "You've heard of wallets, right? They're great."

Izzy coughed up a sound that faintly resembled a laugh.

"Do you think love is like a brain tumour?" He asked his brother. "Does it alter who you are and how you think?"

Mac dropped his smile, granting him a surprisingly level gaze. "It doesn't change who you really are, I don't think. Maybe it helps you access some under used parts of your brain? It's still you, but high on courage and optimism. And you need that, because it's not easy." He looked away. "No, it doesn't change you, but it peels off the layers. You'll see what you really value, what you're willing to suffer for."

"Wow, deep." Izzy tossed him a teasing look.

Mac sneered at him, taking a measured step back. "I meant to say… it gives you a kick in the butt."

Before he realised his mistake, his brother's boot landed on his ass. He should have never turned his back on the little devil and his karate kicks. Izzy pivoted, staring down at his big brother from the considerable height and weight that he had on him, his biceps flexing. “You really want to go there?” He assumed his best warrior stance, his eyes bulging out of his head.

Mac threw up his arms. “Nope. Definitely not. But keep that energy. You’ll fly anywhere, easy as.”

A sad, nervous laughter bubbled out of Izzy’s chest, adrenaline pumping through his veins. Mac was right. Feeling a little unhinged was probably his biggest asset right now.

“I’m going to do it,” he said, half to himself.

Mac came at him with a fist bump. “I know.”

When Mac left, Izzy sat at his computer and replied to Mia’s email.

Everything will work out. Trust me.

All yours, Izzy

Chapter 33

Mia stared at the wrinkled, swollen perfection of her tiny niece, her breath a soft whisper as she slept inside the odd transparent plastic crib, bathed in blue light. An alien creature. She'd come out healthy but a bit yellow, and needed the light to break up bilirubin. Mia shook her head, wondering if she'd ever be in a room like this with her own baby, the one sitting on the bed instead of the corner chair. Right now, the chair was empty as Tommi had left the room to fetch them something to eat.

"I think she looks like me." Kati switched the breast pump from one side to the other like she'd done it a thousand times. The bottle she was pumping to only held a few drops of something resembling tree sap.

"How can you tell? They all look the same this early on." Mia sat at the foot of the bed. "Have you agreed on the name yet?"

Kati looked up, her eyes sparkling with excitement. "Yes! I got my way. I think after Tommi saw how hard I had to work to get her out, he couldn't say no. She's going to be Venla!"

"After grandma? She would have loved that!" Mia smiled, remembering the white-haired lady who'd always eaten dry bread from the back of the cupboard when visiting her flat, to stop it from going to waste. "Are you hoping she'll be equally frugal?"

Kati giggled. "Yes! And love bananas."

"She probably will. Although I think grandma loved them because she thought them exotic. She used to say they didn't have bananas in her youth."

"How do you remember stuff like that?"

Mia shrugged. "I don't know. My brain collects useless stuff."

"Good for writing songs, right?"

It was a throwaway comment, but Mia's insides wobbled. Kati knew she'd dragged her guitar around the world – she'd arrived with the evidence – but she'd never played her music to anyone, not even her sister.

"Yeah, I guess it is."

Kati massaged her breast, sighing as a few more drops fell into the bottle. "This takes forever, but apparently the early stuff is like liquid gold so I have to get it all out." She looked delirious after a long night of labour.

Mia kicked off her shoes and sat at the foot of the bed.

The room felt cosy, less hospital-like than she'd expected. No beeping machines or sounds of panicky footsteps down the hallway. Everyone spoke softly and moved with light-footed purpose. "How does it feel like to be a mum?"

Kati's eyes glimmered with unfocused dreaminess. "It's weird. Like I'm suddenly in plural. Nothing's just me, only us. But you know what's even more weird?" She glanced at the sleeping baby. "I can hardly remember what it was before, and it's only been like a day. Like my mind was wiped and reset."

"It's probably the hormones." Mia smiled, trying to imagine the strange feeling. "But it doesn't sound bad. Being in plural. I like that."

Ever since leaving New Zealand, she'd felt so alone, her heart like a crater left behind by a meteor that had crashed and burned, leaving only ashes.

"Are you okay? What happened on the trip? You haven't told me anything yet." Kati set the tree sap bottle on the night stand, glancing at the door.

"It's not that important. Not like... this." Mia gestured at the baby. "But I think... I'm so sorry, but I have to go back."

Kati's eyes widened, finally fully focusing on her face. "You met someone!"

"Did I say that?" Mia's brow furrowed. Kati was one of the sharpest women she knew, even in her post-labour stupor. "But yes, you're correct."

"Who? Where? Please tell me it was someone on your first layover in Stockholm! I can't have you move far away to—"

"New Zealand." The words cut the air between them, clattering on the floor as she held her breath.

"Well, fuck."

"Yeah."

"Are you sure it's the real thing? Hormones have a lot to do with that stuff, too. Holiday romances..." Kati cast her a sad, hopeful smile.

Mia bit her lip. "How do you know if it's real?"

Kati considered the question, staring at the light curtains softly moving over the wall heater, covering the quadruple-glazed window that gave to the dark street. It was past four p.m. and could have been midnight. Finland, why so cold and dark? With the little snow on the ground intermittently melting away, the overwhelming darkness of winter felt like a prison sentence.

"I think it comes down to your odds of having a future." Kati nibbled on her nail. "You can't sustain the passion. It comes and goes. So there has to be enough of the other stuff to build a partnership."

The sobering thought floated across the hospital bed, landing on Mia's lap. There it was – the stress test of her happiness. "I sent him an email last night when I arrived. It was pretty nonsensical. I just had to talk to him, like he's the only person in the universe who could possibly get it." She looked up at her sister. "I mean, *you* get me, but... you have a life here. A full life."

Kati nodded, quietly waiting for her to continue.

"I can't touch him. I haven't even talked to him. I tried to call, but I must have missed him. The time difference is the worst! My night is his day. The exact opposite."

"Did he reply to your email?"

"Yes. But it was one line and kind of cryptic. He's been making me these playlists on Spotify."

"What? Like a mix tape?" Kati snorted.

"Yeah, pretty much. It's adorable. I'm using his account. His phone. I told you I got robbed in Auckland, right? I only have my guitar and my passport. Izzy bought everything else I needed. I owe him so much! I mean, I paid him back, but—"

Kati stared at her in confusion. "Why didn't you tell me? I would have wired you money!"

"I didn't want to add to your worries. Also, it's really hard to contact anyone when you don't have a phone or a laptop. Anyway, it all worked out." Mia adjusted her legs against the starchy sheets. "Do you think I fell for him because of the... situation? Nothing like that has ever happened to me and I didn't feel like myself. I still don't. It's like I'm under a spell."

"Maybe." Kati shrugged. "Does it matter? You only need to worry about whether it has legs."

"And you hope it doesn't, right?" Mia twisted her mouth. "Because he's so inconveniently located."

"Um... guilty. But I'm okay that you're not with Mikko. He was always so..."

"Boring?"

"I was going to say clenched."

"What?"

Kati's hand flew to her mouth, unable to stop the eruption

of giggles. "He was always... clenching his butt cheeks. I often joked about it with Tommi." She wiped her eyes. "I'm sorry... I shouldn't have said that. He's a smart guy, so driven."

Mia couldn't help laughing along. "I can't say I ever noticed, but he does prefer those jeans that hang loose so it's hard to tell."

"Sorry," Kati hiccupped. "I think I am really hormonal. That'll be my excuse from now on."

Mia threw herself across the foot of the bed, her head half-hanging over the edge. "Can I use the same excuse? Like, on the account of being hopelessly in love?"

"Sure, why not. That messes up your brain. Does he... feel the same?" Kati's voice lowered, gathering gravity.

"He... hasn't said as much, but I think... I don't know. I'm probably delusional because of the hormones, but I'm pretty sure he was going to say something at the airport, but he's not really someone who enjoys crowds, or long-distance travel—"

"He doesn't like travel?" Kati's voice rose an octave and she shushed herself, throwing a cautious look at the baby, who remained asleep. "How's that ever going to work?"

"It's not!" Mia rolled over on the bed, sudden pain searing through her body. "It's a fucking disaster. I honestly feel like my heart's been split open and I'll never be okay. Nothing will ever be okay again." The tears came without warning, shaking her whole body.

Kati leaned forward, awkwardly patting her arm. "I can't reach you with this stomach," she complained. "Get over here."

Mia snuggled up to her sister, resting her head against the cotton shoulder of her hospital gown. Nice and absorbent.

"So, you're crying now?" Kati whispered, stroking her hair. "Wasn't there a time when you... didn't?"

"Yeah. It all happened there. It's all thanks to him. That and the music, the songs... he knew how to play them, he opened my eyes to all that. I want to write more songs, I want all these things... But I don't want any of it without him."

Kati held her for a moment, softly and firmly like a baby. Quiet footsteps echoed in the hallway, passing their room. The street behind the window was getting another dusting of snow.

"Then you probably have to go back." Kati's voice held a tinge of regret, but she topped it with a smile. "It might crash and burn, but if you don't give it a go, you'll be left forever wondering. And that's worse."

Mia sat up, wiping her eyes on her sleeve. "Yeah. Want to hear the worst part?" The thought hit her just as she said those words, solidifying like a bitter taste in her mouth.

"What's that?"

"I have to take a job at Mikko's start-up."

"Why?"

"Because it's the only offer I have, and I need to make some money, quick."

"So, you guys broke up and he still offered you a job?" Kati stared at her in awe. "He's not your average butt clencher, is he?"

Mia shook her head, suppressing a laugh. "No. He honestly doesn't hold grudges, which is admirable, but I'm not sure he ever really loved me so much as appreciated my skills."

"You helped him a lot when he was developing the idea, didn't you?"

Mia twisted in discomfort. "Yeah. But only because you couldn't really spend any time with him without hearing about it. He's just all about... productivity." Mia expelled a sad laugh. "It's exhausting, to be honest."

"Maybe the butt clenching is just ultimate productivity? Maybe he's doing Kegels or something?" Kati's mouth twitched with mirth.

"Men do Kegels?"

"They have a pelvic floor, don't they? But you're right, probably just training the butt cheeks. Sorry, I had a Kegel lecture earlier."

Mia laughed, tears clouding her eyes. She'd missed her sister more than she'd realised.

"I'll keep an eye out from now on. That'll make it more entertaining. Which is great, because if I'm honest, the job terrifies me. He'll make me do all the public speaking because he hates it. They all do. It's like they can't talk to other humans without clenching not just their butts but their faces. It's nauseating. I'll have to pitch for them at Slush, do these presentations... But I don't really have other options."

Chapter 34

Mia stepped through the meeting room doors, cursing at yet another glass wall that wasn't frosted. After three days as the acting head of PR, she'd slipped into something new yet familiar, blood whooshing in her ears as her mind tackled a constant stream of challenges.

To her relief, Mikko had agreed to her asking salary, without the stock options. She didn't need to get rich on the back of this. She just needed money to get the hell out of here. Their negotiations had taken place via email, short and sweet. They'd briefly met in the office, but so far she'd managed to avoid spending any time with him one on one, or running into the Portuguese Carlotte. The flexible hours made it rather easy.

The work had sucked her in like a rollercoaster, filling every minute of her life, invading her thoughts. She needed a moment to herself, right now. It was Sunday and nobody was supposed to be in the office, yet the buzz had only lessened by a degree as they prepared for Slush, the upcoming tech pitching event. Mikko seemed to be working around the clock, and others followed his example out of solidarity, or lack of social life.

Mia sat at the awkward but trendy trestle table, letting out a long sigh. She finally had a decent pitch. It only needed a couple of more user stories and some visuals. She'd tap into the designer after the lunch break.

The open office felt like an aquarium, one currently blasting Rage Against the Machine, where you couldn't make a private phone call without leaving the building. With half the furnishings still allegedly on their way (Whose responsibility was it? Had they dropped the ball?), every step on the hard laminate floor echoed off the walls, sending micro tremors to the giant window overlooking the half-frozen ocean and to the screens displaying the number of users signed up for the new service.

Mia suspected Mikko had attempted to recreate the scene from *The Social Network* and fancied himself the next leader of a multi-trillion-dollar company – an awkward genius with poor social skills and questionable fashion sense. She wasn't sure about the genius part, but the rest seemed accurate.

Mia finished her sandwich, washing it down with something called Brain Booster she'd found in the office fridge. It looked and tasted exactly like blackcurrant juice, but obviously there was some kind of higher science at work. She gathered her rubbish, along with her brand new laptop – courtesy of the job – and headed back into the open office, bracing herself for the loud beat that made the halogen lamps reverberate. The all-male staff (evidently, Carlotte didn't have to work on Sundays) seemed to draw energy from old school metal, enjoying the chance to blast music without headphones when the building was empty of others. Thankfully, that only happened on Sundays.

Scanning the space, she noticed Mikko with two developers. They stood in front of the screen, staring at the number which had frozen at 143,502. Was there a glitch or had the app user base stopped growing?

Her gaze fell on Mikko's ill-fitting jeans and she almost laughed out loud. He did look like he was clenching his butt cheeks! How had she never noticed that before? In fact, he seemed to continuously tense and relax his gluteus muscles. Mia pressed a hand to her mouth, determined to swallow the giggles. If she was lucky, she could sneak out without them noticing. She had so much to do, and whatever was wrong with the screen – or Heaven forbid their sign-ups – would potentially drag her off course and make her day even longer.

Deciding to take her work to a nearby cafe, Mia pulled on her winter coat, wrapped a scarf around her neck and searched the staff lockers for her mittens. Her leather satchel felt heavy with the 15-inch laptop and she went through it to identify anything she could leave behind. Water bottle, definitely. An apple. Izzy's phone? With her new work gear, she didn't need it, but still carried it around.

Mia turned the phone in her hand. She couldn't resist brushing her thumb on the button to wake it up. Her body quivered as she noticed an email from Izzy. The blank message contained only one audio file titled *Night and Day*. It couldn't be. Fingers shaking, Mia plugged in her headphones, pressing them into her ears to block out the background noise. From the first chord, she recognised the song she'd recorded, now beautifully mixed with Izzy's voice singing the harmonies, like they'd done on the river. Mia ripped off her earphones, eyes flooding with tears. She couldn't do this. Not here. She'd dissolve into a puddle on this hideous laminate floor.

Mia wiped her eyes on her scarf, taking deep breaths. Office life had definitely been easier without the tears. With a heavy heart, she hid the phone in her canvas bag and left it in the cubbyhole. If she brought it with her, she'd get nothing done. Hoisting her laptop bag on her shoulder, she snuck down the stairs to the lobby. Being Sunday, the receptionist wasn't around but a young guy from their team, Vesa, manned the desk, glued to his laptop.

"What are you doing down here?" Mia asked, leaning in so her voice would carry above the music.

He looked up, taking a moment to focus. "Mia, hi. Another focus group is coming in this afternoon so I thought I'd sit here." He glanced up the stairs. "It's a bit loud."

Mia smiled. "Yeah. I'm heading to Carousel for a long lunch to send some emails. I can't hear myself think."

The cold wind hit her face as she stepped through the sliding doors. Mia hiked her scarf a little higher, fumbling with her thick mittens as she pushed against the wind towards the shore. No longer under the watchful eye of her colleagues, her mind immediately wandered to the encapsulating heat of New Zealand summer. She could almost smell the jasmine and hear the native birds calling for each other, each with a different sound. Her fingers on guitar strings, her fingers on Izzy's skin… Had it really happened to her, or some distant holiday version of herself?

She'd replied to Izzy's email with a longer one, talking about the culture shock she'd experienced on returning and how much she missed him. He'd replied within minutes with one line: *I need to talk to you.* She asked what was on his mind and waited for more, but nothing arrived, except a new playlist on Spotify with her name on it. And now, the song.

It had been two days, and she promised herself she could overthink whatever had happened between them once she got through work and everything was set up for Slush. She couldn't raise a salary like this without delivering something.

Following the coastal pathway to the waterfront cafe, Mia studied the frozen landscape of greys and whites, punctuated by dark, leafless trees, pale pinks of the art deco buildings perfectly softening the stark landscape. She'd always regarded wintry Finland as dreary and uninteresting, something to escape. But now the familiar scene stirred something inside her. An idea. A song was hiding in there, almost too short a glimpse, a flash behind her eyes, itching like a sprout about to break the surface. Yet she knew if she didn't capture that idea, it would float away and dissolve into the universe, never to be caught again.

A piece of a melody formed in her mind, followed by a few words. She sang softly into her scarf, her heart glowing. There was such beauty in the moment of creation, following the first steps of an idea still fragile and shapeless. It didn't have to work. She could just follow it like a floating feather, to see where it might land.

Mia skipped ahead, her toes aching from the cold. How many of these moments had she missed before? Had there been beauty and wonder in Stockholm, New York, L.A., Honolulu and Melbourne? Maybe she'd missed it all, asking herself pre-determined questions about her future, her mind spiralling around the problem like water circling the drain.

Izzy's words from the airport whiplashed her.

They already did.

Stars aligned when they met. That's what he'd meant. She'd been waiting for a divine intervention to stop her from leaving and in its absence, she'd boarded the plane. But divine intervention had already arrived in the shape of the thief who'd taken her things and led her to Izzy. Stars *had* aligned, and she'd failed to see that. Izzy had more faith – she'd seen an inkling of it, despite his discomfort. It must have taken all his strength to utter those words, to cut through her monologue on finding someone local. Convenience. She'd tried to sell him convenience, and he'd tried to make her see the miracle.

Oh, Izzy. She missed him so much it was hard to breathe.

Chapter 35

Izzy's mind reeled from the cacophony of sounds and sights as he gazed over the crowd of pale blondes. To his relief, Helsinki-Vantaa airport was much smaller and quieter than the one in Singapore he'd navigated on the way. He'd spent most of his 10-hour layover either drunk or working on his screenplay-turned-book, headphones on. He knew he needed therapy, but right now, he had to make do.

Mia had been right. Writing the screenplay as a book had renewed his interest in the project. He was only two chapters in, but already felt he understood the main characters and their motivations better.

After a feverish writing session, hiding at the far end of a dimly lit lounge, he'd spent the last flight snoring against the wing of his headrest, sleeping off the alcohol and exhaustion. Right now, he desperately needed a shower. Instead, he'd stripped in the bathroom and washed his upper body over the sink, ignoring the side-eyes from ghostly white, expressionless blond guys this country seemed to have an infinite supply of. Travelling had pushed him to his limits, but he'd survived.

Izzy rubbed his swollen eyelids, adjusting the guitar case on his shoulder. He'd arrived in Mia's country, finally standing within the same national borders again. Now he had to find her. Thank God for the tracking app on the phone he'd given her. The idea had come to him right before the first flight, granting him the courage to board the plane. He'd downloaded the app and there it was, a blinking map marker in the middle of Helsinki, pointing to the location of his phone.

Mia had kept the phone on, maybe because of the Spotify playlists he kept updating. He'd tried to keep himself busy on the flights by building a new one of songs she might like, but it was difficult in an offline mode, and once he'd started drinking in Singapore, the song selection may have gotten a bit sappy.

As Izzy stepped outside the airport, the cold air hit him like a sucker punch to the lungs. How could anyone breathe in this country? He watched the stony-faced blondes in their thick parkas and woollen accessories lining up at a nearby bus stop, spaced two metres apart. Mia hadn't been kidding.

Izzy checked his phone. According to the tracker app, Mia was in a suburb called Eira, by the seashore. Izzy stared at the street name, cold sweat prickling on his neck. There was no point in even attempting to pronounce it, just like there was no point in trying to take the bus. He had to show the map to the taxi driver, as soon as he located one somewhere.

The middle-aged driver nodded at his Visa card, and Izzy got in. After glancing at the map on his phone, the driver steered away from the airport. The latest model Mercedes Benz with a black leather interior looked identical to the other two taxis available. Izzy wondered if he'd somehow missed the budget options. There seemed to be no airport shuttle or Toyota Priuses. Inhaling a lungful of new car smell, he fixed his gaze at the window, mostly to avoid seeing the running meter.

It was late afternoon and fairly light outside, yet everything in the landscape looked white and grey as if the colours had come out in the wash. The sun hid behind a solid layer of clouds that didn't crack despite the constant wind. Piles of dirty snow lined the roads. He'd landed on an alien planet inhabited by highly evolved beings who survived with the help of technology.

After a twenty-minute drive, they reached the city, the multi-lane highway turning into narrow roads lined with candy-coloured apartment buildings and leafless trees. A couple of times, a green tram clanked past. As they got closer, he caught a peek of the ocean, but the water looked odd. It must have been frozen, or partially frozen. Did sea really freeze? Maybe he should have brushed up on school geography instead of writing a book or mucking around on Spotify. He could have at least learned a couple of phrases in the native language, to seem like he was making an effort.

Maybe that's why the taxi driver seemed so miffed.

The driver had remained quiet for the entire trip, his eyes firmly on the road. Monotonous, foreign chatter on the Radio sounded like someone reading architectural drawings out loud. Finally, the driver stopped in front of a glass-covered office and said something he couldn't follow, gesturing at the building. Izzy checked the tracker app. It was the right address.

"Thank you." Izzy handed over his credit card and winced as his measly travel budget shrunk further.

He had enough for a few weeks, if he decided to never upgrade his computer. But since editing was his only source of income, he needed to keep something in the bank for a rainy day. The old machine could die any day. Financially speaking, travelling to Finland was the most ill-considered decision of his life. But surely there was still time to make worse ones, since he'd clearly lost his marbles.

Taking his suitcase and guitar, Izzy stepped onto the footpath, staring at the office building. Was Mia really here? It was Sunday, and she'd quit her job before travelling. Had she found another one, or were there apartments among the offices? Izzy double-checked the app, which insisted he was at the correct address.

Taking a deep breath, he stepped through the automatic glass doors.

Chapter 36

"Mia!" Mikko ambushed her as she stepped out of the staff kitchen with a cup of tea. "Everything ready for Tuesday?"

Mia jumped backwards, reeling from the sudden run-in. She'd returned to the office in the afternoon, hoping to find it empty. No such luck. Music was still blasting and two developers sat at their desks, hunched over their keyboards.

"Uh, yeah. I'm nearly done with the pitch," she said, avoiding his eyes. "I'm just getting some graphics done by tomorrow. I'll run you through it so you can practise."

"But, you'll pitch, right?" His gaze skittered around the room, his face a picture of abashment.

Mia sighed. "I'll pitch."

"Just make sure you add some excitement. Really sell it."

Guido – Mikko's productivity app – was no Facebook, but it made great promises and hoovered new sign-ups at a steady rate (after the lunch time glitch, the counter on the big screen had been updating regularly). Its sophisticated AI engine learned patterns of successful job and university applications in any given field, and used this knowledge to guide the user towards the career of their dreams, harnessing every moment of their lives to improve their odds. The premise was simple – when studying or applying for jobs, most people lacked self-discipline and focused on the wrong things. They wasted time on unproductive hobbies, derailing them from their original goal. Mikko's app was like a personal trainer who reinforced the user's 'right' behaviours and thought patterns – all in the name of success.

Before her trip, Mia had appreciated the idea, aware of her own procrastination. When she'd tested the prototype, *Guido* had advised her to swap her aimless guitar playing to weight training, to compensate for the gradual loss of muscle mass in her thirties. It made sense on paper, like exchanging chips for salad.

Now, she stared at the same pitch, her faith faltering. What if she needed her procrastination? What if she needed her music? Even if it never amounted to anything resembling a career, her soul would wither without it.

"What's with the face?" Mikko's eyes narrowed to slits. "You always say you love pitching."

"It's not that. I'm wondering about the content... what we're offering. Is it... attractive enough?" She picked at a hang nail, looking out the window.

"Why would it not be attractive? Who wouldn't want success?" Mikko sounded flabbergasted.

"Yeah, that part is great. But our generation... many of us

are already so tired, trying to get ahead. Telling people they're wasting their time, that they have to optimise their life, do more… it sounds exhausting. Maybe it's not the right message? Maybe we should spin it a bit differently, or add something to balance things out, like some mental health checks?"

Mikko blinked. "They tick that box in the beginning, it's basically a waiver."

"No, I don't mean the terms and conditions. I mean, actually asking the user if they are okay. Maybe we could double-check that the goals they've chosen are the right goals for them. Ask them if life feels… meaningful."

"I don't want any 'are you happy' crap." He huffed. "That's not what we're about. We offer results!"

"I didn't say happy. I said meaningful!" Mia scowled. "What good is success if you don't enjoy the journey? And what if you miss your true calling because you're so busy chasing one goal that you don't even notice another opportunity or talent you may have…"

Mikko folded his arms, raising his brow. "Whoa. Good to know the person selling our product doesn't believe in it."

Mia scratched her neck, feeling hot all over. "I'm sorry. I just need to work through these things and prepare for any curly questions the investors might have."

"They're not going to ask about existential issues. They'll ask about revenue streams, the growth rate, the upcoming features… you have all that information, right?"

Mia nodded. He was right. But something about this

bothered her like a tiny pebble in her shoe, hitting a nerve on every step. She took a deep breath, lowering her voice. “You’re right. The investors will probably only care about the financial stuff. But, does it bother you?”

“What?”

“Promoting this goal-chasing lifestyle that gets people to run faster on the hamster wheel. What if they burn themselves out?”

His brow knitted in confusion. “We have an exercise component. If your work or study is high stress, it suggests yoga twice a week.”

“Yeah. I get it. But do you ever wonder what you might miss in life when you’re just chasing one goal?” Mia glanced up, searching for a flicker of understanding in his pale blue eyes. She’d dated this guy. How could he not follow her?

Mikko tilted his head, his sandy buzz cut catching the overhead light. “People who think like that never get there. They get lost on the way smoking weed in their basement, listening to Pink Floyd.”

Fury built in Mia’s chest, swelling like dough. “Get where? What if you die trying – is it still worth it?”

He took a tiny step back, probably wary of the intense gleam in her eyes. “Isn’t it better to try than—”

“Is there a prize at the end?” She felt the heat building in her core as words poured out. “Do you get a stamp on your eternal passport if you achieved your goals and reached your full potential?”

Mikko's gaze flicked to the side like he was actually considering the rhetorical question.

Mia threw out her arms. "No, there isn't! You die. That's the end, Mikko. You can race to the finish line all you want, but that's not the point. The journey is the point!"

As she yelled the words at her ex boyfriend's half-terrified, half-smug face, they sank in. This was what she believed. This was the reason she couldn't do this job. And the reason she couldn't work with him. Or be around him.

The latest song on the office playlist wound down and a distant sound of conversation caught her ear. Someone was speaking English downstairs.

"Who's that?" She shifted towards the staircase. Thanks to the open office layout, the second level opened partially to the lobby, a balcony overlooking the reception.

Mikko followed her, a deep crease between his eyes. "It's probably the focus group. Vesa is down there, he'll look after them."

Mia peered down to the polished granite floor below. She caught sight of the sliding doors closing behind a dark figure who disappeared from view. The picture lasted only a half-second, but it stole the air from her lungs. Izzy. Ignoring, she charged down the stairs, blood pumping in her ears.

He couldn't be here. She'd only seen someone with dark hair and a guitar case on their back. It could have been anybody.

"What's up?" Vesa stood behind the reception desk, a baffled look on his face.

"Who was that?"

"I don't know. He asked for you. I told him you were still out at lunch. When did you get back?"

Mia growled in frustration, running straight out the doors. She'd deal with Vesa later. But as she stepped on the footpath, a tram stopped at the station and opened its doors, spilling a group of commuters from its guts. Mia sprinted down the street, weaving her way through the crowd. By the time she had a clear view of the street, he'd disappeared. It was four thirty p.m. and already getting dark. She couldn't even see into the shadows between the buildings that curved along the road. He could have stepped into one of the side streets. As if on cue, the first of the street lights flickered on, lighting up more snow-covered footpath and strangers.

With no coat, the winter chill bit her skin and Mia shivered. She had to go back and get dressed. She'd figure out how to contact him, if indeed he was here.

Stepping back into reception, she found Vesa flirting with two young ladies with trendy haircuts. They must have been the focus group. She cut in mid-sentence. "Sorry, but I need to know everything he said."

"Who?" Visa stared back, fighting to keep whatever relaxed, magnanimous persona he'd been presenting to the girls.

"The guy who was just here. The one who asked for me."

"Let me see... He had a funny accent, but I understood him since I've spent a summer in New York and got used to all those accents... So it was no problem." He cast a look at the girls, making sure they were listening. "He asked for you. I said you'd gone out to lunch and hadn't come back. Then he asked if you work here, and I said yes."

"And then he left?"

Vesa looked up, scratching his jaw. "No. He asked how you got the job."

"How I got the job?" Mia swallowed, cold spreading underneath her skin. "What did you say?"

Visa pulled a face. "I should have said it's none of his business, right? It was an odd question. But he was so polite about it... like 'oh, really? How did she end up working here?' Like he was just making conversation. So I said you knew Mikko so you've been involved from the start. I joked that you're part of the furniture."

"Oh, my God!" Mia buried her face in her hands, ignoring the strange looks from the young women. "I'm not part of the furniture! We don't even *have* furniture!"

"It's a saying," Vesa argued, clearly proud of himself for knowing a colloquial, English phrase.

Mia fought the urge to slap the smug grin off his face. "Whatever."

She ran upstairs, slipped on her coat and gathered her things.

Mikko reappeared, wearing an angry scowl. "Where did you run off to? I don't think we're finished with that conversation. I know we have history, but I can't have you talking to me like that, especially in the office. I'm the CE, Mia. I know these titles are silly and we all work on the same goals, but I have to keep up certain appearances. I can't have you undermining the product when you should be selling and promoting it."

Mia took a breath, the clarity she'd been searching for months finally arriving like a beam of light. "No, you can't. It's best for both of us that I quit. This is it."

His eyes widened with panic. "But Slush is in two days!"

"I'll email you the pitch. Just follow the script. You can do it."

"No, I can't..."

Mia placed her work computer and phone on a nearby desk, then hoisted the lightened satchel on her shoulder and grabbed the canvas bag with Izzy's phone in it. "I'll give you a tip though. It'll make all the difference."

"What the fuck are you talking about? I don't need tips. I need someone to do the job!" Mikko frowned, his eyes shooting daggers at her.

"Do you want the tip or not?" Mia buttoned her coat, hovering at the edge of the stairs.

Mikko shrugged, huffing out an angry sigh. "What?"

Mia cast him a wide smile. "Relax your butt cheeks. Apparently, constantly clenching them makes you seem like a douche. I heard this from a focus group."

With that, she skipped down the stairs, her heart glowing so brightly she couldn't hear the angry words he hurled at her receding back.

Chapter 37

Izzy wandered down the inner city street, his eyes mindlessly browsing the decorated shop windows, many of them already closed but sporting beautifully lit Christmas displays. Gentle snowflakes had started falling, illuminated by the street lamps. As he reached what looked like the Main Street, their light was overpowered by the hanging Christmas lights, zigzagging overhead. A storybook scene, as magical as anything he'd ever witnessed, but his legs felt heavy, heart unwilling. Mia had gone back to that guy. That's where she was working. Part of the furniture, because she knew the CE. The young guy had said it with a wink, a universal signal of a deeper meaning behind the words, meaning that sickened him to his core.

She needed a job, she needed money. But she was so clever. She could have found work anywhere, he was sure of that. So why in that company?

Since leaving the office, Izzy had walked towards the city centre, more to keep warm than anything else. He could feel the deep exhaustion of the flights catching up with him, along with hunger. He had to stop somewhere. Forcing himself to focus on the colourful lights and signs, he scanned the windows, trying to find anything that was open and looked like it served food.

That's when he saw it. Iguana. With a Mexican theme, the restaurant looked nothing like its namesake in Hamilton, but it was his only connection to her, a lifeline thrown by the universe. Izzy opened the door, wrestling his suitcase and guitar to a corner table. The restaurant was almost empty, with a couple of older guys nursing beers at the bar. An orchestral version of White Christmas pumped through the speakers. A young waitress approached him with a wavering smile. Something about her face reminded him of Mia. In fact, every female he'd walked past since arriving here had given him the same feeling, as if he'd seen them before.

"Sorry," Izzy said as he caught himself staring. "Could you please bring me a beer and a sandwich. Or anything else, really. I don't know your menu."

She gave him an odd look, opened the menu lying on the table right in front of him, and talked through the options with impeccable English. Izzy pointed at a random dish and thanked her, his eyes lingering on the brick arches of the old building. A historical milieu wasted on a Tex-Mex restaurant.

Izzy placed his phone on the table, his finger hovering over the tracking app. Did he need to know where she was? She clearly didn't keep the phone on her. She'd left it behind and gone to lunch.

What could he do? In all his dreams, all the scenarios he'd run in his mind, he'd never considered this. Mia was his. He'd claimed her. He'd fought his demons to travel all the way here. For this. Izzy ran a hand over his face, disguising the pain he was undoubtedly broadcasting.

This couldn't be the end. He couldn't just fly back. No. He'd fight. He'd find her and confront her. Even if he couldn't change anything, he had to see Mia. If he'd wanted to slip away and quietly retreat from her life, he could have stayed in his basement. The alien land with its hostile weather, historical buildings and quiet blondes did nothing to put him at ease, but he'd keep going. If he had another panic attack, so be it. To his relief, he'd noticed the strangers around here didn't make eye contact.

The food arrived, a burrito of sorts covered in cheese, and a tall, frothy beer.

Tired of the Christmas-themed elevator music, Izzy dug up his headphones and opened the Spotify playlist he'd made for Mia. As the list of songs appeared on the screen, an unfamiliar title caught his eye – an artist and song he'd never heard of. Had Mia added it? Izzy tapped the play button, and a soft female voice filled his ears, drowning the noise from around him, pulling him into a wistful melody.

Izzy swallowed against the lump in his throat, a plan taking shape. He'd go back to the office. If Mia wasn't there, he'd lean on that scrawny guy at the door to get her local phone number, address, and anything else he possibly knew. He'd find her.

Chapter 38

Mia ran down Mannerheimintie, towards the main transportation hub of Kamppi, her fingers frozen against the phone screen as she tried to type an email.

Where are you, Izzy?

As she pressed 'send', her gaze landed on the green neon sign. *Iguana.* The word drew her like a beacon in the night, glowing behind the flurry of snowflakes that had started falling. An odd feeling took over her. She could sense his presence, like a faint beeping of a metal detector.

Mia approached the window, leaning in to peer through the glass. She saw a dark shape sitting at the table further down, but couldn't tell who it was. The moment she grabbed the door handle and stepped in, the inner door flung open and she crashed straight onto a wide chest. She recognised his scent before her eyes even travelled up to his face, landing on that scruffy beard and dark eyes.

"Izzy!"

The doors closed, trapping them in the small vestibule that

kept the cold and snow away from most Finnish buildings. A draught lobby.

"Mia?" Izzy dropped his suitcase and raised his hand towards her face, stopping just short of making contact. His eyes searched hers.

Mia bit her lip, her heart flip-flopping between relief and desperation. "I had this strange feeling, like I could sense you somewhere close. And you're here."

His gorgeous brown gaze darkened. "I went to your office, but—"

"I know. I'm so sorry." Mia held up her hand. Every cell in her body called out to him. She wanted to throw herself at that chest before she dissolved in this dark foyer. But the hurt in his eyes held her back.

"You took the job?"

She squeezed her eyes shut and nodded, hating herself.

"I suppose it was a good offer. Millions. Shares. A boyfriend."

Mia buried her face in her mittens. "No! I'm not back with him, and I didn't take the shares. I needed the money and had no other options. Nothing I could just jump into and—"

"So you went back to *him*?" Izzy's voice cracked with emotion, making her heart ache.

"It would have been the fastest way to make money, but I couldn't stand it and today... I resigned. I'm sorry. I should have told you." She peeked at him from behind the wet wool. "Izzy."

"I can't do the long distance thing." His voice was gruff. A strand of hair had escaped his man bun, falling over one eye.

The front door opened behind Mia, and two customers edged past them in the narrow space. Izzy picked up his suitcase and they both stumbled outside onto the snow-covered footpath. The snowfall had eased into a gentle sprinkling of picture-perfect snowflakes that landed on Mia's face like tiny, freezing kisses.

"How did you make it here?" she asked him. "It must have been… so hard." She wanted to reach for him, touch those tense shoulders, do everything in her power to smooth the worry lines crossing his forehead.

Izzy shrugged. "I got drunk in Singapore."

"Good call." Mia risked a smile. She saw the corner of his mouth tug upward and hope lit up in her chest. "I wish I could have been there with you."

Izzy slid the guitar case off his back and set it on the ground next to his suitcase. Mia's gaze swept the footpath almost involuntarily, scanning for trouble. If anyone tried to take his luggage, she'd attack them with wet mittens.

Izzy studied her for a moment and his eyes softened. "So, you're not back with him?"

"No!" She blinked against tears. "There's nobody else. There'll never be anybody else. I—"

His hand cupped her face and he skimmed his thumb across her lips. His voice dropped and eyes burned with meaning. "It's okay. I'd fight them. I didn't come all the way here to give you up." He paused, those dark eyes glistening under the Christmas lights.

"Why did you come here, Izzy?" Mia held her breath, her heart skipping God knows how many beats. "I would have come back to you."

"I fucked up at the airport. I let you go. I didn't tell you..."

"What?"

His thumb swiped a snowflake off her eyebrow and his eyes wrinkled in the corners, his lips curling up. He pulled her closer, his breath tickling her ear. "I'm in love with you, Mia. Head over heels like a fool and I don't care if it's too soon or if it's all doomed because of the distance. I don't know what will happen, but I had to tell you."

He pulled away to look her in the eye, then dropped his gaze to her lips.

Mia gasped as his mouth landed on hers, closing the world outside. The heat from his touch engulfed her, and emotion erupted in her chest like fire crackers, gathering more tears in her eyes. They mixed with the melting snowflakes, her face salty and wet, but she couldn't pull away from him, her brain belting out one thought like a broken record.

Izzy is here. Izzy loves me.

His beard scratched her chin and his fingers sunk into her hair, holding her tight. He tasted of beer and passion, of Izzy. A billow of memories flooded Mia's brain and she travelled ten thousand miles in a fraction of a second, back to their first kiss in his basement. Home. She hadn't felt like home since then, but he'd brought home to her.

Finally, they came up for air and Mia rested her cheek against his puffer jacket. It looked so strange on him, like a Halloween costume. "I love you. You don't have to travel alone anymore. I'll go with you. I'll follow you anywhere."

His beard rubbed against her beanie and he bent down to kiss her forehead, his voice a low whisper. "I'm going to hold you to that."

Chapter 39

Izzy followed Mia through a snowy archway leading to a small courtyard. "This is my sister's place," she said. "I'm staying here until I get myself sorted."

The pale yellow apartment buildings, lit by eerie torches, rose towards the dark sky. The snow fall had ceased, but the alien feel of the foreign city hung heavy in the air, making his head spin. He felt better next to her, his only anchor in this strange place, like some tiny part of it belonged to him via her, as long as he stood close enough and breathed the same, crisp air.

"We're not staying the night, though?" He asked again as she opened a heavy door and led them into an echoey corridor. "Your sister just had a baby."

She turned to face him in the dark. "They're still in the hospital. The baby came early, she had to be under blue light and has trouble feeding... Anyway, let's stay here tonight and we can find somewhere else tomorrow?"

Relief engulfed Izzy as he followed her up the curved

staircase of the historic building – so solid and quiet it seemed to have its own atmosphere with no connection to the howling wind outside.

Mia opened the door and led him inside the modern apartment. They peeled off their winter jackets, beanies and scarves and Mia showed him where to hang them. "Are you hungry?" She asked and he shook his head. "Tired?"

Izzy nodded. He felt so out of his element, but he'd be okay, as long as he kept his eyes on her, his lighthouse in the dark ocean. Sensing his hesitation, she took his hand and pulled him into a small room with a single bed. "This is where I'm staying. There's another mattress that pulls out from underneath. Sorry, it's not flash."

He looked at her and the bed, seasick. He wanted to show her how much he loved her, how much he'd missed her, but his head felt funny. The air was so different here. Everything was different. Dry, solid, echoey. Unreal. Izzy swallowed.

Mia closed the distance, wrapping her arms around his waist, speaking to him in quiet whispers. "Izzy. Isaiah. I love you. I love that you're here. I know it's probably overwhelming. Let me help you. You can sleep if you want to."

She sat on the bed and he joined her, tiredness shaking his body. "I want to be better than this." He hung his head. "I'll get the hang of this place. I'll learn the language and the customs and everything—"

"Shh. You don't have to." Mia's arms closed around him

and she pushed him back on the bed, climbing on top with a warm smile. "Izzy, take me home. I want to go back with you. If you buy me a ticket, I'll make it up to you. I'll start right now." She peeled off her top and dropped it on the floor, smiling victoriously, revealing a black, lacy bra. God, she was beautiful.

"Are you sure?" Izzy stared at the perfect pair of breasts bursting out of a bra he immediately wanted to rip off. "Don't joke about it, because I'll take you. I'll steal you forever."

"You need a date for your brother's wedding. Maybe we can come back here in the summer, for a visit?"

Izzy nodded. Maybe he could do that. Travelling together – it sounded better. "We'll have to make some money." A thought hit him. "Which reminds me..." He unearthed a tight roll of twenty-dollar notes from the pocket of his jeans, stuffing them into her bra.

"What the hell?" She grasped at the bundle of money, laughing. The notes unravelled themselves into a flurry of green plastic, spreading all over the bed.

Izzy flashed her a cheeky smile. "I told you I didn't want your money. So I came to return it."

Mia huffed, still chuckling, and gathered the notes. "Your money looks ridiculous, like some fake boardgame money." She placed the notes on her nightstand. "But if you insist on giving it back, I'll put it towards my flight ticket."

"The best use I can think of." His eyes lingered on her bra, warm relaxation flooding his guts, draining blood from whatever overactive part of his brain was currently freaking out and transporting it down to his groin. “I have enough for our tickets, and I can always earn more—”

“We’ll do it together! We can produce and edit videos. I’ll find us some better paying gigs. I’m good at that stuff. And you’re way under-priced.” Her smile sparkled with faith.

Izzy couldn’t help smiling back. “I thought I couldn’t love you more, but I think I was wrong.”

Mia removed her bra and threw it on the floor. “I honestly don’t care about money. I thought I did, but when I look at you…”

“Sorry? Did you say something? Your boobs were talking.” Izzy pulled a silly face, feeling a million pounds lighter, and increasingly hard.

“Ha-ha.” Noticing his excitement, Mia reached down to unbutton his jeans. “We can talk later. I’ve missed you too much.”

“Same here.” He gathered her in his arms and turned her over on the tiny bed, his mind flooding with memories.

As he lowered his mouth on the woman he craved, he noticed the absence of something. The sense of urgency had disappeared. His heart beat a little slower and his mind rested, knowing they could take their time, slow down and enjoy every second of being together. They’d make it work – in any time zone, any city, any room.

She was his other half, day to his night, and he’d never let her go.

three weeks later

Mia watched in wonder as Shasa and Mac stood under a bursting arch of flowers, kissing for the first time as husband and wife. With Lilla flitting around them in her lacy, white dress, they all radiated happiness, captured by the subtly moving photographer. A view of endless rolling hills spread behind them, glowing in late afternoon golden light, framing them like a movie poster.

As their kiss went on, anything but chaste, the small wedding party cheered. Mia had noticed some of the aunties arching their eyebrows as Shasa had walked down the makeshift aisle – the grassy path leading to the flowery arch – barefoot, her mustard yellow wedding dress flapping in the wind. But after hearing their heartfelt vows and seeing the love and adoration on their faces, even the most hardcore traditionalists had jumped onboard, celebrating their commitment.

As Mac and Shasa led the way towards the party tent, dancing wildly to 'Fly me to the moon', Izzy squeezed Mia's hand. She looked up at his smiling face, noticing the rising moon in the sky, right above his shoulder, ready for the magical night.

Izzy's muscles strained the suit he'd bought for the occasion. He was Mac's best man, his tie the same mustard yellow as Shasa's dress. The same golden tones repeated in the flowers and decorations all around them. As promised, it was relaxed, yet gorgeous.

The official part finished, Mac and Shasa announced they would head out to take a few photos, and the guests trailed for the drinks tables. Happy chatter filled the air, rising above the playlist of classic love songs Izzy had compiled, scouring soundtracks of Shasa and Mac's favourite movies.

Mia was about to join the queue for drinks, but Izzy held her back. "Let's check on Casanova."

Deke had borrowed a van to transport Casanova's cage to the wedding. The parrot had been an instant hit with the children, but they'd had to move him further out for the ceremony as he was getting quite loud, as well as inappropriate.

Mia suspected Izzy hoped to avoid the swarming crowd of aunties and uncles and their questions, particularly the ones about their future plans (why was everyone obsessed with where they would 'settle down'?) and was more than happy to comply. She followed Izzy around the main tent to where Casanova's cage had been left on top of a small camping table.

To their surprise, the bird was neither alone, nor in its cage. Deke stood next to a pretty woman in a purple dress, holding Casanova on his shoulder.

Mia grabbed Izzy's hand. "Wait," she whispered. "I don't think he needs help."

They retreated quietly into the shadow of the tent, observing the scene. The woman held up her arm and Deke helped Casanova climb on her shoulder, croaking "Gorgeous!!"

The woman laughed, staring at Deke starry-eyed.

"Who is she?" Mia hissed.

Izzy shook his head. "No idea. Must be one of Shasa's friends."

She had a similar bohemian vibe –no shoes and long, tangled, dark hair with purple highlights framing her face. Almost blue, Mia thought with amusement. So perfect. She glanced at Izzy, who smiled back knowingly. They returned to the wedding party, leaving Deke, the woman and the bird to get acquainted.

The rest of the party went by in a blur of delicious food, wine, dancing – and giving more vague answers about their future plans to Izzy's nosy relatives. When darkness fell, the fairy lights turned on.

As the first guests started excusing themselves and disappearing into the night, Izzy found Mia outside the main tent, nursing a glass of wine. "Are you ready to go?" He gestured to the carpark.

"Are you sure? The party's still going. Won't it be rude?" Mia asked, fighting a yawn. It had been a long day. She'd spent the morning researching visa applications, while Izzy worked on his novel. If she wanted to stay here for longer than three months, she had to get her paperwork sorted.

"No. I talked to Mac. He's fine."

Accepting his reply, Mia followed him to the carpark. "Wait! Are you okay to drive?" She definitely couldn't. The world gently swayed around her. New Zealand wine was far too drinkable.

"I had one beer hours ago." Izzy opened the car door for her. "I made sure I'm good to drive. I have a surprise for you."

"A surprise?"

He flashed her a secretive smile, getting behind the wheel. He drove in silence as Mia sang along to her favourite playlist, *Mia 5* (Izzy kept discovering more treasures, although certain favourites remained). Coming closer to Hamilton, she noticed he missed the turn to his house, heading instead towards the river. "Where are we going?"

"You'll see."

Izzy turned to a small, gravel driveway that ended at a closed gate, and parked the car. Confused, but too happy and content to worry, Mia followed him down a slope towards the water's edge. It was so dark she could barely make out the shapes of the trees and bushes, and another dark shape in the water.

"Wait here." Izzy ran ahead of her, and in a moment, lights came on. Hundreds of fairy lights twinkled from the trees, revealing a small clearing right by the water. Mia recognised the dark shape in the river as the dock they'd moored at during the boat trip. The fallen tree had been cleared away, but the wooden structure still appeared broken, inaccessible from the shore.

"Oh, my God! Did you do this?" Mia approached the lights, and the man she'd lost her heart to. "How?"

Izzy took her hand, pulling her in the middle of the clearing, under the lights. "I had to find this place again. I drove around and asked the owner if I could use this spot for one night. He agreed."

"Use it? For what?"

"For this." Izzy stuck his hand into his pocket and unearthed a ring. It was a simple gold band, wide and flat with a brushed surface. Scandinavian, she thought, the drunken stupor clearing from her mind as she stared at it.

"Will you marry me, Mia?"

Mia blinked, words deserting her. She stared at the ring, then at him, searching for a counter argument. "You've only known me for..." She tried to calculate the days and weeks. Did it really matter?

"It doesn't matter," Izzy said, as if reading her mind. "I want you. For life."

"You mean here? Or in Finland?" She wanted it to not matter, but struggled to imagine their future. Everything felt new and scary, like forging a path where no human had gone before. Which sounded dramatic, and likely wasn't true.

Izzy's eyes shone with hope, challenging her doubts, capturing the thousands of fairy lights. "How about both?

We don't have to settle anywhere for the rest of our lives. Let's leave it open. I'm only asking you to choose us."

Hope flickered in her heart. Could they approach it like that? Getting married would allow her to stay in New Zealand, but she wouldn't marry only to get permanent residency. She wouldn't settle for something practical. Not anymore.

"You're not just thinking about the visa issues?" She bit her lip. "Because I'm sure I can get that sorted..."

"No!" Izzy grabbed her shoulders. She could see the muscles in his forearms twitching as he held back from squeezing too hard. "I'm thinking of you. You've upended my life. You saved me. Let me spend the rest of my life being there for you. We won't make millions, but we'll get by, and I'll make sure you always have time to write your songs, because I want to hear every one of them."

His eyes captured her with unbridled adoration, like a gentle punch landing in the middle of her heart. Tears burst out of her eyes without a warning, blurring the twinkly lights into overlapping blots. "Goddammit, Izzy. Are you going to make me cry for the rest of my life?" She smiled through the salty film.

"It's the price you pay for being fully alive," Izzy whispered. "So, are you in?"

"I'm in," she sniffed, her heart so full there was no room for anything else, every cell of her spoken for. His. She closed her eyes, letting the tears roll. She felt him slide the ring on her finger before he bent down to kiss her cheeks.

"These taste different." His voice held a playful spark. "Like tears after a good choice."

Acknowledgments

This book would have never been written without my sister Aini. She wrote a song for me, releasing it on my birthday and making me cry all day. I live in New Zealand. She lives in Finland. With the whole world in-between, it's hard to stay in touch, but we decided to make an effort by doing something together (we're doers, not idle chatters – it might be a Finnish thing). I wrote a book and my sister wrote music. She helped me shape the story, lending many ideas, personality traits and details (she once had a butt-clenching colleague) and in turn, I wrote my favourite song of hers into the story and begged her to record an English version of it. She did! Thank goodness she also knows a lot about the Helsinki start-up scene I love easy research! This has been my favourite book to write, ever.

Secondly, a huge thank you to my friend and fellow Kiwi author Jen Morris for her endless support, as well as referring me to her wonderful editor Rachel Collins, who fit me into her busy schedule and both improved my work and greatly encouraged me. A massive thank you to my beta readers Jamee Crosby, Kirsty Butler, JL Peridot, Gabriela Steier, Erin Branscom, Emma Grocott, and, Frida Johansson. Your feedback was invaluable!

Thank you to my husband Sami for introducing me to countless amazing indie artists and helping me find the perfect songs for the book playlist. And thank you to Nathan Higgins both for the private tour of the Waitomo glow worm caves and the fascinating facts that made their way into the story.

I'd also like to thank all my ARC readers for jumping on board, reading faster than I knew was humanly possible and delivering thoughtful, beautiful reviews. Launching this book in the middle of moving countries and dealing with multiple personal challenges has been a crazy ride, and I'm so grateful for every single person who's helped me along the way.

I hope you enjoy Izzy and Mia's story as much as I enjoyed writing it. This story has been my refuge in the last few months, offering the perfect escape from everything in life that's trying to drag me down. May it do the same for you!

Love, Enni

Thank you for reading!

If you enjoyed this book, please tell your friends and leave a review on Amazon! Referrals and reviews help wildly unknown indie authors such as myself get discovered.

To find out about my upcoming books,
sign up for my newsletter at
enniamanda.com

Lightning Source UK Ltd.
Milton Keynes UK
UKHW041330070223
416605UK00004B/294